Benita Renee Jenkins:

Diva Secret Agent

Benita Renee Jenkins:

Diva Secret Agent

Lorisa Bates

www.urbanbooks.net

Urban Books, LLC
300 Farmingdale Road, NY-Route 109
Farmingdale, NY 11735

Benita Renee Jenkins: Diva Secret Agent

ISBN 13: 978-1-64556-257-3
ISBN 10: 1-64556-257-3

First Mass Market Printing October 2021
First Trade Paperback Printing November 2020
Printed in the United States of America

10 9 8 7 6 5 4 3 2 1

Distributed by Kensington Publishing Corp.
Submit Orders to:
Customer Service
400 Hahn Road
Westminster, MD 21157-4627
Phone: 1-800-733-3000
Fax: 1-800-659-2436

To Mom and Dad—the prettiest flowers in God's garden.

Acknowledgments

First and foremost, I give thanks to God for providing me with the gift of telling stories. Without His inspiration, I would have never been able to complete this body of work. Secondly, words cannot express how appreciative I am for all the love and support I received from my family, friends, and folks in the publishing world.

About the Author

Lorisa Bates has always had a zest for telling stories. As a young child, while children her age were playing with dolls, she was developing characters and writing short stories. As she got older, her love for writing only grew. She started her career in the entertainment business over a decade ago, and her experiences include writing, producing, directing, and editing for film. She has also written several plays focusing on family and relationships, and they were part of several play festivals throughout New York City, Detroit, and Washington, D.C.

Prologue

It was nearly midnight when Carl "Holiday" Johnson drove through the dark and desolate warehouse district in the southern part of Brooklyn. He pulled up in front of warehouse 117 and blew the horn a few times, expecting Nick, his main guy, to open the oversized garage door and let him in. But no one showed up. He laid on the horn, hoping someone from his crew would raise the gate, growing more pissed by the second when no one did.

He shook his head in disbelief and thought about firing Nick when he saw his incompetent ass. He looked in his rear-view and side-view mirrors, almost expecting to see some assholes approach his two-hundred-fifty-thousand-dollar 458 Italia Ferrari, stick a gun in his face, and carjack him. He rubbed his sweaty palms on his pressed white polo shirt and his pair of dark designer jeans, looking down at his new Nike Air Jordans.

Ever since he made it big in the music industry, he'd been forced to protect himself from overzealous fans and vengeful, jealous enemies. But tonight, he'd made the decision to come out without his bodyguards. He had business to take care of and wanted to do it without a lot of eyes watching. He trusted no one, not even the guys paid to protect him.

He squinted at his fifty-thousand-dollar Hublot Big Bang watch and snapped, "Fucking Nick! I'm gonna kill you." Dialing his cell, he drummed his fingers on the steering wheel, waiting for Nick to pick up.

After three rings, Nick answered.

"Nick, where the fuck are you? I been blowin' the fucking horn for fifteen minutes. Open the goddamn gate."

The gate opened, and Carl slammed on the gas and sped toward his jackass employee, who leaped out of the way. Carl jumped out of the car and grabbed Nick by his neck, pinning him against the wall.

"I should fire your fucking ass. You must be one of the dumbest muthafuckas on the planet."

Nick was about to respond, but Carl cut him off. "I'll fucking rip your lips right off your face if you attempt to speak. Close the damn gate. I'm not gonna have somebody come up in here and steal my fucking ride. You understand?"

Nick nodded quickly, and Carl released him and walked toward the back of the warehouse.

Three burly men stood in a semicircle, waiting for Carl to arrive. They'd been there for hours, watching over a little guy who sat in a chair, looking nervously around the building.

Although the majority of the enormous warehouse was empty, Carl had still invested thousands of dollars on a high-tech alarm system and video surveillance equipment. He had become obsessed with protecting his properties after his first house was vandalized. He would never forget how it felt to see the damage that had been done to his empty brownstone in Bed-Stuy, Brooklyn. It had infuriated him, and he grew even more upset when the police couldn't find the culprits. He vowed to always protect his assets, no matter what.

Carl loathed disloyalty. He paid top dollar for it, and if he didn't get it, he would become angry. An uncontrollable rage would overtake him, and he wanted to hurt somebody.

Carl remembered when he was a kid, he and his sister were harassed by the neighborhood bullies. His mother encouraged him to ignore the boys, but that didn't stop the teasing, and his father commanded him to watch over his sister. Things finally came to a head when Carl's sister was knocked to the ground by one of the bullies. Carl's father grabbed him by the arm and dragged him down to the playground.

"Carl, the only things we got in this world are family, loyalty, and respect. You never ever let somebody hurt your family. It's time for you to be a man and stand up for what you believe in. I want you to go over there and take care of that asshole. Make him respect you and your family."

The ringleader, a kid nicknamed Big Boy, had been teasing Carl and his sister for months. Now Carl had to defend his sister, and he was mad about it. He was mad because he'd been charged with protecting his little sister and even madder because he'd been the butt of many jokes. But what he hated most was being called a little runt by his tormenter. That day, Carl's anger got the better of him, and it was time for Big Boy to pay.

Small Carl strutted up to the monster-sized bully and stood toe to toe with him, looking up at his ugly mug. Big Boy laughed in Carl's face, but before he could open his mouth, Carl took a swing and punched him in the nose. Blood spurted everywhere. Carl moved at warp speed and punched the enormous kid in the stomach and kicked him in the shin. Big Boy toppled over like

Goliath, hitting the ground with a thud. Carl kicked him uncontrollably, and it was only after his father pulled him off that Carl returned to his senses.

From that point on, Carl never backed down from a fight. He protected his sister and did whatever it took to make his father proud. Carl promised he would always stand his ground. He developed a reputation for attacking first and asking questions later.

He always remembered the day his father made him avenge his sister's honor. He would do anything to make his father proud and would protect his family—no matter what.

When Carl was fifteen, his father died in a car accident, and Carl got angry. He hung with the wrong crowd and got into fights because it was the only way for him to release his emotions. After Carl spent a few years selling drugs and terrorizing some of the younger neighborhood kids, his father's brother came into his life. He had just finished serving a twenty-year stint in prison. He'd been one of the biggest drug dealers in Brooklyn, but he was a changed man who pushed Carl to do something better with his life than being a gangbanger like he used to be.

Carl began focusing on music as a way to calm the inner demons that had built up inside of him. He managed several local groups and produced their albums. However, one particular music group named 718 (after one of New York City's area codes) would become his ticket out. By twenty-five, Carl's career had catapulted when the group won a Grammy for Best New Artist in the late nineties. His fan base grew, and the media took an interest in him. He navigated the music world, working with 718 on his path to huge success. Carl also launched the careers of a girl group called Brooklyn Baby Girls, who became an overnight sensation.

He found his calling and discovered he had the Midas touch. The more successful Carl became, the more the media loved gossiping about him. They reported everything he said or did. He was a talented young music maven, but what hurt him was his unpredictable behavior, and they labeled him "Brooklyn hothead."

No matter how hard Carl tried to control his temper, he eventually landed in jail on two different occasions. The first time, just after his twenty-eighth birthday, Carl had become annoyed soon after the release of his debut album, *Free to Live, Free to Die,* when "shock jock" Pete Rimmey criticized the album during his live show on 97.1 FM. Carl and his buddy Bruce were listening to Rimmey bash his album.

"Who the fuck he think he is? He's on the damn radio telling people not to waste money on my shit."

"Holiday, we should go down there and bash his skull in, man," Bruce said, egging him on. "You know what I'm saying?"

After listening for a few more minutes, Carl jumped up from the couch and headed to the door. "Let's go. We got a date with a DJ."

The two men jumped into Carl's Lexus GS460 and headed to Chinatown to confront Rimmey. Thirty minutes later, Carl double-parked in front of the building and made his way inside. He called in to the radio station and was able to speak to Rimmey on the phone.

"Mr. Johnson. So glad to hear from you."

"Really, Rimmey? Because from what I hear on the radio, you seem to be having a good time dogging out my new album."

Rimmey goaded the rapper mogul. "Carl, I'm only speaking the truth. You may wanna stick to managing groups instead of producing your own work. Stick to your God-given talent. Well, Carl, I gotta let you go. More listeners to talk to." Rimmey hung up and continued to give his listeners an earful, not knowing Carl was pacing the lobby.

Carl waited patiently until Rimmey got off the air. He slipped past an intern who was leaving the floor from a locked door. The receptionist tried to stop him, but Carl's friend Bruce stopped her from calling security.

"Wait here," he yelled at Bruce, but Bruce quietly followed.

Carl wandered the floor until he found Rimmey's office. He burst in and slammed the door. "Man, you talked a whole lot of shit today. And you know what? I think you need a serious ass-whooping."

Rimmey reached for his phone, but Carl grabbed it and threw it across the room. He then leaped across the desk and shoved Rimmey hard in the chest. Rimmey toppled over the chair and landed on his ass. His head hit the floor with a loud thud.

Carl grabbed him by his collar and pulled him off the floor, slamming him down into his swivel chair. "You think my albums suck? I'm about to show you what garbage really smells like, dumb-ass muthafucka." He hauled off and punched Rimmey across the face. Still holding Rimmey's collar, he hit him again. "Who the fuck do you think you are? God?"

"Calm down, man," Rimmey sputtered, wiping blood from his beaten face. "Can we just talk about things?" The man was near tears. "C'mon, man. We're adults here. I . . . I know you're pissed, and I'm sorry." He frantically searched the room, most likely for an escape route. "Man, you know it's radio. Nothing personal." He spat out a couple of teeth. "It's all about ratings and shit. Man, can we—"

But Carl's eyes grew wild, and he balled his fist so tight his fingernails dug into his skin. "Nothing personal? You're messing with my life, you fucking idiot. I ain't gonna let any fuckin'-ass clown mess with my money. I'm gonna fuck you up." He picked up a chair and held it over Rimmey's head.

Rimmey screamed and covered his head with both arms to lessen the blow, but Bruce grabbed Carl from behind and dragged him out of the office.

"Get offa me!" Carl yelled, struggling to get out of his grasp, but Bruce was bigger and stronger.

"No way, man. You wanna go down for murder? We gotta get out now."

Of course, Rimmey called the police. Carl was arrested and eventually spent thirty days in jail for assault. He also received five hundred hours of community service and one hundred hours of anger management counseling for his bad judgment.

Carl promised himself and his mom he would never end up in jail again. The first thing he had to do was learn to control his temper, or his successful career in the music business would disintegrate. As soon as he got out, he saw a therapist to help him get his anger in check.

It had been a long time since Carl had lost his temper, but tonight, he was losing control. He was livid after finding out—thanks to Benjamin Mahoney, his brilliant number-two guy who handled all his legitimate (and illegitimate) financial dealings—that his dumb-ass employee Malik Williams had been stealing from him. Carl never doubted Benjamin's loyalty and trusted his judgment. Benjamin was crunching numbers and discovered a discrepancy between the number of CDs in the warehouse and the number Malik was reporting to his boss.

Two of Carl's men snatched Malik off the street and brought him to the warehouse in Red Hook. Carl didn't usually get his hands dirty—it was beneath him, and it was dangerous, considering his rap sheet—but he couldn't resist one last conversation with this piece of shit. He had left his Tribeca apartment in Manhattan, hopped in his sports car, and practiced his breathing techniques while driving over the Brooklyn Bridge. But as soon as he saw Malik, his anger exploded. He wanted to strangle the guy with his bare hands. He wanted him dead.

Carl sat in an empty chair across from Malik, who looked terrified. Clapping his hands together and rocking back and forth, Carl tried to compose his thoughts. He moved in closer, staring at Malik with his cold, dead eyes. Malik turned away.

Carl grabbed Malik's chin and stared at him before releasing his grasp and wiping his hand on his jeans. "How long you been working for me, Malik?"

Malik's eyes pleaded for help, but he didn't have any friends here. "Eight months," he whispered.

Carl leaned back against the gray metal chair and stretched out his legs. "Eight months. Haven't I treated your family well?"

Carl knew there were rumors about him being a sociopath, and now here he was, sitting across from a man who was scared to death to be near him. Carl could practically see Malik's heart pounding against his shirt, and that secretly brought him pleasure.

"Carl, man, I don't know why I'm here." Malik started crying, but he couldn't wipe away the snot bubbling in his nose because his hands were tied behind the chair.

Carl flashed a devious smile and looked up at the extra-large, muscular men standing next to him. "He thinks I'm stupid. I don't fucking believe this. Why you insulting me, Malik?"

Malik vigorously shook his head. "No, no, Mr. Johnson," he cried. "I'm not. I'm just saying—"

"The fuck are you sayin', Malik? You sayin' you don't know why you sitting here in this fucking warehouse, man? That what you sayin'?"

"Y–you got the wrong guy," he stammered. "I'd never do nothin' to dis you, man."

Carl stood up and threw the chair across the floor. "Muthafucka, I know you been stealin' from me, and this makes you a punk-ass lyin' bitch." Carl smacked Malik so hard across the face he knocked him and the chair over.

"I'm sorry, Mr. Johnson!" Malik screamed, cowering, unable to protect himself from Carl's attack.

"You sorry?" Carl kicked Malik several times in his side and face while Malik lay helpless on the ground.

Carl looked at his men. "He sorry. Everybody's always fuckin' sorry. I'm sorry too. Sorry I gotta kill your muthafuckin' ass."

"Please," Malik begged, "please, man. You got a right to be mad. I stole from you. But I was desperate, man. My ma's in a bad way, man. It's her heart. She real sick, man. I can get you all your money. Please gimme a chance. Whatever I gotta do. Please, Mr. Johnson. Give me another chance."

Carl wiped a smudge on his expensive watch using the bottom of his shirt. "Your ma's in a bad way?"

Malik nodded, but the movement was limited. He was apparently in a lot of pain from the short attack, and blood poured from various head wounds.

"Well, Malik, my friend, one thing I respect is lookin' out for your family, man. Protectin' them no matta what. And your ma bein' bad an' all . . ."

"Yes, Carl."

He started laughing. "You lyin'-ass, muthafuckin' piece of shit. Yo' ma's not in any bad way. I saw her at Foxwoods a week ago. Ain't nothin' worse than a piece of shit usin' his own mother to save his ass. Look at you, lyin' in my face. Beggin' for forgiveness. Shut up, you raggedy-ass piece of shit. You're a fuckin' dead man, Malik. You gonna pay me back, all right—with your fuckin' life. I'ma get every red cent outta yo' ass."

Carl grabbed the chair he'd thrown across the room. He screamed at the top of his lungs and pounded his chest as if to release the pain bottled up inside as he continued yelling, startling everyone in the warehouse. For what seemed an eternity, Carl kicked Malik over and over again in the stomach, ribs, and head, rendering him a bloody mess on the floor.

"Fuck you, Malik! Fuck you! I'm gonna rip your fuckin' balls off. Punk-ass bitch."

Carl took long, deep breaths, finally regaining his composure, and said calmly, "Clean up this blood before you throw out the trash. Make sure he don't get up."

Carl stepped into his car and backed out of the warehouse without saying a word to Nick. He put the car in park and searched for his artist Prince Bobby G's latest CD. He played his favorite song, "I'm the Fucking King G," and closed his eyes, mesmerized by the rap beat.

Tired and wanting to sleep, Carl drove to his penthouse apartment at the newly built sky-rise off Eastern Parkway and Grand Army Plaza in Prospect Park, Brooklyn. Once upstairs, he took a long, hot shower, slipped between his soft Egyptian cotton sheets, and slept like a baby.

Chapter 1

Benita Renee Jenkins had always loved the fall because it offered relief from long, hot New York summers. This year, there'd been a record number of days over ninety degrees. She loved how the leaves turned from deep forest green to golden brown to burnt orange. Fall brought a time of rejuvenation and new beginnings. Benita felt focused, energized, and happy.

After she completed a rigorous semester at John Jay College of Criminal Justice in Manhattan while also working full-time as a hairstylist, the summer had been a much-needed break. It was taking a long time to complete her bachelor's degree, but she was determined to finish and work in law enforcement. Grace, her grandmother, always told her she just needed to keep her eyes on the prize, to work hard, and God would take care of the rest.

It was 6:45 a.m. when the alarm clock started beeping. Barely hitting the off button and almost knocking the clock off the table, Benita rolled on her back and looked at the ceiling. She sat up and stretched out her lean body, throwing back the wrinkled pink-and-brown floral comforter. Swinging her feet onto the floor, she landed on the furry brown rug. It was time for her morning ritual of making her bed and arranging the oversized pillows across the headboard.

"Time to make the donuts," she mumbled, rubbing her sleepy eyes. Opening the window allowed her to breathe in the morning air. The young woman closed her eyes and thanked God for another beautiful day.

Benita walked over to her closet, where her clothes were arranged by style and color. Running her fingers over the hangers, she searched for the perfect outfit. It would be a long day, and she needed something stylish yet comfortable to go between classes, work, and jiu-jitsu training. A full-length mirror bolted inside the closet door allowed her to take a long look at herself while rubbing her bright pink manicured fingers over her face and neck.

Damn, I forgot to wash my face last night.

At least she'd wrapped her hair in her favorite blue satin scarf. Now she removed it and retied it over her hair.

She rubbed her face and pointed a finger at the mirror. "Not good, Benita. Bad habits will ruin you. They're not allowed in this house. You can do better. Always do better." She chuckled. "Oh, great. Thanks, Gram. Now those words are stuck in my head." A smile spread across her face.

Thanks to her martial arts training, she had abs and legs of steel, which was great, since she loved wearing clothes that accentuated her curves. She worked out hard to stay fit so she could enjoy her grandmother's food. Grandma Grace made the best fried chicken, corn pudding, collard greens, and macaroni and cheese. But her coconut cake was more like kryptonite than dessert, and it killed Benita's workouts. Whenever she went overboard and overate, Benita would push herself to the max to burn the fat. She didn't want to see her butt expand beyond recognition. She had a small frame, and the last thing she needed to be was a chubby fashionista who studied jiu-jitsu.

Benita placed a white tank top and army-green cargo pants from her closet across her bed and her dark brown peep-toe booties on the floor. She then opened the top drawer of her white armoire and found her favorite wide gold belt and oversized gold hoop earrings. She searched for a sassy cropped-cut blonde wig and placed those items on the bed before jumping in the shower.

When she was dressed, she perfected her makeup and adjusted her wig. She looked in the mirror one last time and then grabbed her oversized Juicy Couture bag to make sure she had everything she needed for the day. Picking up her Android phone from its charger, she glanced at her watch and rushed out. She didn't want to be late for her first day of class.

Benita made sure the front door to the two-family home she shared with her grandmother and brother was locked before heading south on Ralph Avenue. She had walked this route a thousand times, and she never tired of her neighborhood. She couldn't imagine living any-where else. Bed-Stuy had a certain vibe and energy that attracted a diverse group of people to the neighborhood. Spike Lee had filmed *Do the Right Thing* and *Crooklyn* in the area, and Chris Rock's *Everybody Hates Chris* was set in Bed-Stuy. Well-known hip-hop artists like Jay-Z, Biggie, Lil' Kim, Mos Def, and Fabolous rapped about their experiences in the neighborhood.

Benita walked past the nearby park and noticed two young boys playing a competitive game of basketball. "I hope they're getting ready for school," she mumbled.

The sun felt so bright on her face, and she was over-whelmed with happiness. Whatever the universe planned to bring her way, she was focused and ready. She smiled as she made her way down the subway stairs and headed into Manhattan.

Chapter 2

"Ooooooh, Mrs. Wiggins, can I just say you look gorgeous? I've outdone myself this time," Benita raved as she put the finishing touches on her client's hair.

Mrs. Wiggins squealed with delight. "You think so, Benita? I can't wait to see your masterpiece."

"Uh-huh. I think you're gonna love it." Benita handed Mrs. Wiggins a small oval mirror so she could view the back of her head.

Mrs. Wiggins examined her new wine-colored, cropped hairdo with a watchful eye. She rubbed the back of her neck and held onto the mirror as if her life depended on it.

Benita stood back, crossing her arms and waiting for her client to comment on her new look. From Mrs. Wiggins's expression, Benita knew the woman was happy. Benita was pleased with herself for convincing Mrs. Wiggins to remove the braids she'd been sporting for the past two years and letting her cut her hair into a new style.

Benita whipped the chair around, facing the mirror. "Check out your bangs. See how I angled them? Just long enough. Now you can comb them forward or move them to the side."

Mrs. Wiggins cooed. "Benita, I just love it. Love it. Love it. Love it. Is there anything you can't do?"

Deon Wright, the owner of the salon and Benita's cousin, sashayed over to the two ladies wearing a bright blue satin shirt, skinny jeans, and black boots. He placed his hands on the side of his oversized stomach and stomped his feet.

"Work it, girl. Benita's always been an exceptional child. She inherited her mama's gift for hair. I'm sure she's looking down from heaven, happy and proud of her little baby girl."

Benita gave Deon a hug and a kiss on the cheek. "I couldn't have done any of this without you."

"You're so right," Deon answered.

Mrs. Wiggins commented, "Well, you betta never lose this one, Deon. 'Cause wherever Benita goes, I go."

"I'm in high demand."

Gloria Gaynor's "I Will Survive" began playing on the radio. "Ah, sukkie-sukkie now. This is my song. Sheila, turn the radio up, girlfriend. I'm about to get my swerve on right now." Deon danced to the beat.

Sheila, Deon's receptionist, turned up the volume and blasted the music. She shook her head in disgust and tried to ignore Deon and his dancing. "Deon, you betta slow down, 'cause I don't wanna have to rush you to the hospital when you break a bone or somethin'. Plus, I just got my nails done."

Benita and Mrs. Wiggins laughed at Sheila's comments. Deon grabbed Benita's waist, and they started dancing.

"Don't worry about me, Sheila. I still got my moves, don't I, Benita?" Deon swirled Benita around to the vibrant beat. He was singing the chorus: "I will survive, hey-hey!"

Raven Sanborn, African American "princess," walked into the salon, stopping dead in her tracks. Rolling her eyes and placing her hands on her hips, she yelled, "Excuse me. I thought this was supposed to be a hair salon, not *Soul Train*."

Deon turned toward Raven. "Ms. Sanborn, I'm so sorry. We were just having a little fun."

"Whateva. I came to get my hair done, not stand around watching y'all dance."

Benita rolled her eyes at Raven and walked over to her workstation. She mumbled under her breath as she brushed a few strands off Mrs. Wiggins's shoulders. "Oh, hail, it's Queen B. in the house. My day was going so well."

Raven whipped her head around in Benita's direction. "Benita, you have something to say?"

Benita turned around and faced Raven while rolling her neck. "Well, actually, yeah. I just don't understand how a rich bitch like you can be so ghetto."

"Who you calling ghetto?"

Deon jumped between the two girls. "Raven, what do you need done today? Why don't you follow me to the back of the salon? Benita, don't you have work to do?"

Raven walked past Benita and whispered, "Bitch."

"Well, you would know, wouldn't you? It must be hard being the biggest bitch living in Brooklyn."

Deon's eyes pleaded with Benita not to get into a fight with his customer as he escorted Raven to the back of the salon so she could get her hair washed. Benita rolled her eyes at her cousin and sucked her teeth.

Mrs. Wiggins used her fingers to comb through her hair. "Ms. Princess needs a royal ass-whooping."

Benita chuckled. "Yup, and I'd love to take her on as my personal project."

It was 7:30 p.m. by the time the last customer left the shop. Benita cleaned up her station while Deon emptied the cash register and grabbed receipts from the reception area. Plopping down in her swivel chair, Benita removed her booties and rubbed her feet before slipping on gold sequined flats.

"My feet are killing me," she whined.

"Nobody told you to wear those high-ass heels all day long. Why you women never listen? Comfy shoes, Benita. Comfy. You're killing your back, and trust me—when you get older, your dogs are gonna suffer."

"Whatever, Deon. You know I need to look good."

"For real? 'Cause I don't think you feel good with you rubbing those feet. You ladies kill me with all your flossin'. You need to focus on protecting them dogs because they be howling." He started howling like a wolf.

Benita laughed at her crazy cousin. He was one of the funniest people she knew, even when he wasn't trying to be funny. He was also one of the most talented hairstylists she'd ever known. Graduating at the top of his class and working for Hair Styling by Joseph, a well-known Black-owned hair salon in Manhattan, Deon built his reputation as the go-to stylist, transforming the most damaged hair into bouncy and healthy locks. The first time Deon did her hair, she wanted to be just like him.

"Can you teach me how to do a weave?" Benita had asked.

"Why you wanna learn how to do weaves?" Deon teased.

"'Cause the girls at school want me to hook them up."

Deon saw a lot of talent in Benita and eventually sent her to cosmetology school, where she learned to do hair and makeup. She also graduated at the top of her class and had been working for Deon ever since. Benita loved doing hair, but she loved working beside her cousin even more.

"Deon, are we still on for Saturday? There's this new Malaysian weaving technique I'm dying to learn. It's supposed to take hair-weaving to another level."

"I heard about it. There's a latch hook you twist on the hair that acts as an anchor for the extensions. Do you know how much time we'll be saving doing all of those broads' weaves? We'll make a killing."

"You sure do try to keep your clients happy. Gotta keep the moolah rollin' in, okay?"

"Right. Happy clients keep coming back. Even the bitchy ones. By the way, thank you for not kicking Raven's ass earlier. She may be a royal pain, but her dollars help keep the lights on."

"Puleez," Benita answered. "You got at least ten clients like her and a slew of hood rats coming in every day. I think you'd be okay if she never came back to this establishment."

Deon sighed. "You're missing the point. I care about all my clients and don't want to lose any of them over some foolishness. You feel me?"

"Yeah, yeah. I feel ya. Ooh, I'm gonna be late for jiu-jitsu. Gotta go."

"How can we squash all this animosity you have with this girl?" he asked.

"Since the first grade, we've never liked each other."

Deon shook his head. "She acts like you've done something terrible to her."

"I couldn't care less about that gold-diggin' bitch. She thinks she's the cat's meow. Ever since she hooked up with that big-time music guy."

"And I hear one of the biggest criminals as well," Deon commented.

"Yup, a real loser. Who cares about Raven and her loser boyfriend? She bites. She gonna catch me on the wrong day, and her teeth may land on the floor."

"Girl, you're crazy. You need to stop with martial arts and find you a man."

"D, you act like my life is lost if I don't have a man. Plus, I'm not finding a man—he needs to find me."

"Go on with your bad self."

"I'm bad and don't you forget it. Whatchu doing tonight?" she asked.

"Oh, I don't know. Maybe try to find some trouble," he replied.

"You go, boy." Benita kissed him on his forehead. "Bye, Deon."

"Later, baby."

As Benita walked out the door, she was almost knocked down by two thugs as they entered the salon. She stopped for a moment and turned back around to see Deon talking to these men. An uneasiness came over her, and she was about to walk back inside, but the bus was coming, so she rushed to catch it. She made a mental note to speak to Deon about it the next time she saw him.

Chapter 3

For the past ten years, Executive Director Jeremiah Nathan Bolden had been in charge of the Domestic Terrorism Crime Unit, or DTCU, a joint venture created by the CIA and the FBI to handle high-profile assignments that needed to stay under the public radar. DTCU was a vehicle to protect officials who had a bad habit of participating in unorthodox tactics that would be political suicide if the media got wind of them. Avoiding bureaucratic red tape and the observant eyes of government watchdogs was a major part of DTCU's mission.

Bolden was committed to building the solid infrastructure needed to increase productivity and assigning dangerous and challenging projects to his highly trained agents, who were relentless in their charge to eliminate the enemy. He was a badass in his own right, having been a Green Beret for more than twenty years. He was the perfect person to run the organization because he had a reputation for recruiting the best of the best, and he had no problem dropping any weak links. This wasn't a job for the faint of heart; it was a job for someone who could create a clear line between right and wrong and not have second thoughts. One bad move and an agent's life could be over in a flash. He was the ultimate commander in chief, and he owed it all to his Green Beret training.

Serving his country with passion and vigor, he had retired as a high-ranking official responsible for training and recruitment of the new crop of Green Berets. He was proud to build a team of elite soldiers committed to serving their country with the same drive and commitment he'd shown. However, he had a hard time dealing with disorganization and chaos, and he went from being well-controlled to biting someone's head off at the drop of a dime.

This morning was no exception. At ten o'clock, he arrived at his office, pissed off from having spent two hours being grilled by the board of executives—or what Bolden referred to as the executive team—over the status of the organization's cases. They wanted to know how many were still open, how many were close to being completed, and how many new jobs were in the pipeline.

These meetings always put Bolden in a bad mood because he had to justify his team's existence. His agents worked their asses off and didn't shy away from taking on dangerous assignments, which were handed off to them when the CIA or FBI refused to take them on. But still, the executive team never wanted to address his agents' lack of support. They had more assignments than any other agency yet fewer agents doing the work. If this team wanted a higher success rate, then they needed to put their money where their mouths were—in other words, give him more money to increase the number of DTCU agents.

Bolden entered his office, turned on the light, and placed his coat on the hook behind his door. A fresh pot of coffee simmered on a small table opposite his mahogany desk between the large bay window and the door. He never liked to have his back to a window or door. From this position, he could always see what was happening.

He filled his cup and sat in his oversized black leather chair. The ex-military officer closed his eyes and took a much-needed break. He'd gotten riled up during his early meeting and now had to prepare for the day at hand. But he wasn't expecting to get bombarded with numerous calls relating to a murdered informant found in the East River. He stood up from his chair, stretched his stiffening neck, and walked his super-lean six-foot, three-inch frame over to his assistant's desk and slammed his hand on it.

"Pri, what the hell's going on? Find Perkins and Stratsburg now."

Priscilla Thompson, who was a middle-aged former beauty queen, had worked for Jeremiah Bolden for more than five years. It was rare to see her boss get irritated about anything. She knew his history and knew he prided himself on demonstrating complete control and professionalism. But there were those rare occasions when he would lose it, and it scared her. She was afraid he would rip someone's head off, and no one would be able to stop him.

Today she saw a man who was about to lose control. She felt something creep up in her throat, and she sipped her herbal mint tea before phoning agents Miguel Perkins and Alex Stratsburg. She'd seen them earlier and suspected they were in one of the conference rooms in the north wing of the building.

Upon hearing Perkins's voice, she told him Executive Director Bolden wanted him and Strasburg in his office immediately. She got off the phone and took another sip of her herbal tea. Multiple lines lit up, and she started answering them one by one.

***

"So, let me get this straight. I've been getting a shitload of calls this morning about a thug who was dragged from the East River last night—a guy who just happened to be one of our informants. You know how I feel about coincidence, right? Now you're telling me you dropped him because he was hustling DTCU and was double-crossing his boss? Is that what you're telling me?" Bolden snapped.

Agent Miguel Perkins thought about what he'd planned to say to keep Bolden from blowing a gasket. Although most people had seen the calm, authoritative side of his boss, he had experienced his volatile side. Bolden fought Miguel on everything. He apparently felt the need to keep a tight leash on what he considered was a walking time-bomb.

Perkins really wasn't looking forward to speaking to his boss because he had to explain why the case on Carl Johnson still wasn't closed. This was yet another setback because even with surveillance and eyewitnesses, most of whom turned up dead or went missing anyway, Carl was untouchable. Perkins needed to find someone who could infiltrate Carl's business so they could finally shut down his operation. Malik had failed them miserably, and now the shithead was dead.

"Director Bolden, Alex and I've been working overtime on the Johnson case. We had a final meeting planned with Malik Friday night, but he never showed."

"Well, the little punk ass got himself killed. Who approved this clown as an informant?"

Miguel and Agent Alex Stratsburg glanced at each other, and Miguel answered. "You did, sir."

Jeremiah stood up and glared at them. "Perkins, are you trying to test me? I swear to God I'll reach over this table and throw you both out on your asses." He sat back down and grabbed the file on his desk. "So, instead of sending this little jerk to jail, you thought it best to recruit him as an informant. How'd that work out for ya? This doesn't make me happy. Not one damn bit."

Alex spoke up this time. "May I say something?"

"What the hell do you wanna say? Do you know how much flak I'm getting about this little punk? I want you to close this Johnson case already. Do I make myself clear? Now, get the hell out of my office."

They walked down the hallway toward their offices.

Stratsburg was pissed off that he hadn't been allowed to share his opinion. "Bolden's a fucking lunatic. We've been working like hell to get the goods on this guy, but does he appreciate what we do? Hell no. Just barks at us like we're stupid."

Perkins gave Stratsburg a half glance. "Johnson is a piece of shit who's been flying below the radar for a while now. The sooner we get him off the street, the sooner we can get Bolden off our asses."

Chapter 4

Deon held a cold compress on his right eye and looked in the mirror. He removed the cloth and squinted when he touched the bruised area on his face. "Assholes," he mumbled. This was the third week in a row they'd come into his shop to shake him down for money. He wasn't sure what to do because he didn't want to make things worse. If he kept paying them, he might have to close down his business. He was doing well, but his new arrangement was becoming terribly expensive.

They were growing more violent with each visit. He knew Benita had seen them enter the shop, and he breathed a sigh of relief when she hadn't come back to see what was going on. He didn't want her to get hurt. He had to figure out how to get out of this complicated situation before something really bad happened.

Hakeem Gibbs and Terrell Frantz had been working for Carl for the past six months. They'd been hired to convince small-business owners to either sell their business to Johnson Holdings or move out of the neighborhood. Either way, Carl got what he wanted, and the business owners got nothing.

Deon's Hair Salon was on their list, and Deon was an easy target for Terrell to harass. He pushed the owner around and even backhanded him across the face. Terrell wasn't worried about his victim going to the police, and he planned on dragging out the torture for as long as he could.

Hakeem and Terrell were also paid to investigate any shady business within Carl's inner circle. When one dealt with people who were not of high moral fiber, it was easy to point them out in a crowd.

One such person was Malik Williams. Terrell had known Malik since they were kids, and they used to be friends before Malik stole his girlfriend. Ever since then, Terrell hated Malik, and revenge caused him to drop a dime on him when he found out Malik was double-crossing Carl. When Hakeem found out Malik was dead, there was no doubt in his mind that Terrell had set the crime in motion. He needed to figure out an exit strategy before he ended up in the East River like Malik.

Miguel Perkins had discovered through a source that two local wannabe gangsters were working for one of Carl's real estate companies. They were responsible for intimidating small-business owners. They were also collecting weekly insurance payoffs on the side, and Miguel knew that was a big no-no when affiliated with the Johnson enterprise. He contacted Stratsburg and another agent to set up surveillance at a local establishment to track the two criminals.

It was about nine p.m. when Miguel entered Ray's Place, a local hangout heavily frequented by the Brooklyn locals, including gangbangers and young college kids. He sat in a chair away from the door, sipped a Corona for about an hour, and watched a mixed martial arts match on the TV suspended behind the bar. He'd familiarized himself with their photos on his phone. He didn't want to miss them when they came in.

When Terrell and Hakeem were done with their daily grind, they made their way to Ray's Place. They showed up close to ten and plopped themselves in a booth opposite Miguel. A young waitress walked over and took their order, but not before the tall, skinny one grabbed her arm. She jerked away from his grasp and stormed off toward the bar.

Miguel paid for his drink and walked past the guys as he made his way to the bathroom. He pressed a button on his jacket and snapped a few photos while the guys were laughing and drinking in the booth.

Miguel walked out of the building and headed across the street to an unmarked van, where agents Stratsburg and Carlos Santos were waiting. They would follow the two thugs once they left the bar, no matter what time they left.

Chapter 5

Fifty-year-old Leroy Jones walked around the packed jiu-jitsu class observing his sparring students. He paid close attention to Benita, one of his top students for the past five years. She wore her new belt, which was placed around her traditional white uniform, as a kyū rank. If she committed herself to training hard over the next six months, she would proceed to the next level and receive the shodan, the first dan, a first-degree black belt.

Sparring with her partner Martin Jackson, Benita kicked him in the leg, knocking him to the floor. She placed her foot over his chest with her hands in a defensive position and shouted, "Kiai!"

"Excellent, Benita. Excellent." Leroy placed his hand on her shoulder and then walked around the room, observing his other students.

Benita bowed. "Thank you, Sensei Leroy."

Humiliated, Martin stood up and whispered mockingly in Benita's ear, "Thank you, Sensei Leroy."

"Whateva, Martin. You always hatin'. Wanna try again?"

Leroy looked at his watch and raised his hand to let his students know the class was coming to an end. They moved into formation and looked at their master teacher in silence.

"Class, the International Jiu-Jitsu Tournament is coming up in four months, and I'm expecting many of you to score high among your peers. I'll be adding additional classes on Saturdays and Sundays for those who need extra time to train. You've all made me proud. Not only have you been training to be top athletes, you're learning to be champions. You're the epitome of what the philosophy of jiu-jitsu is all about."

He bowed, and the students returned with bows.

They yelled in unison, "Honesty, discipline, and respect. Kiai!"

"Class dismissed."

As the students walked out of the classroom, Leroy stopped Benita to discuss the competition. "Have you thought about competing?" he asked her.

"Sensei Leroy, between work and school, I don't think I can do it. I barely have time to train for the next belt level."

"I've watched you excel into an extraordinary athlete, and I know you have what it takes to win. You're one of the most talented students I've ever trained. I know you're busy, but would you please think about it?"

Benita nodded, picked up her water bottle and towel off the floor, and walked to the locker room, where her friend Kimberly Scott was anxious to speak to her.

Kimberly said, "Well?"

"Well, what?"

"Don't play with me. Are you going?"

"Girl, I don't know. I've got a lot on my plate right now."

"But you gotta go. We could be roommates and have a blast."

Benita thought Kimberly was one of the coolest white chicks she'd ever met. Kimberly had moved to Brooklyn from Indiana to attend the Pratt Institute. During her first week at school, she was mugged. So, she decided to sign up for a self-defense class at Leroy's jiu-jitsu school and met Benita. They were instant friends, hanging out all over Brooklyn. Benita taught Kimberly how to fit into the hood without sticking out like some tourist, and Kimberly convinced Benita to pursue her degree in criminal forensics. They complemented each other, and Benita was grateful for this spunky little Midwestern girl from Indiana.

"I told Sensei Leroy like I'm telling you. I don't think I can do it, but I'll think about it. So, you're gonna compete?"

"Hell, yeah. And I'm gonna win. I wanna kick some serious jiu-jitsu ass."

Benita chuckled. She loved how Kimberly had become so fearless. She'd changed a lot in the last five years. Now she would walk late at night in some of the shadiest neighborhoods in New York City. She was always prepared, and she was always looking for a fight. Benita didn't know if it was a good thing or a bad thing, but it was a funny thing.

Placing her arm around Kimberly's shoulder, she walked with her into the women's locker room. "Kimberly, if I decide to compete, you'll be the first to know."

Benita and Kimberly walked out of the school together, gave each other a hug, and walked in opposite directions. Martin was waiting for Benita on the corner. When she walked past him, he tapped her on the back of the shoulder.

"Hey, Benita. Where's the fire?"

Without missing a beat, Benita kept her stride. "What do you want, Martin?"

"How about we go for a drink? We're near Ray's Place. We can stop by there and catch up."

"Not tonight. I gotta get home."

"Come on, Benita. Why are you always turning me down?"

She stopped and faced him. "Sorry. It's been a long day, and I'm tired."

"What's it gonna take for you to go out with me?"

"Let me think about it for a little bit and get back to you."

"One day you're gonna wake up and realize you're letting the best thing slip through your fingers. I ain't always gonna be around waiting for you to get at me."

Benita tapped Martin's cheek with her hand. "Have a good night, Martin." She took off across the street.

Martin shoved his hands down his front pockets and walked in the opposite direction.

Benita looked back to see if Martin was still watching her. When she saw him walking away, she headed toward the bus stop. He was tall, dark, and cute, with a head full of curly black hair. He had an amazing smile, but Benita would never give him a chance—maybe because she had always been attracted to confident and laid-back guys who were not intimidated by her aggressive personality. There was not a person alive she wouldn't stand up to or fight if she had to. She had a bad temper, and it didn't take much to set her off. She was passionate and vocal about things she believed in, and if someone did her wrong, she'd let that person know. No holding back. She was a diva and didn't apologize for it. Little Martin couldn't handle her personality, especially since he was nothing more than a pushover. He acted like a lovesick puppy, and she didn't have the heart to tell him he'd never have a chance with her.

Benita was too busy for any kind of romance, but her family thought she was just avoiding relationships to protect her heart. In high school, she had dated Andre Grant for three years and had fallen in love with him. When he got another girl pregnant, Benita had never felt so much pain. She was heartbroken and never forgave him. She promised she would always put her feelings first, and if it meant not dating while she pursued her dreams, then so be it.

Benita was twenty-five and had plenty of time to fall in love. For now, she focused on her goals. She smiled when she thought about Martin's persistence. But when she saw the bus speed past her, her smile turned into a frown. She crossed the street and waited in front of the bus stop. If the bus didn't come in twenty minutes, she would walk over to Fulton Street and hail a gypsy cab.

She pulled out her iPod and placed the earbuds in her ears. She looked around and noticed a black van parked across the street. It was the only vehicle on either side of her. The area was desolate, and Benita felt a little uneasy when she saw two young guys walking toward her. She stepped back against the building, making sure she kept a clear vision of them once they passed. She had learned a long time ago to always be familiar with her surroundings. As she watched from the corner of her eye, they smiled at each other and then looked back at her. She prayed they would keep walking.

Instead, they stopped near her. They whispered to each other and smiled at Benita. The skinny one pulled out a wad of money and started counting it in front of her before putting it back in his front jean pocket. The other one stepped off the sidewalk and looked in the direction of the bus route. When he didn't see the bus, he turned back around and grinned at Benita. Both men followed her lead and propped up against the building.

"You been waiting long?" one of them asked.

Benita tried to focus on her music. Without missing a beat and without removing her earbuds, she said, "Nope." She hoped the conversation had ended.

"So, what's a pretty girl like you standing out here by yo'self. You ain't got a man to pick you up?"

Benita was appalled by his question and wanted to respond, wanted to verbally slap some sense into his empty head, but she really just wanted to be left alone. Here he apparently thought he would impress her with his wad of cash, but instead, it just annoyed her. And now this guy's corny approach was annoying her even more.

He apparently wasn't getting the hint. "Hello? Foxy lady? You listening to me? What's your name, baby?"

Benita finally removed her earbuds and put her iPod in her bag. She crossed her arms and faced Mr. Skinny. "I don't know you, and my grandmother always told me not to speak to strangers."

"Come on, girl. Why you trippin'? Look, my name's Terrell. This here's Hakeem. Now you know us. Satisfied?"

Terrell took two steps forward, but Benita blocked him with her hand. "Step back, man."

"Listen, ma. I think we got off on the wrong foot. Me and my man ain't bad dudes. We just trying to be friendly."

"Well, Terrell, you need to back the hell up."

Hakeem snickered at his boy getting dissed by the lady. "She trying to tell you something, T."

Benita shoved her hand inside her jacket pocket and pulled out a box of breath mints. "How about you take one of these Tic Tacs and keep it movin'? I just want to wait for my bus in peace."

Hakeem laughed. "Come on, man. We gotta go. Leave the lady alone, will ya?"

"Shit, she ain't no lady. She ain't nothin' but an uppity Brooklyn bitch."

Benita ground her teeth and crossed her arms. She attempted to walk past the guys, but Terrell blocked her path. When she moved in the other direction, Terrell moved and blocked her again.

"Please move."

"Terrell, let her pass, man."

"Hakeem, you stay out of this shit, okay? This is between me and the little bitch."

Benita attempted to push past Terrell, but he grabbed her arm. She jerked her arm away and stared at him.

"You ain't got nothing to say, bitch?"

Benita took two steps closer to Terrell and stood eye to eye with him. "Who you calling a bitch, bitch?"

Terrell opened his arms and started doing a dance. "I don't see nobody else standing here but you, bitch."

He grabbed her by both arms, but Benita quickly pulled away. "I got your bitch right here." She smacked him across the face.

Terrell clenched his jaw. He wasn't letting this broad get away with assaulting him, or more importantly, embarrassing him in front of his boy.

The three DTCU agents sitting outside Ray's Place were mesmerized by the interaction between a young woman and two guys across the street. Agent Santos was wearing oversized headphones, trying to hear the conversation from about a hundred feet away, but it was difficult. However, he was able to get a clear view. Miguel was reading a report when Stratsburg tapped him on the arm and suggested he watch the video screen. Stratsburg was interested in what was happening outside the van.

"Perkins, you gotta see this. Gibbs and Frantz are causing trouble for this young lady."

Miguel looked up from the file and watched the monitor. He was surprised when the young woman slapped Frantz across the face.

"Damn, she got some serious balls on her," Stratsburg commented.

"Or is she just crazy? Yowza! Carlos, can you zoom in closer?" Miguel asked.

Santos zoomed in on the exchange, and the agents watched with great anticipation. Although there was some bit of concern, the agents couldn't break surveillance.

"Santos, call 911. I would feel guilty if something bad happened to that girl," Miguel remarked.

"Terrell, man, you gonna take shit from some chicken head? You may wanna let her know who's in charge."

"This bitch ain't gettin' away with nothing. She gonna pay." Terrell reached for Benita's arm again, but she stepped back and spin-kicked him in the groin. He dropped to the ground in pain. She kicked him again to make sure he didn't get up.

Shocked by this girl's skills, Hakeem tried to bum-rush Benita, but she elbowed him in the neck and punched him in the stomach. As he keeled over, she kicked him in the butt, and he went flying across the pavement.

Benita readjusted her workout bag and stepped over them. She thought for a few seconds and turned back around, looking at the men. "The next time a lady—not a bitch, not a chicken head, but a lady—asks you to leave her alone, you need to listen. You never know who you're gonna meet, and the next one could land you in the hospital." Benita tapped Terrell on the cheek while he cupped his groin. He couldn't speak through the pain.

Benita walked away from the men on the ground. When she got to the corner, two cop cars with sirens blasting and lights flashing flew by her and stopped in front of the men. She flagged down an off-duty cab looking for extra fares and jumped in, heading home.

Benita looked back at the scene and shook her head in disappointment, saying to the cops, "Always late. Where were you when those creeps were harassing me?" She turned around and focused on getting home. It had been a long day, and she looked forward to diving into her bed and getting a good night's sleep.

Miguel, Stratsburg, and Santos watched in utter amazement as the young lady kicked the guys' asses, taunted them, and walked away without a care in the world. Miguel wanted to know who this beautiful woman was.

"She sure seemed prepared," Alex commented.

Santos said, "I've met a few girls like her before, and they're brutal. They attack first and ask questions later."

"It's fascinating when you think about it. They fight for survival. They defend themselves and aren't willing to walk away. Do you think she knew those guys?" Alex asked.

"I don't think so. That skinny one was trying real hard to impress her, but she just ignored them. Then she slapped the shit out of him. She's lucky he didn't pull a gun or a knife."

"She was fearless. They could have really hurt her, but she didn't even break a sweat. Quite entertaining," Miguel Perkins replied.

"Didn't look like they could've hurt her, if you ask me." Alex changed the subject. "What next, boss?" he asked Miguel.

"Since our bad boys will be in jail, let's call it a night."

Miguel reviewed the footage and noticed the words *Leroy's Jiu-Jitsu School* on the woman's bag. He made a mental note to do some research on this fearless badass and find out just who she was.

Chapter 6

It was after eleven when Benita finally walked into the house she shared with her 65-year-old grandmother, Grace, and her 20-year-old brother, Wes. When she heard TV sounds coming from the living room, she tossed her keys in a small bowl sitting on a table by the front door and peeked around the corner. Her family was engrossed in a show about monkeys.

"I'm home."

Grace perked up when she heard Benita's voice. "Hey there, baby. We were getting worried. You don't usually get home this late after practice. You need to call when you're gonna be late."

"Yes, ma'am. I'm sorry. I missed the bus, and the next one didn't come for a long time, so I ended up taking a cab."

Grace gave her granddaughter a huge hug. "Baby, you look so tired. You coming down with something?" She placed her hand on Benita's forehead to check her temperature.

"Between school, work, and jiu-jitsu, I'm just worn out, Grams."

Wes was leaning against a bunch of pillows on the couch and rolled his eyes at his sister. "Grammy, she's all right. That's what happens when you act like you got superpowers or something."

With her hand on her right hip, Benita walked over to Wes and slapped him upside his head. "Look here, Wes, I'm not in the mood for you tonight." She slapped him again.

"Owww! Benita, have you lost your mind?"

Benita and Wes started arguing, and Grace shouted in protest. "Lawd, Lawd, Lawd. Stop bickering, you two. I don't wanna hear it. Not in this house. Now my blood pressure has gone up. Y'all gonna make me have a heart attack."

Benita looked at her grandmother. "Grams, I'm sorry, but Wes started it."

"Yo, Grammy, I was just sitting on this here couch, minding my own business. Then Benita hit me. Not once, but twice."

Grace walked into the kitchen. "Oh, shush, Wes. You're all right. Benita, come on in here and eat your dinner. It's warming up in the oven."

"Thank you, Grams. I'm starving." Benita hit Wes again and left the room before he pushed her away.

"Ow! Benita, stop hitting me."

Grace yelled from the kitchen, "Benita, stop hitting your brother. I don't want him losing the little sense he has left. Takes so much after his father, and he wasn't the brightest bulb in the light fixture."

Benita walked into a clean little galley kitchen, where Grace was busy washing the few remaining dishes. She pulled out a plate of fried chicken, black-eyed peas, and yams from the yellow oven and placed it on the dining table.

"Grams, you know this is too much food. I don't want to be too stuffed when I go to bed."

"Didn't you say you were starving? You don't have to eat all of it. You can take it to work with you tomorrow and have it for lunch. But I need you to eat. I think you're getting too skinny. You need some more meat on them bones."

Benita dug into her meal as they talked about their day. After she finished eating, Benita rubbed her belly in appreciation of Gram's cooking.

As she walked down the long hallway past her brother's bedroom, she peeked in to see if he was sleeping. She laughed when she heard him snoring. Even as a kid, her brother had been such a loud snorer that some of the neighbors would call her grandmother and threaten to call the police if the noise didn't pipe down. How could such a scrawny kid have made so much noise? Nothing much had changed. At twenty, his snoring could still wake the dead.

Although Benita was only five years older, she oftentimes treated him like he was still a kid. She was protective of him, and he often complained she acted more like his mother than his sister. Ever since their mother died, she felt a sense of obligation to make sure he stayed on the straight and narrow. Benita hated Wes's friends and warned him they would ruin his future. Two of his high school friends had already been given hefty sentences for selling drugs, while another became paralyzed when members of his crew were targeted during a drive-by shooting. There were plenty of times Wes told her to mind her own business and let him live his life the way he wanted. She promised herself she would stay on him until he got it through his thick skull. He couldn't depend on their grandmother to take care of them. In fact, they needed to take care of Grams for a change.

Benita flipped on the light switch and glanced around her room, dropping her bag on the floor. She walked to the closet to get her hot pink robe, matching slippers, and a shower cap. She desperately needed a shower to wash away the day's grime and was looking forward to hitting her pillow.

Her cell phone rang, and she retrieved it from the side pocket of her gym bag.

"Hey, girl. Whatcha doing?"

"Hey, Nikki Taylor. Just got home."

"Lemme guess—from karate practice?"

"Uh, you mean jiu-jitsu. But seriously, Nikki, I had a run-in with two thugs harassing me while I was waiting for the bus."

"What happened, girl?" Nikki asked.

"They got outta pocket, and I beat them down."

"What? Why is everybody straight-up crazy?"

"Amen, Nikki. This is what I'm always saying to Wes. Stop hanging out with those criminals. They'll lead you down the wrong road. But he don't listen to me."

"Well, he needs to get it together."

"You know Wes. He's hardheaded."

"Just like his sister."

"You ain't funny, Nikki. What's going on with you?"

"Workin'. I'm getting a little cabin fever. I was calling to see if you wanted to hang out tonight."

"Nah, I'm dawg tired. I was about to take a shower and hit the sack. I can't keep my eyes open."

"Okay, but let's make a plan for this Thursday. I'm pissed off at my mom and her new man. They've been kissing in front of me. How she gonna have a man and I don't? Straight up not fair. We need to find us some hot boos before the winter hits."

Benita laughed at her friend. "Let's focus on you finding a boo, 'cause I'm good."

"You always good, Benita. Never want a boo in your life. I hope you're not still holding a torch for Andre. He's so tired."

"All right, Nikki. I'm getting off the phone now."

"Okay, holla atcha later."

Benita hung up and placed the phone on her side table. Nikki had just put her in a bad mood by mentioning Andre. Maybe she was right, but it was too late to think about it.

Benita took her shower, moisturized her face and body, and put on her pajamas. She climbed under the covers and closed her eyes, curled up in a fetal position, and drifted off into a deep, relaxing sleep.

Chapter 7

Grace stared out the kitchen window. Benita grabbed a bowl from the cabinet and poured herself some cereal and milk, opened the silverware drawer and got a spoon, then sat down at the table. Grace was still looking outside.

"Uh, Grams, what are you looking at?"

"There's a van outside, and I'm trying to see what it's doing out there."

Benita stood next to Grace and saw a white utility van parked across the street. She sat back down to finish her cereal. "Grams, it's just a utility van."

"For the past thirty minutes, I haven't seen any workers coming out of it. I'm telling you, something's not right."

"Oh, I see. And this means what?" Benita asked her paranoid grandmother.

"I think the neighbors across the street are under surveillance."

"You mean the white couple with the little baby? Do you think they're terrorists?"

"Hey, anything's possible."

Benita placed her empty cereal bowl in the sink, but Grace shooed her away when she attempted to wash it.

"Well, Grams, I gotta go. We can talk about it tonight."

Without missing a beat, Grace pulled out her binoculars to get a closer look at the van. "All right, baby. Have a good day. Tell Deon he needs to come visit his family."

Benita kissed Grace on the cheek, grabbed her lime-green oversized Juicy bag, and walked out the door.

When Benita arrived at the salon, she tried opening the door, but it was locked. Pulling out her cell phone, she called Deon.

Deon was walking at a slow pace when he eventually opened the door, wearing sunglasses. He wasn't his usual loud and boisterous self. Something was clearly wrong with him.

"Good morning, D. Seems like somebody had a late night," Benita joked.

"Yup. Late night," Deon responded.

Benita noticed Deon holding his right side. "Deon, what's going on with you? Why you holding yourself?"

"Oh, I had a little accident."

"Right. Accident. Listen, I know when something's not right with you. What's going on?"

Deon removed the sunglasses covering his bruised and swollen eyes.

Benita gasped. "Oh my God, Deon. What happened to your face?"

He walked over to a small mirror hanging on the wall and touched the swollen area. He tried laughing, but his face throbbed. He sat at his desk and took a few deep breaths before sharing his story.

Benita remained silent as Deon told her about being the target of a shakedown. They had been coming by his salon for the past month, asking him for a weekly payout. But each week, they increased the amount, and yesterday, the beating started.

"What did they look like?" Benita asked.

"One is tall and skinny, and the other one is short and chubby."

"What are their names?"

"Terry, Teshawn, Terrell? That's it. Terrell."

"Oh, so it was those little shits that did this to you?"

"Benita, you know them?"

"I ran into those clowns last night after practice. If I had known they were harassing you, or better yet, beating on you, I would have put a bigger hurting on them."

Deon gave his cousin a worried look. "Wait, you got into a fight with them?"

"Yes, Deon. They came at me when I was waiting at the bus stop, and I had no choice but to put them both down."

"Oh, no. Benita. You can't be doing that. These guys are dangerous. You gonna get yourself hurt out there in these streets. Please be careful."

Comforting Deon, Benita took his hand.

"Deon, don't worry about anything. I'll make sure no one bothers you again. Okay? Now, why don't you go in the back and rest? I'll take care of the clients today."

"Okay, I think I'll take you up on that offer. Didn't get much sleep last night."

Deon slowly got up from his seat, put back on his sunglasses, and walked to the back of the salon.

Benita slammed her hand on the desk.

"Those little pricks are gonna pay for what they did to him."

Pulling out her phone, she made a call to Nikki's brother. If there was anyone who could stop these guys without blinking an eye, it would be Ted. She hated contacting him, but she would do anything to protect family.

Chapter 8

After jiu-jitsu, Benita walked past the bus stop on Livingston Street and headed to Ray's Place. She looked around to see if T-Bone was waiting for her, but she had arrived before he did. She looked at her watch and then moved to the bar, where she saw her old friend, Joe Lewis.

"Hey there, hot thang. What are you doing here?"

Benita reached across the bar and gave him a hug and kiss. "Joe, sweetie pie. When did you get back?"

Joe flashed his pearly whites and poured her a Bud Light, sliding it over. "About two months ago. I finished my tour in Afghanistan, and I'm out for good. I needed a job, and Ray hired me. Work here six days a week."

Benita took a swig of her beer. "Oh, you're in plenty of trouble, mister. I can't believe you didn't call. You must've inhaled too much dust over there, because my number hasn't changed. My feelings are hurt."

Joe touched her hand to comfort her. "I'm sorry, B. I just needed some time to get my mind right."

"I forgive you this time. Now you've got to make it up to me. Come out with me and my girls next week. Ladies' night."

"Maybe. I'll let you know."

"What's it been, like, two years since I've seen you last?"

"Something like that." He smiled at Benita.

"What?"

"You look good."

"Thanks. You look good too."

"What are you doing here so late?"

Benita shifted her body toward the front door. She didn't want to miss T-Bone coming in. "I'm meeting Ted. Have you seen him?"

"T-Bone? Nah. Dude's bad news. What you've gotten yourself into?"

"Some people are roughing up my cousin Deon. Harassing him for protection money. Just wanna find out if T-Bone knows them."

Joe poured drinks for two of his patrons at the end of the bar. He slid them down and continued looking at Benita. "Why not go to the cops?"

"'Cause Deon's not gonna talk to them."

"B, T-Bone's dangerous."

"Don't worry about me. I can take care of myself."

Joe suddenly looked up. T-Bone walked through the door. "Speak of the devil . . ."

When Benita saw T-Bone, she pulled out her wallet, but Joe dismissed her efforts. She stood up and bumped into a gorgeous guy wearing a baseball cap. They apologized at the same time. Benita gave him a quick glance and then hurried over to T-Bone.

T-Bone smiled when he saw Benita. He gave her a huge bear hug that almost cut off her circulation.

"Ted, man, I can't breathe."

He released her and gave a hearty laugh. At six feet, three inches and three hundred pounds, he was massive and didn't realize his own strength. "Sorry, sweets."

She didn't like T-Bone much and definitely didn't trust him, but he was her only link to finding out about the guys harassing Deon. T-Bone was a bad seed. There was no doubt about it. He'd gone to jail for attempted murder and gun trafficking, but there were two people he treasured—his mother and sister. And since she was his sister's best friend, he loved her too.

"You lookin' good, B. Girl, you better be glad you're my little sister's best friend or else I may have to get a little somethin'-somethin'."

If it were anyone else talking to her this way, she would have dropkicked him in the throat. But she just sat back and dealt with T-Bone's vulgarity, even though it was hard for her. "You'll never change, will you, Ted?"

He winked at her and pointed for her to sit beside him. "Now, miss. What kind of trouble you in?"

"Some dudes are hitting Deon up for money. I was hoping you could ask around and find out who these assholes are."

"Huh, I see. And why you think I could help? You think I'm into some harassing bullshit?"

"Come on, T-Bone. If anybody can get to the bottom of things, it's you. You're a legend."

T-Bone took a gulp of his beer and touched her hand. Like a vulture circling his prey, he put a disturbing grin on his face. "What do I get in return?"

Benita removed his hand. "Ted—or T-Bone or whatever the hell you go by—why does it have to come down to what somebody can do for you? This is Deon. He was there for you when you needed his help. And you can't be there for him? Forget it. I'll find another way to help my cousin."

She stood up and was about to leave the bar when T-Bone stopped her. "Wait. I didn't say I wouldn't do it. Damn, girl. And here I thought my sister was tough. I'll ask around about these dudes. A'ight?"

Benita softened her look and smiled a little at T-Bone. "Thank you. I appreciate it."

"Yeah, yeah. Bitch me out and then you all nice again. You got a name for me?"

"All I know is some dude named Terrell."

"Terrell, huh? Okay, that's a good start."

"Great. Thanks."

"Listen, B, if you change your mind about hooking up . . ."

Benita picked up her bag and shook her head at T-Bone. "You'll never change, will you?"

"For you, I'd change the world."

Miguel was sitting across the room and watched the heated discussion between the beauty and the beast. When he got a closer look, he realized it was the same woman from the other night, the one who'd dropkicked the two hoods. Miguel flipped open his cell phone and texted his surveillance team. He put one of the headphone pieces in his ear and clicked to another application on his phone, connecting him to the conversation between the couple from across the room.

Miguel was more curious about this woman and her affiliation with this big guy. He took a few photos of the couple and of the gym bag she had with her. He paid for his drink and rushed out of the bar.

Outside, Miguel leaned against the building and pulled down his cap. He wanted to get a better look at the young woman as she exited Ray's Place. He hadn't yet gone to the karate studio to ask about her, but that was next on his agenda. He wanted to know who this woman was, and he wasn't going to let her slip through his fingers.

Benita said good-bye to Joe, who was still mixing drinks. He warned her again to be careful when it came to T-Bone because he was bad news. She reassured him everything would be okay. But she had no idea what it meant to make a deal with the devil. Her life was about to change, and she didn't even know it.

Chapter 9

It was eight o'clock in the morning when Leroy unlocked the door to his studio. He had followed the same routine for the past ten years, waking up at five-thirty and working out for ninety minutes. He practiced his techniques of takedowns, escape positions, and submissions. He was a true warrior and a champion. At fifty, he was in tip-top shape and lived by the jiu-jitsu philosophy of respect, discipline, and self-control.

He was caught off guard when he saw a young man wearing a navy blue suit and sunglasses trying to enter his establishment. Leroy blocked the man's way.

"May I help you?

The young man removed his sunglasses and handed him a business card. "Mr. Jones, I'm Agent Miguel Perkins. I was wondering if I could speak to you for a few minutes about one of your students."

Leroy looked at the card and moved aside, letting Perkins enter. "I'm not sure how I can help you."

"I wanna know about a young lady who attends your school."

Leroy crossed his arms in a defensive position. "Which young lady are you referring to?"

Miguel noticed rows of framed pictures enclosed in a trophy case. He walked across the room and stood in front of the case, scanning the photographs. He spotted the young woman from the night before and pointed to a picture of her holding a trophy.

"This woman right here."

Leroy looked at Perkins without expression. "No disrespect, Agent Perkins, but you haven't explained to me why you're here."

"Mr. Jones, I know you used to work for DTCU. From one fellow agent to another, you're obligated to help me."

"I don't give a damn if you were sent here by God. I'm not gonna help you without proper protocol."

Miguel reached into his pocket and pulled out a sealed envelope, handing it over to Leroy, who tore it open and read the words *Kojak - 25765* on a small card.

Leroy balled it up as he took a deep breath and ran his hand over his chin. "Okay, Agent Perkins. What information do you want?"

"Let's start off with her name."

"Benita Renee Jenkins."

"Background?"

"Twenty-five. Extraordinary student, one of my best. Been coming here to my school for five years. She's close to mastering the sport. She's disciplined and works hard at her craft."

"What about school? Employment?"

"Both. She's a full-time hairdresser in Brooklyn and attends John Jay part-time."

"Status? Kids?"

"Unmarried. No kids." He paused. "Her mother died when she was a teenager, and she and her brother were raised by their grandmother. She's a hard worker. Not the type to get into any trouble."

Miguel finished typing information on his iPad and flipped the cover closed. Since this wasn't official business, he needed to tread lightly with this former agent.

"Thank you, Mr. Jones." He exited the school and made his way to the corner and called one of his agents.

"Rodriguez, I need you to research a woman named Benita Renee Jenkins. She lives and works in Brooklyn. Mid-twenties, African American. Works as a hairstylist. She studies jiu-jitsu at Leroy's Martial Arts Studio and is a student at John Jay College."

Miguel ended his call, grabbed a muffin and a cup of coffee, and headed to the unit's satellite office in Cobble Hill, Brooklyn, to prepare for a ten o'clock conference call with his boss. The pressure was mounting for him and his team to close the Johnson case. Although the group was working overtime, it never seemed enough for Bolden.

After the meeting, Miguel was pissed he'd had his ass served to him on a platter. He hated when he had to justify to his boss why his team was working at a snail's pace. It was ironic that Bolden was the hardest on him because Miguel had closed more cases than any other field agent. At thirty-two, Miguel had moved up the ranks at DTCU during his ten-year tenure. He had never let Bolden down before, and he wasn't starting now.

He opened an e-mail Agent Luciana Rodriguez had sent him earlier in the day. He scanned the personal information relating to Benita, but other than confirming what Leroy had said, there was nothing new.

He examined several photos of Benita and scrutinized her stylish clothes and her devilish smile. She wasn't your typical Brooklyn girl. Confident, poised, and beautiful, Benita could bring any man to his knees. He wanted her for his team, and he would do whatever it took to recruit her—whether she liked it or not.

Chapter 10

Dressed in a white, off-the-shoulder T-shirt with a sketched self-portrait silk-screened on the front, black cargo pants, and black platform shoes, Agent Luciana Rodriguez was one of the first customers to walk into Deon's Hair Salon that morning. Her jet-black, shoulder-length hair was swooped up in a loose bun on top of her head, held in place by an oversized clip. As she entered Deon's shop, she looked for the young woman she was assigned to meet.

Luciana had noticed Perkins's excitement over this new recruit, but it wasn't his typical reaction. She hadn't seen any official paperwork on Benita being recruited as a new agent, but then again, her job wasn't to track that info. She just focused on doing the job she'd been assigned. Today, her boss wanted her to do a preliminary background check and observe Benita in her surroundings, and that was what she was going to do.

Luciana smiled at the colorfully dressed man gliding toward her. She noticed he had stopped what he was doing and greeted her with an oversized grin.

He offered his manicured hand and greeted her. "Hello, I'm Deon. I'm the owner of this establishment. May I help you?"

Luciana smiled and shook his hand. "I'm Luciana. I just moved into the neighborhood, and I need to get this mop washed. I've got a meeting later this afternoon, and I just don't have the energy to do it myself."

"Well, you've come to the right place. You'll be more gorgeous than you are now after we get done with you. I'm finishing up a client's hair right now, but if you don't mind waiting, I can take care of you."

"Oh, I'm sort of in a hurry. Is there someone else who can help me?"

Deon looked over at Benita's empty station.

"You know what? I'll see what Benita's doing. She's one of my best stylists. Let me see where she is. Why don't you have a seat, and I'll be right back."

"Gracias."

Rodriguez watched him walk away. He headed to the supply room, where Benita was unpacking hair supplies.

"Benita, can you come take care of a walk-in? She's in a hurry, and I'm still doing Willona's hair. And you know it's gonna take me at least another hour to finish up."

"I don't know why she refuses to perm her hornet's nest. You should tell her the straightening comb went out in the nineties."

"Oh Lawd, I can't tell her that. She's way too hard-headed to listen to anything I say. But in the meantime, I got some serious work to do. I hope my fingers don't lock up after I'm done."

"Okay. Just need a few more minutes to finish up stocking."

"Don't worry about the inventory. Let's get her happy. You know we need the money."

Benita and Deon walked to the front of the shop, and Benita met the stunner who was flipping through a magazine. "Hi, I'm Benita. What can I do for you today?"

"Hi. I'm Luciana. I need a wash and a blowout. I've got an important interview in a couple of hours."

"Oh, sure. I'm here to make you beautiful. But it's not like you have to try hard. Follow me, please."

Benita escorted Luciana to her workstation, where Luciana noticed several photos of Benita and Mary J. Blige, Lil' Kim, and rapper Fabolous. There were also photos of Benita's high school graduation. The other photo that caught Rodriguez's eye was one of Benita with two women and a younger male.

"Oh, I love your photos. Look at you, hobnobbing with the superstars. Impressive."

After Benita removed the hair clip from Luciana's head, she examined the texture of her hair. "Fabolous grew up in my neighborhood. He's mad cool. And smart, too. Love him. Lil' Kim is also from around the way. She just showed up one summer and hit up one of our block parties. A bunch of us were just kicking it, and Kim ate some of my gram's apple pie. Mary J. is my absolute favorite singer in the whole wide world. I met her at one of her listening parties. We just hit it off. She wanted me to do her hair full-time, but I didn't want to travel all over the world and back with her. So, if she's local, then I hook her up."

"Traveling around the world? Why on earth not? That sounds like a dream job to me."

"Yeah, I know, but I didn't want to leave my family. My grandmother isn't getting any younger, and my little brother really needs me. Plus, I'd miss my friends and my clients."

"So how long you've been doing hair?" Luciana asked.

"Since I was twelve. Started off washing hair, then got my cosmetology license, and I've been working here at Deon's ever since."

"Well, you seem to enjoy what you do."

"Yup, I do. Girl, this hair needs a deep condition and a trim. When was the last time you had it done?"

Luciana looked in the mirror at her hair. She just shrugged. "I don't remember. It's been at least a year. I was working in another state, and I guess I didn't find anyone to take care of me."

"Well, you've come to the right place. I'm gonna hook you up, Ms. Luciana. Let's go over to the washing area."

Benita got down to business and washed Luciana's hair with vigor. She pulled out a Moroccan hair shampoo made from grapeseed and Moroccan oils. She finished up by using a keratin protein pack to seal in the moisture and shine.

Luciana had been neglecting herself ever since she went on her last assignment. She'd been working in a small town fifty miles from the Mexican border in Texas. Her objective was to break up a trafficking ring that was transporting migrants across the Mexican border into the United States. She didn't have time for any type of beauty regimen.

Benita washed Luciana's hair with so much care that Luciana almost forgot she was on assignment. Luciana liked Benita's great personality. She closed her eyes and wondered why Perkins wanted her to meet with Benita. She knew he had his reasons, but after four years working together, it didn't do any good trying to get a straight answer from him. In the meantime, she enjoyed being pampered. She couldn't remember the last time she'd been this relaxed and happy.

It was almost noon when Benita finished styling Luciana's hair. The salon, which was empty when Luciana arrived, was now filled with loud chatter from the other hairstylists, Pinkie Baby, Gerard, and Andre. While they were busy taking care of their clients' hair, they shared stories and would break out in laughter at any given time. Clearly, everyone loved coming to the salon because it was a haven for women to relax and enjoy the overall experience.

Benita smiled when Deon touched her shoulder. It was his sign to have her move things along. She didn't mind, because he was efficient and had built a reputation of staying as close to schedule as possible. She was always amazed by how efficient he was. He managed to finish multiple clients while the others were still working on one.

Benita handed Luciana a mirror and swirled the chair around so she could get a full view. Luciana ran her fingers through her new silky jet-black hair.

"Wow! Benita, I don't think my hair has felt this soft in a long time. You know your stuff, don't you?"

Deon yelled across the room to Luciana, "She's been doing hair since she was five years old. Started styling her Barbie. She got talent from her mama, and that woman was a straight-up genius. It just comes natural for some folks."

"Benita, you've got the Midas touch, and you know how to make a woman look and feel beautiful. You can do my hair anytime."

"Thank you, Luciana. I hope you come back soon. One time is not enough to keep your hair healthy. You're way too hot to have such raggedy hair."

Luciana kept staring at herself in the mirror. "Thank you so much. You did an amazing job. I'll hit you up again."

Benita handed Luciana a slip and a business card. "Here ya go. I'm here six days a week in the afternoons. I take classes in the morning. Just call the salon and set up an appointment. But don't wait too long. You need to nourish your hair, my dear. Hope you don't mind my saying, but it looked like you spent a bunch of time on a dry-ass ranch or something. Your hair sure lacked a bunch of moisture."

Luciana smiled and placed the card in her small cloth bag. "I'll be back. Thanks, Benita."

Benita watched Luciana pay her bill and leave the salon. She liked Luciana and could picture hanging out with her. She hoped she'd be back. Benita motioned to Sheila to send over her next client.

Luciana walked out of the hair salon and turned left onto Fourth Avenue toward a black van parked near the fire hydrant. She opened the side door and climbed in.

Miguel was annoyed about having waited more than two hours for Rodriguez, but when he noticed her long and flowing hair, his annoyance subsided. In fact, he was speechless.

Stratsburg was the first to respond. "Wow, Luciana, you look hot."

Luciana smiled and ran her fingers through her hair. "Thank you, Alex. But I can't take the credit. Ms. Jenkins is amazing. She's a genius. If nothing else, she can do hair."

Miguel regained his focus. "Well, what did you find out about her?"

"Besides doing hair since she was a little girl, she has a knack for fashion. She's observant, intuitive, and smart. Book smart and street smart. Her peers respect her. She's getting her degree in forensic science. She loves taking jiu-jitsu classes. Loves movies. She's into music. She loves her family and friends. She dreams of having a fulfilling life."

Miguel listened to Rodriguez brief him and Stratsburg on his new recruit. "Do you think she's trustworthy?"

"I think so. She's focused and has a plan for her life."

Miguel turned on his iPad and started typing Rodriguez's assessment. He needed to think about how he could convince his boss to let him pursue this woman as a new recruit.

For the past five years, he had followed his instincts and recruited some of the best talent in the business. He had singlehandedly created a system to follow top candidates in the CIA, FBI, Homeland Security, and NCIS and recruit them to be part of DTCU. Although most of the recruits had completed their bachelor's degree, Benita was currently enrolled at John Jay College of Criminal Justice. She had demonstrated the ability to take care of herself in a dangerous situation.

Miguel just couldn't shake his excitement when it came to Benita. His gut told him she would work well at the organization, but she was still quite raw. But with the right training, Benita could transition from her "round the way" persona and become a sophisticated, poised, and effective agent.

Perkins would have to create the perfect scenario, guaranteeing Benita would work for DTCU and leave her family and friends behind. He now had to convince his boss to bring Benita into the fold.

Chapter 11

Benjamin Mahoney was always nervous when he had to meet with Carl about financial matters. He hated discussing financial losses with him and being the bearer of bad news, because Carl's mood was unpredictable, and he would explode at the drop of a hat. Benjamin had been Carl's financial consultant for the past seven years, and twice when he wanted to resign, Carl threatened to kill him if he tried to leave. Afraid for his life, he did what he was told and prayed that one day Carl would either land in jail or end up dead. But as long as Carl walked around free, he would continue to make Benjamin's life miserable.

Today was no exception. Carl had summoned him to his office, wanting updates on a Mexican deal gone wrong, and the news was going to push Carl over the edge. As Benjamin sat across from Carl, he wished his evil boss would drop dead right there on the spot.

Carl rubbed his chin with his right hand, tapping his customized Mont Blanc pen on his oversized mahogany desk. "So, how much did I lose in the Mexico deal?"

Benjamin took off his black, square-framed eyeglasses and cleaned off the speck of dirt stuck to his lens with his thumb. He usually kept a white handkerchief in his jacket pocket for this purpose, but today he'd left it home. Placing his glasses back on the bridge of his nose,

Benjamin scrolled down to the bottom of the spreadsheet to the grand total on his iPad.

"One point five million."

"Damn. A lot of pesos. Muthafuckin' asshole stole my shit and caused a big-ass hole in my pocket." Carl threw the pen across the room, and it flew past Benjamin's ear. "This shit doesn't make me happy, Mahoney. How long will it take for me to recoup?"

"Six months or longer. But if you're planning on investing any more money, we need to set up another offshore account to hide your assets."

"Fine, handle it. I didn't know I could make so much money from selling bootleg DVDs and CDs in Mexico. Did you know the United States loses more than three hundred million dollars a year to Mexican bootleggers? Shit, then it hit me. All I had to do was hook up with some of those bootleggin' fuckers to make twice the amount of money I was making here in the States. I'm a muthafuckin' genius. Sometimes I surprise myself."

Benjamin sat there listening to Carl rant about how smart he was. He never interrupted, no matter how much he wanted to. The one time he interrupted Carl, the maniac jumped over the desk and choked him, forcing him to apologize. From that point on, he kept his mouth shut.

"All right, Mahoney. Thank you for the updates, but now it's time for you to get the fuck out of my office. Time is money, and I got a lot of money to make."

Benjamin stood up and made a beeline for the door. He wanted nothing more than to get the hell away from his deranged, homicidal boss.

T-Bone hated Carl. He wished he'd killed him years ago when he had the chance, when they both worked for

D Rod. Carl had positioned himself to be the drug dealer's number two. In fact, Carl and D-Rod became so close that he loaned Carl money to jump-start his music career. T-Bone slipped in the ranks and eventually took the fall for a botched drug deal. Carl was responsible for the drug deal gone wrong, and T-Bone wasted no time beating the shit out of him.

T-bone was later arrested on class A and B felony possession drug charges and was sentenced to eight to twenty years in the New York State Penitentiary. While Carl was becoming a successful businessman, T-Bone was rotting in prison. He served hard time in maximum security and made some serious enemies and friends alike.

At six feet, three inches tall and 300 pounds of pure muscle, he could bench press more than 400 pounds without breaking a sweat. He was a man without a soul who wasn't afraid to hurt anyone who got in his way. He was a scary dude, and even the meanest of criminals were scared of him.

The first day he started serving his time, he was jumped by two inmates, but he picked them up and threw them against the wall. He broke the neck of one man and cracked open the skull of the other guy. By the time the fight was over, both men were in the infirmary, while T-Bone was sitting in isolation. Afterward, no one messed with T-Bone.

He ended up serving only five years of his sentence, but he never forgot how Carl had been responsible for landing him in jail. What brought him joy was his obsession with bringing Carl down. He started making anonymous phone calls to the feds about Carl's illegal dealings. It was just a matter of time before Carl would slip up and end up in jail. T-Bone hoped he'd see the day Carl's empire went up in smoke.

Thanks to those little fuck-ups Terrell and Hakeem, T-Bone found out Carl was behind the small-business shakedown in Brooklyn. Although he promised Benita he would warn these little assholes to stay away from her cousin, he had bigger plans for the information he beat out of their punk asses.

Earlier in the evening, T-Bone had gotten word that Terrell and his partner, Hakeem, had been released from jail and were headed over to Ray's Place for a quick drink. He had two members of his crew, Baby Boy and Pretty Ricky, wait by T-Bone's Chevrolet Tahoe and grab them before they entered the bar.

As the fellas approached the entrance, Pretty Ricky yelled for Terrell to come over to where they were standing.

"Yo, Terrell. What up, dog?"

Terrell apparently didn't recognize either man and gave the one who spoke a quick acknowledgment.

"Yo, Terrell. I said what up, dog?"

Terrell turned toward the guy and spread out his arms as if ready to fight. "Nigga, whatchu want? I don't know you. I think you better keep it movin'."

Pretty Ricky turned to Baby Boy, who tapped his buddy in the chest. "Do you believe this little nigga? Talking smack after getting beat up by a Brooklyn chick. His mama probably proud. You know what I'm saying?"

Terrell turned to Hakeem, steamed by the diss. He charged toward Pretty Ricky, but Baby Boy punched him in the face, sending Terrell flying backward. Hakeem looked on in horror but charged at the oversized bullies. Baby Boy grabbed Hakeem by the T-shirt and pushed him into the door of the Tahoe. Hakeem fell to the ground, and T-Bone's crew picked the guys up and threw them in the back seat. They shut the door, got in the car, and drove down the street to an abandoned building underneath the Brooklyn Bridge.

Terrell and Hakeem looked at each other.

"What the fuck are you guys doing? We ain't got no beef with you," Terrell screamed.

Pretty Ricky turned around and backhanded Terrell across the face. "Shut the fuck up."

Pretty Ricky dialed a number. "We got these clowns in the back seat. Yup. We'll be there in about ten minutes."

The Escalade pulled up to a dead-end street, and Baby Boy and Pretty Ricky pulled Terrell and Hakeem out of the car, dragging them toward T-Bone.

"Gentlemen, so glad you could make it. I'm sure you're curious why my crew is fuckin' with you. Well, it has come to my attention that you're making trouble for small-business owners in my territory, and that don't sit too well with me."

Terrell said, "Excuse me, but who the hell are you?"

T-Bone started laughing and nodded at Baby Boy, who walked in front of Terrell and punched him in the stomach. Terrell bent over, but Baby Boy punched him in the gut again, causing him to drop to the ground.

"I'm T-Bone."

"Oh, shit. You're T-Bone?" Hakeem asked. "What the hell you want with us? For real, we ain't got no beef with you. We're just trying to make a living, playa. That's all."

"First of all, I ain't your playa. Second, you absolutely got beef with me. Who you workin' for?"

Hakeem didn't answer, and Pretty Ricky hit him hard in the side. Hakeem folded and fell to the ground.

"Now, I'm gonna ask you again. Who the fuck you work for?"

"Hask—" Hakeem sputtered, catching his breath.

"No, man. Don't say nothing," Terrell said.

Baby Boy kicked Terrell in the face.

Looking horrified, Hakeem answered T-Bone. "A dude named Mahoney."

"Hmm. Never heard his name before. Who's he work for?"

"Don't know."

"I don't believe you. I think you know, Hakeem. You got one more chance before you end up in the East River. You don't want that, do you?" T-Bone calmly asked.

"He ain't answering nothing else, you piece of shit." Terrell staggered to his feet and held on to his side. His eye had already swollen shut, but that didn't stop him from being defiant.

"Terrell, man, chill," Hakeem said, shaking his head. "You makin' it worse." To T-Bone, he said, "Mahoney work for Holiday Johnson. Man's into real estate now and wants to build up his property. That's where we come in."

T-Bone bent down close to Hakeem's face and tapped him on the cheek. "Now, was that so hard? Listen, one other thing. I need Mahoney's number because as of today, you two are out of the protection business."

Hakeem and Terrell looked at each other in complete confusion, too petrified to move.

"Hello? The number, please?"

Baby Boy grabbed hold of Hakeem and shook him. Hakeem pulled out his phone and found Mahoney's number. T-Bone grabbed the phone from him and texted the number to his smartphone.

"It's probably a good idea if you two left town tonight, because if I find out you still here after tomorrow? Baby Boy and Pretty Ricky here are gonna make sure your bodies are buried in concrete." T-Bone pulled out five hundred dollars from his wallet and dropped the bills on the ground near Terrell's feet. "You hear me? There's a new playa, and I've just taken over your territory. Understand?"

They nodded.

T-Bone and his crew left them in pain, but not before hitting them a few more times. T-Bone took out his phone and snapped a photo of Hakeem and Terrell as they lay writhing on the ground. He smiled and placed the phone in his jacket pocket. The picture would come in handy when he met with Hakeem and Terrell's immediate boss.

"Y'all niggas need to count to a hundred and don't move till we gone."

Benita was walking out of her class when her phone buzzed. She looked down and read a text from T-Bone.

Your cousin won't be bothered again. It's taken care of.

Benita breathed a sigh of relief. She couldn't wait to share the good news with Deon. Closing the phone, she placed it back into her orange patent leather tote bag. She headed toward the subway downtown to catch the train that would take her to Brooklyn.

Chapter 12

Miguel Perkins had been up all night, putting together a thorough and extensive file on Benita Renee Jenkins. The more he reviewed his research, the more he liked her, and the more he liked her, the more he was convinced she would be a perfect fit at DTCU. However, he had to convince Bolden to bring this unpolished girl onboard. After flipping through the file one last time, Miguel was ready to fight for his new recruit.

It was seven o'clock in the morning when Miguel stood in front of Bolden's closed door. Just when he was about to walk away, he noticed Bolden and Evan walking down the hallway, laughing and joking with each other. The two men were dressed in identical tailored white shirts, blue paisley ties, and dark-blue dress pants. Mr. B. looked more like a proud father ushering his son to work than the hardcore, in-your-face ex-military operative boss cutting you down at the knees.

During Miguel's tenure at DTCU, he had rarely seen a smile on Bolden's face, let alone seen him laugh. But today was one of those rare occasions. Miguel's stoic and rigid boss was cheerful and happy, walking with Evan, the mailroom guy.

Bolden spotted Miguel waiting in front of his office. He was caught off guard and seemed annoyed. He'd always demonstrated nothing but a strong, serious side to his employees, but this particular morning, Miguel had seen a cheerier side of him, and Bolden was clearly irritated.

"Perkins, what the hell are you doing here so early? Aren't you supposed to be closing your cases?" Bolden gave Evan a quick nod, opened the door to his office, and walked past Miguel.

Miguel took a deep breath, walked into the office, and shut the door.

Bolden was already sitting behind his desk when Miguel entered. "What is it, Perkins?"

Miguel dropped a file on his boss's desk. "Benita Renee Jenkins. She's got the makings of a great agent."

Bolden opened the file and quickly reviewed the contents. "Am I reading this correctly? A damn hairdresser? Is this some kind of joke? You playing me for a fool, Perkins?"

"No, sir. She's the perfect person to infiltrate Johnson's organization."

"Perkins, take this and get out of my office."

As Bolden tried to hand the file back to him, Miguel sat down in the chair facing his boss. "Sir, let me explain."

"Go ahead, Perkins, but make it quick."

"She's focused and smart and wants to work in law enforcement. She's aggressive and tough. I've seen her handle herself under extreme pressure. She's trained in martial arts. She's the kind of recruit you've trained me to spot."

"Yeah, yeah, yeah. But I don't see anywhere in your report she wants to work for DTCU or any of our affiliations. Hell, she doesn't even have her degree."

"Yeah, well, this is why I'm here. I need to convince her."

Bolden took a long, hard look at Perkins before commenting. Perkins had shown amazing judgment in the past when it came to choosing recruits, but this possible recruit troubled him. In fact, it made him nervous when he thought about bringing in some young woman who was a damned hairdresser. What in the world was Perkins thinking?

He picked up the file and glanced at the report. Perkins saw something in this recruit and was hell-bent on getting this woman to work at DTCU. "Fine, Perkins. Do what you have to do."

"Thank you, Mr. B."

"But, Perkins, if you fail—"

"Have I ever let you down, Director?"

Jeremiah grunted and kicked him out of his office. He liked Perkins, maybe because he reminded Jeremiah of himself when he started in his career. They butted heads because they both were both headstrong, and Perkins sometimes had a hard time following authority.

Shrugging off his uneasiness, Jeremiah looked through the file again. He raised his eyebrows when he saw the name Leroy Jones. *Well, I'll be damned*, he thought. *Perkins just might be right about this Benita Renee Jenkins.*

Benita was cleaning up her workstation when Deon walked past her on his way to lock the door. He'd been in a much better mood since the shakedowns had stopped. He was back to his happy self and seemed to glide across the floor.

"Well, well, well, Deon. Aren't we in a good mood?"

Deon smiled and sat in the chair beside Benita. "I can't tell you how much I appreciate your help. You've saved me, my little Benita."

"Ah, Deon, you know I'd do anything for you. You're family."

"Now, you didn't do anything illegal, did you?"

Benita rolled her eyes at Deon and placed her hands on her hips. "Come on, Deon. How you gonna ask me that?"

"I'm just saying. I don't want you to get hurt or end up in jail."

Benita smiled as she packed up her bag. She had to get home and change for her ladies' night out with Nikki and Kimberly. She kissed Deon on the cheek, unlocked the door, looking around to make sure no one was hanging around outside the shop, and headed toward the bus.

Chapter 13

Benita had been so busy with work, school, and jiu-jitsu that she couldn't remember the last time she had been out partying with her friends. That night, she was meeting up with Nikki and Kimberly at Le Petit hosted by DJ Master Mic. It was nine o'clock by the time she arrived at the club, and the line was around the corner.

Wearing a super-skintight black halter top paired with white short-shorts and black-and-white platform shoes, Benita's rock-hard body glistened under the streetlights. While waiting in line, she pulled out her silver monogrammed compact mirror and checked out her reflection. She gave herself a little smile before putting the mirror away in her small Marc Jacobs clutch.

Benita turned around when she heard Nikki calling her name. She couldn't believe Nikki was wearing an über-short red dress and thigh-high black boots. The outfit looked good on her, but Nikki's hair was a mess. She also wore too much makeup.

"Benita, your outfit is slammin'."

"Thank you, Nikki. I'm loving your boots."

Nikki stuck her right foot out toward Benita so she could get a better look. "Guess who's performing tonight. Bobby G!"

"What? How do you know?"

Nikki smiled. "I got my ways."

Benita answered her vibrating phone. "Hello? Kimberly, where are you? What? You're already in the club? Okay."

Benita hung up and crossed her arms. "Damn. I'll bet you Kimberly was the first person here when the doors opened. But I ain't complaining. She got us on the list."

"Look what our little white girlfriend can do. She hooks us up. Work it, girl," Nikki commented.

The two made their way to the front of the line and walked over to a petite brunette who was holding a clipboard. Benita gave the girl their names, and then they entered the club.

Brothers Joe and Herb Clarke had transformed Le Petit into a classy and swanky cocktail lounge. With the windows covered with crisscrossed bamboo, the design screamed urban, exotic, and chic. It sported high ceilings, a large dance floor, and an extra-long mahogany bar. The owners had created a place for a mature crowd, and they required their patrons to dress to impress. There was a strict dress code: du-rags, baseball caps, sneakers, hoodies, or athletic wear were not allowed in the club. Tight security helped manage the crowd to keep the bad element out. If Le Petit was going to be successful, people had to feel safe to have a good time.

Benita and Nikki made their way through a large crowd to find Kimberly waiting at the bar. They gave each other hugs and kisses.

Nikki placed a hand on her hip and pointed her finger at Kimberly. "Kimberly, you white girls sure are punctual."

Kimberly smiled at Nikki and placed her arm around her shoulder. "Right. And this white girl got you on the VIP list and saved you a seat at the bar. You betta recognize."

"Go 'head, girl. I ain't hatin' on you," Nikki said and then faced Benita. "This place is exactly what this neighborhood needs. A hot spot to compete with Jay-Z's 40/40 Club."

Benita nodded in agreement. "Uh-huh. This place is smokin'. I like it. I'm glad we got in, and it's already packed. Thank you, Kimberly. Hell, without you, we'd still be outside. And y'all know how much I hate lines."

"You ladies are my peeps. You know I always got your back," Kimberly replied.

A gorgeous chocolate bartender with a bald head asked the ladies if they wanted something to drink. Kimberly's back was turned to him, and she flipped her shoulder-length hair to the side when she twirled back around.

"We'll have three Spellbounds, please."

"You got it, pretty lady." He walked away, leaving the ladies to drool over him.

"Damn, Kimberly, you got game up in this piece," Benita commented. "I ain't gonna lie. Dude is fiiiiine. You need to get those digits before we leave tonight."

"What makes you think I don't already got those digits?"

"Well, excuse you. I forgot you ain't a typical white chick. Sassy."

The ladies laughed and looked around the club. While Kimberly and Nikki were commenting on the song rocking in the background, Benita noticed a gorgeous man staring at her. He was wearing a fitted baby-blue V-neck T-shirt and khaki pants. She couldn't place him, but he looked familiar.

Nikki followed Benita's gaze and noticed the attractive man staring at her. "Damn, he's fine. Benita, do you know him? Because if you don't know him, you need to get to know him. For real."

"No, I have no idea who he is."

"Well, it looks like you may have your chance," Kimberly said.

The attractive man approached and flashed a million-dollar smile. "Hello, ladies." He turned to the bartender and threw up three fingers. "Mike, put their drinks on my tab."

"Sure, no problem."

He smiled at the ladies and walked toward the back of the club.

Benita fanned herself and took a long, deep breath. "Damn! Where in the world did he come from? Can't live around here."

Nikki commented, "Well, you need to make it happen. He's interested. And if you don't jump on him, then your girl Kimberly will. Right, Kimberly? Flip your hair again."

The bartender placed three drinks on the bar. "Enjoy," he said before making his way to the other side of the bar.

Benita, Kimberly, and Nikki raised their glasses and toasted to having an amazing night at Le Petit.

DJ Master Mic had been spinning nonstop for the past two hours, and the place was rocking to old-school rap, hip-hop, and gangster rap. Master Mic left no stone unturned. He had an art to his spinning, and every club in town wanted him for their own personal DJ. He commanded big dollars and had no problem turning down clubs who didn't want to pay him his rate.

Master Mic introduced Prince Bobby G Jackson, who performed his first-ever hit single, "Life on the Streets," from his debut album, *Brooklyn G*. The album had reached number one on the Billboard 200 chart and sold more than two million copies. His follow-up album, *Brooklyn Justice,* was number seven on the Billboard 100 and still rising.

While Bobby G performed for the audience, he focused his attention on Benita, Kimberly, and Nikki. They screamed and clapped while mouthing the words to Bobby G's rhymes.

They danced to a few more songs before Benita started complaining. "My feet are killing me."

Nikki looked down at Benita's feet and teased her. "You know every pair of high-heel shoes has an expiration. Those you're wearing, oh, they gave out about an hour ago. Why didn't you bring another pair to change into?"

"I didn't want to bring my big bag. Too corny."

Benita spotted Martin from jiu-jitsu school walking through the crowd toward them. "I didn't know Martin was coming."

"Hey, Benita. What's going on, ladies?"

"Martin. You lookin' kind of cute tonight," Benita replied.

"Thanks. What's up, Kimberly?"

Nikki smiled and interrupted Kimberly before she answered. "Hi, I'm Nikki. Benita's best friend."

"Nice to meet you. You ladies want something to drink from the bar?"

"Sure. Three Kamikazes," Nikki yelled.

Benita noticed the handsome, drink-buying man standing by the restrooms, watching her again. "Uh-uh. A Corona Light for me, please. I'll be back. And oh, thanks, Martin."

Benita disappeared through the crowd and walked up to her admirer, who was leaning against the wall facing the stage.

"Hey," Benita cooed.

"Hey yourself," the man replied as he sipped his drink.

"Okay, you've been staring at me all night. You look familiar. Have we met before?"

He took another sip and looked into Benita's eyes. "I don't think so. I'm Miguel."

"Benita."

"I'm sorry if I've been staring. You're beautiful. I'm sure I'm not the only man in here checking you out."

Benita smiled and shook her head. "Well, thank you. I don't know. You look familiar. You sure we haven't met? I can't remember where I've seen you before, but I never forget a face. Not a face as fine as yours."

"Maybe we should have a drink and talk about where we could have met."

Miguel's phone vibrated in his pocket, and he pulled it out to read a text message. "I'm sorry. I gotta make a call. Can we pick up where we left off?"

"Maybe, if I'm around."

"I'm a betting man. I'll take my chances."

Benita watched Miguel walk away through the crowd, and she made her way to the restrooms. She waited in line as the ladies went in and came out of the bathroom stalls.

When Benita finished, she unknowingly stood next to that snotty bitch Raven Sanborn as she was putting on her lipstick.

"Oh. I thought this was a private event. What the hell are you doing here?" Raven snapped.

"Whatever, Raven. I'm here just like you."

"I doubt it. I was invited. I got plenty of reasons to be here. You probably crashed."

"Raven, you have serious issues."

Raven smirked at Benita and turned back around to the mirror, checking her makeup one last time before bumping into Benita as she left the bathroom. Benita stormed out and walked back over to the bar, where her friends were waiting.

"Benitaaaaaaaaaaaaaaaaaa. I saw you talking to Mr. Wonderful," Nikki commented.

"We had a serious connection. Things were moving right along until he had to make a call. Hopefully I'll see him before we leave. Guess who I saw in the bathroom? Raven."

"For real? She's such a bitch," Nikki said.

Kimberly changed the subject and turned her attention to Martin. "Benita, Martin got us an invitation for an after-party at Carl Johnson's house. We can hang out with Carl and Bobby G."

Benita pushed her bangs out of her eyes. "Nice, but I don't think I can go. I have a busy day tomorrow."

Nikki whined. "Come on, Benita. This party's gonna be off the chain."

Martin touched Benita's arm. "G and I go way back. We used to throw parties back in the day. Carl's place is da bomb. You ladies will have a great time."

"All right, let's do this," Benita responded. When her phone vibrated in her bag, she pulled it out and saw a text message from Joe. She said to her friends, "My boy Joe is outside trying to get in."

Nikki's eyes quickly lit up. "Now, that's a fine glass of chocolate milk. I could slurp him up all day."

"Nikki, if you don't stop—what's wrong with you? Why are you so man crazy?"

"Because I ain't got one. Listen, can you put in a good word for me?"

Benita smiled and looked around for Miguel but was disappointed when there was no sign of him.

The girls took a shot of tequila Martin had ordered, and Benita's phone buzzed again.

Kimberly commented, "Damn, you are one popular broad tonight."

"You know it, woman."

Benita saw the text and was shocked. It was from her brother, Wes. It read: Deon's in hospital. Me and Grams going to Kings.

Benita headed toward the door, but not before Nikki stopped her. "B, what's wrong?"

With tears in her eyes, Benita answered. "Deon. He's in King's County hospital. I gotta go."

"What happened? I'll go with you."

"I don't know what happened. But you stay here, Nikki. You guys go to the party. I'll be okay. I'll talk to you tomorrow, okay?" Benita hugged her friends and headed out the door.

As she was walking out, she ran into Joe.

"Whoa, where you off to?"

Benita started crying. "Deon's in the hospital."

"Let's go. I'll drive you."

"No, I'll be fine. You're already at the front of the line."

"Benita, stop. Let's go."

Benita and Joe walked across the street to the parking garage where his Ford Mustang was parked. Joe paid the attendant and opened the door for Benita. After he slid into the front seat, he held Benita's hand as she cried hysterically.

"Hey. Your cousin's gonna be okay."

"How do you know?"

"Because I'm psychic."

Benita smiled and wiped the tears from her face.

Miguel, who had been standing in front of the club talking on the phone with one of his agents, spotted Benita walking across the street with a tall guy. He watched them get into a red car and zoom down the street. He texted the license plate number to Stratsburg. He needed to know what kind of company the Brooklyn girl kept.

Chapter 14

Benita and Joe rushed into the hospital room, where Grace and Wes were sitting quietly by Deon's side. Shaken when she saw Deon lying motionless, Benita hugged her grandmother.

"Grams, what happened? How is he?"

"He was attacked leaving his salon. The doctor said he has a few broken ribs and a black eye, but he'll be okay. The nurse just gave him a sedative to help him sleep."

Benita couldn't stop crying, and the guilt took over. "Grams, this is my fault."

"Oh, sweetie, you couldn't have known this was gonna happen. You can't blame yourself. Listen, why don't we take this outside and let Deon sleep."

Outside in the waiting area, Benita took a few minutes to pull herself together. She had almost forgotten Joe was there.

"Grams, you remember Joe Lewis? He was nice enough to bring me here."

"Hello, Ms. Jenkins. It's been a long time since I've seen you. You're still as pretty as ever."

"Of course I remember you, Joseph. You're the spittin' image of your grandfather. Handsome and smart. Benita told me you were back from Afghanistan."

"Grams, what happened?"

"Deon was closing up the salon when he was jumped. One of the other business owners saw what was happening and called 911. I got a call that Deon was rushed to the hospital."

Benita couldn't help but think about what might have happened had she gone to the police instead of taking things into her own hands. If she had, Deon might be okay. She wanted to know what "done" meant when Ted let her know he'd handled things. She looked over at Joe, who was holding her grandmother's hand. She should have listened to him and not gotten involved with T-Bone.

Wes was quiet, and Benita put her arms around her brother. "How are you doing, kiddo?"

"I can't believe somebody beat up Deon. What did he do to deserve this?"

Benita didn't have an answer. "I don't know why this happened to Deon, but I can promise you I'm gonna find out who did this to him. Believe it."

Wes nodded. He fought back tears as he pulled away from Benita. He plopped down on the couch beside his grandmother.

Benita went into Deon's room and sat next to him. She held his hand and started crying again. Her heart was breaking as she watched her broken and bruised cousin lying in the hospital bed. If anything happened to him, she would never forgive herself. She needed to fix it. She leaned back in the chair and drifted to sleep.

Two hours had passed when Deon woke. He opened his eyes and turned his head toward a sleeping Benita. He winced in pain, and Benita woke up and leaned toward him.

"Hey, cuz. How you feeling?"

Trying to get comfortable, he just grunted. "Why am I in the hospital?"

"You don't remember?"

Deon flinched when he repositioned himself. "I came out the shop, and two big guys tossed me around like a rag doll."

"Did you recognize them?"

"No, they were big and scary. I've never seen them before."

"Big and scary, huh?"

Benita asked Deon a few more questions, and then he drifted off to sleep. She kissed him on his forehead before leaving the room.

Grace and Wes had fallen asleep on the two couches, and Joe had gotten two cups of coffee. He handed one to Benita, and she thanked him before taking a sip of the nasty beverage.

"Gosh, what do you have to do to get a decent cup of coffee in a hospital?"

"I don't know. Maybe sell your soul to the Devil."

"Ha, funny."

Benita and Joe sat on the windowsill. Joe touched Benita's hand and looked in her eyes. "This wasn't your fault."

Joe was trying to make her feel better, but Benita wasn't having it. "I should have listened to you and never asked Ted for help. He told me he handled things, but I just don't know how he did it. I think he had something to do with Deon getting beat up."

"It doesn't make sense that he would hurt Deon. You can't go around accusing him of doing something like this. He's dangerous, and he'll hurt you if he finds out you're trying to put this on him."

"I just don't understand it. Ted told me he talked to those losers, and I thought everything was taken care of. But then my cousin just happened to get beat up? Something ain't right. Like you said, he's a dangerous dude, and I don't know anyone who would go against him. So, either he lied to me or he put them up to it. Either way, I'm going to find out what's going on."

"Listen, do me a favor. Let me ask around and find out what T-Bone's been up to. Okay?"

"Joe, I don't want you to get hurt too."

"Don't worry about me. I wanna help."

Benita smiled and laid her head on Joe's shoulder. She was happy he was there for her, and right now, she needed him more than she thought.

Two detectives came to the hospital to speak to Deon about the assault, but he was still sleeping when they arrived. Since they were not able to speak to him, they spoke to Benita and her grandmother, who had awakened from her short nap.

"So, did you follow up with the business owner who had called 911?" Grace asked with a stern look on her face. Benita knew her grandmother didn't trust the police because there were many times they didn't do a good job investigating crimes in the black neighborhoods.

"Unfortunately, the owner couldn't provide us with a description of the assailants. When he came out of his building, they ran away without him seeing their faces."

Benita crossed her arms and tapped her right foot. "So, you didn't even get a simple description? Were they tall? Short? Fat? Skinny? White? Black? Nothing? You didn't get any description you can work with?"

One of the detectives tried to defuse the situation before it got out of hand. "Miss, we're following up on every lead. We'll continue with our investigation. Since Mr. Wright is still sleeping, we'll come back later. Have a good morning."

Two hours later, the on-duty nurse came out of Deon's room and notified Benita that if they wanted to see him, they could, but only for a little while because he needed his rest. Benita glanced over at her grandmother and brother, who were stretched out on two of the couches in the waiting room.

She quietly whispered in her grandmother's ear. "Grams, Deon's up."

Grace blinked and looked up at her granddaughter. She slowly pushed herself up and sat up on the couch. "He feeling all right?"

"Why don't we go check on him? Joe, would you take my grandmother in to see Deon? I'll be right in."

Joe helped Grace to her feet and escorted her into Deon's room. Benita sat beside Wes. He was in a deep sleep, with his mouth hanging open. He was the only person who could sleep anywhere, even on a hard pleather couch that was too short for his long, skinny frame.

"Hey, sleepyhead. Deon's awake." Wes didn't wake up immediately, so Benita tugged on his arm. "Come on, Wes. Wake up."

Wes sat up and almost knocked Benita off the couch. "Something happened to Deon? What's going on?"

"Come on. Let's go see our cousin."

Benita and Wes walked into Deon's room and rallied around his bedside. He was in good spirits and seemed to be in less pain than he had been when he first got to the hospital.

"Hey, whatchu all doing here smiling at me?"

Grace said, "Boy, you scared the Devil out of us. Whatchu doing getting beat up? Who you piss off?"

"Just being my fun-loving self, I guess. When am I getting outta here? I got a business to run."

"Nephew, this is what's going to happen. Benita's gonna run the salon while you recover, and you're gonna stay with us after you're released from the hospital. Take time to heal, baby doll. Take time to heal. We got you covered."

"Okay, Auntie Grace. I hear you loud and clear." He knew better than to argue with his aunt. When she put her mind to something, she was like a pit bull gnawing on a leg. He would never hear the end of it if he disagreed with her.

After about an hour of visitation, the nurse kicked the family out of Deon's room because visiting hours were over. He would be staying in the hospital for a few more days. The family said their good-byes and promised to visit him the next day. When Grace asked Benita to call an Uber, Joe volunteered to take them home.

There was little traffic on the road, and ten minutes later, they pulled up in front of the house. Grace and Wes thanked Joe for dropping them off, and they made their way across the street.

Benita stayed behind so she could talk to Joe a little longer. "Thank you for staying half the night with me and my family. I can't tell you how much it meant to me."

"I wasn't gonna let you go through this alone."

Benita reached over and kissed him on the cheek. She got out of the Mustang and waved to him before disappearing into the house.

Joe waited until Benita was out of his sight before pulling away.

Chapter 15

Benjamin was sipping black coffee, looking at the shady characters in the Red Hook Diner as he waited for a man named T-Bone to arrive. He was unsure about how the meeting would go. The "consultants" he hired to get things done for him no matter the cost usually did their jobs and got paid a lot of money to keep their mouths shut. But when this T-Bone character called wanting to discuss future dealings, Benjamin got nervous. He had agreed to meet him at the Red Hook Diner, which was off the beaten path.

As Benjamin finished his coffee, T-Bone and two of his cronies entered the nearly empty diner. He walked over to where Benjamin was sitting and plopped down in the booth across from him.

A petite brunette waitress came to the table and placed a menu in front of T-Bone. "Welcome to Red Hook Diner. What can I get you?"

T-Bone scanned the menu. "Ummmm, let me have the number two and a large OJ."

"Okay, the number two and a large OJ. Anything else?"

"Nope. Thanks, sweetheart."

"Would you like some more coffee?" she asked Benjamin.

"Yes, please."

The waitress finished writing on her pad and did an about-face toward the back of the diner to place his order.

T-Bone turned sideways to stretch his extra thick legs under the table. "So, you're the man who's running shit, huh? Funny, I thought Holiday would've found somebody a little less wimpy."

"So, Mr. T-Bone, how'd you come across my business associates?"

"Oh, you don't need to worry about that. All you need to know is they have retired, and I'm taking over their shit."

Benjamin took another sip of his almost-empty cup of coffee. "I see. Well, Mr. T-Bone, they never mentioned anything to me about a change of ownership. How do I know you're telling me the truth?"

T-Bone's laughter filled the diner, and he didn't care who heard him. He shook his finger at Benjamin. "Ha! You're hilarious, Mahoney. I don't have any reason to lie. Now, we can do this the hard way or the easy way."

"Okay, what do you want?"

When the homely waitress placed a plate of scrambled eggs, sausage, and home fries in front of T-Bone, he smiled at her. She refilled Mahoney's coffee.

"Thank you. Ah, ma'am? Could you bring over some hot sauce? I just love hot sauce," T-Bone said.

She pulled out a small bottle of hot sauce hidden in the pocket of her apron and placed it on the table before walking away.

He turned back to Mahoney. "What do I want? I'm thinking five hundred gees."

"I think you're under the wrong impression about the job Terrell and Hakeem were hired to do."

T-Bone slid his smartphone, with a picture of a bloody Hakeem and Terrell, over to Benjamin. "If I don't get my money, I'll make a few more visits to the business owners, and I can't promise who might end up in the hospital. Then I'll call the police, directing them to you and the Johnson Holding Group. I'm sure your boss won't like having his name dragged through the mud. You know what I'm saying?"

Mahoney couldn't help but think T-Bone was enjoying making him sweat—and he was now sweating bullets.

"You got until Sunday noon to make certain arrangements to get me my five hundred grand."

"I will need more time."

T-Bone smiled. "Sunday, my friend. And oh, you can have this plate. I already ate. About to grab me a bottle of Moët. It's time to celebrate our new business arrangement."

T-Bone and his crew left the diner, leaving Benjamin to figure out his next move. This whole situation was getting out of hand, and if Benjamin didn't resolve this problem, Carl's threats to kill him would come true.

Chapter 16

It had been two weeks since Deon's beating, and he was recuperating at Benita's house. She had taken a leave from school to run her cousin's business. As she looked through Deon's paperwork, she had found a single business card with the words *Gold Starr Corporation* and an e-mail address on it.

She picked up the phone and called Deon. "Hey, question for you. What's Gold Starr Corporation? Is it one of your vendors?"

"No, that skinny thug Terrell gave me the card the first time he came by the shop."

"Oh, okay."

"You haven't seen them come to the salon, have you?"

"No, no. Everything's quiet. I've got everything under control. How are you feeling today, Deon?"

"I'm doing better, but Aunt Grace is staring hard at me. I gotta go. See ya when you get home."

"See ya later.

Benita hung up and started researching Gold Starr Corporation on the computer. "Damn it. What kind of nonsense is this? The website doesn't have anything on it."

Sheila knocked on the office door, and Benita looked up from the laptop.

"Benita, can you take on a walk-in?"

"I'm pretty swamped back here. I don't know how Deon does it. Can you get somebody else to take on the client?"

"A Luciana is asking for you."

Benita closed the laptop and walked to the front of the shop. "Luciana, how are you?"

"I'm sorry it's short notice, but I need your assistance."

"No worries. Come on over to my workstation."

Luciana removed her wool cap, and her hair fell to her shoulders.

Benita examined the condition of her hair. "Let me see. Hmmm . . . much better, my friend. Much better."

Luciana smiled back at Benita as she sat in the swivel chair. "You gave me some real solid advice. I've been conditioning my hair a lot more since."

"Good. So, what do you want done today?"

"Just a wash and blowout."

Benita was much quieter than the first time they'd met.

"Is everything okay? The place is less chatty. What's going on?" Luciana asked.

Benita bit her lip as she combed Luciana's hair with her fingers. "It's been a rough two weeks. My cousin is out on medical leave. I guess everyone is sad he's not here."

"Oh, I'm sorry. Is he okay?"

"Yeah. Thank goodness."

"If you don't mind my asking, what happened?"

"He was attacked after closing up the salon. The attackers got away, and my cousin was rushed to the hospital. It was scary to see him all black and blue. I swear, if I ever get my hands on the ones who beat him up, they're gonna get a serious beat down."

Luciana listened to Benita rant about the unfortunate circumstances. She also asked Benita questions, probing her for more information. "Why would anyone want to attack your cousin? Has this been happening in the neighborhood?"

Benita generally didn't divulge too much personal business with her clients, but she just needed to vent. She'd been ignoring Nikki's calls because she didn't want to discuss T-Bone's involvement. It must suck to have a criminal brother. She knew Nikki would just defend him and chew Benita out for not having any real proof.

"Some thugs have been going through the neighborhood, extorting money and taking over folks' businesses. My cousin got caught in the crossfire."

"Wow. What are the police doing about it?"

"Nothing. Not a damn thing."

"Just terrible."

"Yeah, but I'm not gonna let anything happen to my cousin."

"What are you going to do?"

"I'm not sure. Right now, I got a few leads that I'm working on. I won't stop until I find out who was responsible for putting him in the hospital."

Benita's cell rang, and Joe's number popped up.

"Excuse me for a minute. I need to take this."

"Hey, Joe. Uh-huh. Uh-huh. Yup. I'll be there. Sunday at two. At the bar. Okay. Thanks so much. I owe you. Yeah, I'll make it up to you. Lata."

Benita ended the call and went back to blowing out Luciana's hair. Twenty minutes later, she was done.

"Okay, you are good to go."

Touching her locks, Luciana said, "Wow. My hair looks—"

"Gorgeous?" Benita interjected.

Luciana continued running her fingers through her hair. In fact, she couldn't stop looking at it. "Yeah! Oh, here you go."

Luciana handed Benita a twenty-dollar tip and a business card.

"Oh, thank you," Benita replied.

"You're welcome. Let me know when you have time to grab a drink. My number is on the back of the card."

"Thanks, Luciana. I may just take you up on it. It's been a long week, and it's not even over yet."

"Well, okay. I gotta bounce. Thanks again. See you."

"Bye. Sheila, can you send over the next client?"

After Luciana left the shop, she called Perkins, updating him. Benita was in over her head, trying to track down the bad guys who beat up her cousin. Miguel agreed about Benita's safety. They both knew the more she dug into this situation, the more dangerous it could be for her. They needed to keep a closer eye on Benita.

Chapter 17

Joe unlocked the back door to the bar and headed into the office. He had left the door unlocked for Benita. As he walked toward the front, Joe was punched in the stomach. He collapsed to the floor. Someone kicked him in the side, causing him to cry out in pain. He closed his eyes, groaning, and heard a baritone voice coming from above him.

"What the hell are you doing here so early? Damn, you weren't supposed to be here for another hour, Joe."

Joe opened his eyes and saw T-Bone standing over him. "What the hell are you doing here?" he croaked. "Ray didn't tell me you'd be using his bar for your own personal meeting place."

T-Bone roared a hardy laugh and crossed his oversized arms. "Ray lets me do what I do, no questions asked. And you, my friend, are interrupting my meeting."

After casually asking around the bar about T-Bone, Joe had discovered the gangster was working on extorting money from some real estate guy who was buying up property in the neighborhood. He'd also heard the previous dudes had skipped town. Joe had taken it upon himself to go through Ray's security tapes to see if T-Bone could be linked to Hakeem and Terrell. The last image he saw of the two thugs was when they were about to walk into the bar but stopped and turned around, never making their way inside. He never did see T-Bone with them, but he did see T-Bone's sidekicks, Pretty Ricky and Baby Boy, leave the bar thirty minutes before Hakeem and Terrell arrived outside. He could only imagine what had happened to those guys after T-Bone and his goons got hold of them.

"Take him in the back and make sure he stays quiet," T-Bone ordered.

They dragged Joe away by his arms and then kicked him until he passed out on the office floor.

Meanwhile, Benita entered through the back door to meet Joe. She peeked inside and heard moaning coming from the office. She swung open the door and saw Joe curled up on the floor, holding his side. He tried to prop himself up when he saw Benita.

"Joe, what happened?" Benita rushed to his side and tried to help him sit up, but she was having a hard time lifting him.

"T-Bone and his boys," he said, wincing. "They're up front, waiting to conduct some freakin' business."

"Did he mention any names? Maybe he's meeting with Hakeem and Terrell."

"I don't know. They didn't say. Just started punching and kicking. Then his two asshole sidekicks threw me back here. We gotta get out of here."

"No, we can't move you. Something might be broken. Sit tight. I'll be right back."

Joe grabbed Benita's arm. "I know what you're about to do, and I can't let you go out there by yourself. Those animals are dangerous, and I can't protect you."

Benita kissed and rubbed Joe's forehead. "Don't worry about me. You stay put and don't move. I'll be right back."

Joe's breathing was shallow, and he didn't have enough strength to stop Benita from leaving his side. He let go of her and held his side as if it helped him breathe better.

Benita stood up and pulled out her cell phone. She dialed 911 and reported that the on-duty bartender had been attacked at Ray's Place off Livingston. She placed her phone back inside her bag and walked to the front of the bar.

She passed the kitchen and the bathrooms and stopped in her tracks when she heard T-Bone's deep voice coming from the bar. It was hard for her to hear what was being said since the music was blasting. She peeked around the corner at the end of the hallway and tried to remain quiet.

Baby Boy was coming out of the bathroom and saw Benita. He sneaked up behind her and wrapped his big arms around her body, holding her so tight he lifted her off the floor. She kicked her feet and squirmed, trying to get away from his strong grip. She threw her head back and hit his chin, but the only thing she accomplished was causing herself a headache.

"Let me go, asshole," she demanded. "Let me go!"

Baby Boy laughed at her and carried her to the front of the bar. "T-Bone, look who I found sneaking around."

As Benita continued struggling, she felt completely helpless, and that scared her more than anything else. Adrenaline rushed through her body, causing her to move uncontrollably as her heart pounded. Her mind raced as she thought of ways to get out of this man's grip.

"Stop moving, bitch. You ain't gettin' away. I gotchu. I gotchu tight."

"Put me down, you fucking clown." She steadied her breath, trying to calm down, but all she wanted was to

break free and run. Benita stopped moving when she saw
T-Bone. Anger replaced her fear.

The shades on the windows were down, and she
feared that with the music playing, no one would hear her
if she screamed. She looked around the bar to see what
she could use to fight with, in case things got out of hand.
But in the meantime, she thought about her escape route.
Since the men blocked the front door, she would make a
run out the back door.

"Ted, get your goon off me."

"Girl, you better watch yo' mouth. I ain't no goon."

"Yo, Ted, did you hear what I said?"

T-Bone, who was sitting in a booth, stood up and
walked over to Benita. Flashing a huge smile, he touched
her face. "Whatchu doing here, Benita?"

Benita jerked her head back to get away from his
touch. The only thing keeping her from having a break-
down was that she knew the cops were on their way.

"I should be asking you the same thing, Ted. Why you
here?"

"Hmmmmmm. You smell good. You're a fine piece of
ass, you know that?"

If Benita had been free, she would have slapped
him across the face. He was one of the most disgusting
individuals she had ever met. How could he be from the
same bloodline as Nikki?

"I'll make sure I pose that question to your sister and
mother," she snapped.

T-Bone's demeanor changed, and he stepped away
from Benita. "Let her go, man. She ain't worth it."

As Baby Boy released her, she moved away, creating
space between them. She glared at T-Bone, wanting to
knee him in his nuts and kick him in the throat.

"What the hell is wrong with your crazy ass? Why did you have to beat up Joe? Don't you have anything better to do than attack innocent people? I swear. You never should've gotten out of jail. You're just plain old cray-cray."

T-Bone made it a point of not hitting women, but today might be an exception. "I'm not fucking crazy. But you are, bitch. I should snap your little neck in two. You better be glad you're my sister's best friend, because boy, I'd have some real fun with you."

"Ah, save it, Ted. You're nothing but a two-bit hood-lum who fucks up everybody's lives. Your grandmother's probably rolling over in her grave."

"Baby Boy, take her ass in the back and lock her up with that clown Joe. You hear me? Go!"

"I'm not leaving till you tell me what the hell's going on. What happened when you spoke to Hakeem and Terrell? I thought you were the big man in the hood, because it sure seems they didn't listen to you. Deon still got beat up."

"Hey, I did my part. I told them to get out the business and leave town before they ended up incapacitated. That's the last time I seen those niggas."

"Did you have anything to do with Deon getting beat up?"

"It's all a part of the business, baby girl. Nothin' per-sonal." He turned his back to Benita. "Baby Boy, didn't I tell you to take her in the back?"

Baby Boy made a step closer to Benita, but she grabbed an empty beer bottle, smashed it against the side of a table, and pointed it at him. "You come near me, I'll rip your balls off, and you'll be talking two octaves higher than you do now."

Baby Boy turned to T-Bone. "Man, this bitch is insane enough to do it. You want her in the back, you handle her."

T-Bone rolled his eyes and bit his lip. "Whatchu tryin' to do, fuck up my deal?"

"I want answers. Why did Deon get beat up?"

"Because he was collateral damage. That's why."

There was a knock on the front door, and T-Bone looked back at Benita. "Shit. Benita, I swear, you are a pain in my ass."

Pretty Ricky, who had been quiet most of the exchange, spoke up. "T-Bone, want me to open up the door?"

"In a minute." He turned back to Benita. "Girl, get the hell outta here. You don't wanna be around these muthafuckas. I seriously don't want you to get hurt."

"Fine, I'll leave, but you and I ain't finished."

"Whatever, just leave."

Benita walked past Baby Boy while still holding on to the broken beer bottle. She wasn't taking any chances in case he tried to give her another bone-crushing bear hug.

There was another knock on the door, and Pretty Ricky opened it. When T-Bone and Baby Boy turned, Benita doubled back and hid behind the bar. She pulled out her phone and was ready to hit record when T-Bone's meeting started. He was clearly involved in some shady business, and she wanted proof. If she couldn't get him on Deon's beating, she would get him another way.

She peeked around the corner and saw three guys wearing black hoodies and faded baggy jeans enter the place. These guys looked as bad as T-Bone and his two sidekicks.

T-Bone recognized the leader, another hoodlum from a rival Brooklyn gang.

"T-Bone, what up, man?"

"Grimey, whatchu doing here? You representin' Mahoney at Gold Starr?"

"Yeah. That's right."

"Cool. Where's my money?"

Grimey reached into his pocket, pulled out an envelope, and slid it across the bar. "Mahoney said to tell you he's making a one-time offer. Take it or leave it."

T-Bone picked up the envelope and looked inside at fifty thousand dollars. "Man, this ain't what we agreed on. You go back and tell that muthafucka this ain't good enough. I want my fucking payout."

"I don't know what agreement you made with Mahoney, but this is the counteroffer. Take it or leave it," Grimey replied.

T-Bone picked up a stool and threw it in Grimey's direction. "Well, fuck you and your boss. I leave it."

Grimey pulled out his gun and pointed it at T-Bone. "What the fuck? You threw a chair at me? I should smoke your ass right now."

T-Bone walked up to Grimey and placed his chest against the gun. "Then do it. Pull the trigger. Pull the trigger. Muthafucka, pull the goddamn trigger."

Baby Boy and Pretty Ricky pulled out their guns and pointed them at Grimey and his sidekicks, G-Money and Prophet. T-Bone punched Grimey in the face, and he fell to the floor. Prophet, who was standing closest to the bar, reached over the counter, grabbed a half-filled bottle of vodka, and threw it at T-Bone. T-Bone yelped as it hit him in the back. Baby Boy leaped at Prophet, and the two of them fell over a bar chair and landed on the floor. G-Money tackled Pretty Ricky, and they stumbled toward the back of the room near Benita, who had been crouching behind the bar.

The next thing Benita witnessed was a bar filled with vicious attacks among the six men. Benita tried to crawl from behind the bar and head toward the hallway, but she stopped when a glass broke in front of her. She cried out in pain as a shard of glass became embedded in the palm of her hand. She doubled back behind the bar to see if there was anything she could wrap her hand with. She pulled out the half-inch sliver of glass, grabbed a bottle of Jack Daniels, and poured it over the wound. She wrapped a white napkin around the injured hand. She had to get out before she ended up in the crossfire. Where the hell were the cops?

Pretty Ricky was on top of G-Money, pounding him with his fist. Benita heard a gunshot, and when she peered around the corner, the two men were struggling for a loose gun. When Pretty Ricky tried to pick it up, G-Money accidentally knocked it in Benita's direction.

Benita came around the corner and attempted to grab the gun, but Prophet kicked her in the side. He reached for the gun, but Baby Boy grabbed him from behind and sent him flying across the room. Benita saw that Grimey had shot T-Bone in the shoulder, but he was still fighting the scrawny thug.

Benita picked up the gun and slowly stood up, gaining her composure. She pointed the gun toward T-Bone and Grimey. "Hey! Stop fighting! The police are on their way."

"Who the hell is this bitch?" Grimey asked.

"Your worst nightmare," Benita responded.

"Benita, why don't you just get out and let grown folks handle their business?" T-Bone yelled.

"Bitch, give me that gun." Prophet charged at her, but she kicked him in the knee and then hit him with the gun. He went flying forward and hit the ground.

From the corner of her eye, she saw Grimey pointing a gun in her direction, and she leaped behind a table that had been turned over during the battle. T-Bone pushed Baby Boy out of the way, saving Benita from getting shot.

She heard her name and turned her head to see Joe standing by the hallway. As she turned toward the sound of his voice, G-Money shot Joe in the chest, causing him to fall backward. Benita looked over at G-Money, who was now pointing the gun at her. She pulled the trigger, causing G-Money to tumble over a table and chair, where he collapsed dead on the floor.

She ran over to Joe, who was holding on for dear life. She cradled his head and started crying. "Joe, you're gonna be okay. Joe!"

She started shaking him to keep him awake. Blood trickled from his mouth. He passed out in Benita's arms, and the police came rushing into the bar with their guns drawn. Benita was still holding the gun when one of the police officers yelled for her to drop her weapon. She dropped it and continued cradling Joe's head.

Chapter 18

Detective Henry Phillips tapped his pen on the table while Benita sat in the interrogation room, wiping away tears. She was upset about Joe and had been at the police station for what seemed like an eternity. Phillips had written down Benita's version of what happened, but he was having a hard time believing her.

"Okay, Ms. Jenkins, please tell me again just how you ended up at the bar with a gun in your hand."

Benita sighed from exhaustion, way too tired to answer any more questions. "Obviously you didn't understand the first three times. Again, Joe asked me to come by to see him before he started work, but when I got there, I ran into Ted Taylor and his crew. They had beaten Joe up, and then I called the police. The next thing I know, all hell broke loose when Ted got into an argument with the skinny kid named Grimey."

"Do you mean the one you shot and killed?"

"No, I shot the other dude, who shot my friend Joe. How many times do I have to tell you I was protecting myself? You know what? I'm not answering any more questions until I speak to my grandmother. I wanna speak to her now."

"Are you sure you don't wanna clear up a few more things?"

Benita glared at the detective with hatred in her eyes. He wasn't listening to her. He was trying to get her to confess to something she had no control over, and she wasn't taking the rap for T-Bone's illegal activities. Ted was blackmailing someone, and "someone" apparently wasn't letting him get away with it.

"Why don't you go talk to Ted? He can clarify some things for you. Especially since this was his fault."

Benita became somber when she thought about Joe. She had no idea if he was alive or dead, and the detective wasn't willing to answer any of her questions.

"Detective Phillips, is Joe gonna be okay?"

Detective put down his pen and crossed his arms. "Don't you care about Ted? Wanna know how he's doing?"

"I don't care about Ted. I wanna know how Joe's doing."

"He's still in surgery. He's got a real fight on his hands."

Benita breathed a sigh of relief over Joe. "When can I get out of here?"

"I need to verify your story first. You just need to sit tight." Phillips got up from his chair, leaving Benita alone in the room.

Agents Stratsburg and Santos had been headed to Ray's Place to set up surveillance when they saw several Brooklyn cop cars and ambulances blocking the next corner. Santos pulled the van into a small entryway, and the two agents walked down to the corner to get a better look.

"Damn, this bites, man. We've got a shitload of work to do to set up these cameras—"

Stratsburg interrupted Santos. "Wait, is that Benita Jenkins being put inside a cop car?"

"What's she gotten herself into?" Alex asked.

"I don't know, but Miguel is not going to like it," Carlos commented.

Alex expected to have voice mail pick up and was about to leave him a message for his boss when Miguel answered.

"Listen," Stratsburg said, "I thought you might want to know Benita Jenkins might be in some trouble."

"What's happening?"

Alex filled him in, though he didn't have many details yet himself. He added, "I see your buddy Detective Phillips. He must be running the show."

"Thanks."

Miguel hung up with Alex and left a message for Phillips. They'd worked together last year when Phillips's partner, Detective Kevin Michaels, was brutally killed by a gangbanger named Luther "Baby Boy" Ortiz while Michaels was off duty. Phillips had been there with him when they were leaving a local bar. Ortiz got off due to a technicality. Ortiz seemed untouchable, but DTCU stepped in and got him on other charges. He was arrested and sentenced to 325 years in federal prison for interstate drug trafficking and conspiracy to commit murder. After that, Phillips was more than willing to help Miguel with any open drug and murder cases.

An hour later, Phillips returned Miguel's phone call. "What's up, Perkins?"

"I hear you're investigating a shootout at Ray's Place."

"News travels fast, huh? What's up?"

"I'm calling about a young lady who seems to have gotten in the middle of some serious shit. Trying to figure out how she's connected."

"Don't really know how all the pieces fit just yet, but I can say the young lady you're referring to is lucky she didn't get herself killed."

"How many injured?"

"Three people shot. One dead. A young bartender named Joe Lewis is in critical condition. Not sure if he's going to make it. Another guy named Ted Taylor, goes by T-Bone, was shot twice."

"Is he gonna make it?"

"Looks like it. Just got out of surgery. He's recovering at King's County Hospital. I'm sending over two of my detectives to talk to him before we take him to the prison infirmary."

"Do you mind giving me a few hours before you talk to him?"

"You know I can't do that, Perkins."

"Henry, you've got my word I'm not interested in interfering with your current investigation."

Phillips reluctantly agreed to Miguel's request. "Okay, two hours."

"Thanks, man." Miguel hung up with Phillips and made his way over to the hospital to interrogate T-Bone about Benita's involvement.

Chapter 19

It was almost nine o'clock by the time Grace arrived at the police station with Deon and Wes. Her friend Thomas Matthews, a former civil rights attorney, met them at the station. Grace demanded to see her granddaughter. Benita had been there almost five hours by the time she'd been allowed to call her grandmother, and Grace was furious.

The young female police officer looked up to see who was yelling at her. "Ma'am, I suggest you calm yourself before you end up in jail along with your granddaughter."

Grace placed one hand on her hip and banged the top of the counter with her other hand. "Let me tell you something, little girl. You betta learn to respect your elders. Just because your scrawny little tail is looking down on people like me doesn't make you better than any of these people sitting up in here. Now, if you don't want a lawsuit filed against you, I suggest you let my attorney see my granddaughter. You can't just keep her held up in some room. She got rights. You understand, officer?"

The young policewoman picked up the phone and left a message for Detective Phillips. She hung up and went back to flipping through her magazine. "Have a seat, ma'am."

"Look at this—little girl rather read a damn magazine than do her job." Grace was about to continue with her rant, but Wes escorted his grandmother to a seat.

"Grams, you gotta calm down. They know we're here. Mr. Matthews will get her out," he said.

"I can't relax. Not until I see Benita. The nerve of these folks. Have no kind of home training whatsoever."

When Benita had called from jail, Grace knew the girl was in serious trouble. She called her friend Thomas, who agreed to meet her at the police station. They may not listen to Grace, but they knew the power of the words "lawsuit" and "attorney."

Detective Phillips was in the interrogation room with Benita when his phone vibrated. He read a text message, letting him know Benita's attorney was waiting to speak to his client. Phillips looked over at Benita, who had stopped being helpful about an hour ago. He had pushed her too hard, and she was now a lost cause.

He excused himself and headed to the lobby, where he met the attorney and Benita's grandmother, Grace Jenkins. "Good evening. I'm Detective Phillips."

"Thomas Matthews. I'm Benita's attorney, and this is her grandmother, Grace Jenkins. I want to see my client."

"Why the hell do you have my granddaughter? Are you planning on arresting her?" Grace snapped.

Matthews took control. "Grace, please, let me handle this."

"Follow me," Detective Phillips said.

Thomas turned toward Grace. "I got this covered. This shouldn't take too long. Okay? I'll be right back."

Matthews and Phillips disappeared through a set of double doors leading to an interrogation room, where Benita was waiting.

When she saw Thomas, she got up and smiled. "Mr. Matthews. Where's Grams? Did she come with you?"

Thomas had her sit back down. "Your grandmother is in the waiting area. I'm afraid she may end up in a holding cell if she hauls off and smacks a particular female officer. How are you holding up?"

"Tired. That detective keeps asking me the same questions over and over again. Fifteen different ways. I stopped answering his questions and demanded my phone call."

"Good girl. From this point on, you don't speak to anyone without consulting with me first. Got it?"

"Got it. When am I getting out of here?"

"First, I need you to tell me what you told Detective Phillips. You didn't sign anything, did you?"

"No, sir."

"Okay, now tell me what you told him."

Benita recounted her story.

"Okay, let me find out what's going on. You sit tight and behave yourself."

Benita gave her attorney a devious little smile and nodded.

Thomas knocked on the two-way mirror and motioned for the detective to let him out of the room. Phillips opened the door, and Thomas exited to speak to him in private.

"Are you planning on charging Benita with anything? Because the way I see it, she shot her attacker in self-defense."

"She can go, but we're not finished with our investigation. Make sure she doesn't leave town."

"Oh, she's not going anywhere, except out of this place."

Detective Phillips opened the door and motioned for Benita to leave with her attorney. Benita gathered her belongings and walked out without speaking to Phillips. She held Matthews's hand, and they walked to the waiting area, where she met up with her grandmother, brother, and cousin.

Benita ran to her grandmother and started crying, unable to hold back the tears any longer. "Oh, Grams, I'm sorry. I'm sorry."

Grace held her granddaughter close and let her cry in her arms. "It's okay, baby. Let it out. You've had a traumatic day. Let it out. It's gonna be all right. Everything's gonna be all right."

Chapter 20

T-Bone was sleeping when Miguel arrived at the hospital. Miguel had reviewed T-Bone's rap sheet and was surprised he was out of prison after almost killing a fellow inmate. But once he turned state's evidence, he had gotten a "get out of jail free" card and was running around Brooklyn, terrorizing the community. Sometimes Miguel hated having to make a deal with the devil, and it was clear T-Bone was nothing short of being a devil's soldier.

Miguel had also researched Benita's relationship with this bad boy, and he found out T-Bone was the brother of Benita's best friend, Nikki. He had met Nikki that night at the club when he bought them rounds of Kamikazes.

When Miguel saw T-Bone lying on the bed, he was concerned with Benita's involvement with this character. He knew Benita wanted T-Bone's help to find out information about the criminals who had beaten up her cousin. He just wasn't sure how deeply involved she was with this man. It was clear he was a dangerous character who would do anything to save his own skin.

Miguel entered the room and tapped T-Bone on his bandaged shoulder.

T-Bone slowly opened his eyes, still groggy from the drugs he had been given to help him sleep.

"You awake, Mr. Taylor? How you feeling?"

Closing his eyes, he responded. "I've felt better."

Miguel pressed hard on T-Bone's shoulder. "Uh-uh-uh. You can't go back to sleep. We need to clarify some things before the detectives come and haul your ass off to jail."

"Who the hell are you?"

"I'm your worst enemy. You don't wanna fuck with me. I'm gonna ask you a series of questions, and I expect you to answer them. Understand?"

"Whatever you want, man. I need some more drugs."

Just as T-Bone was about to pump morphine from his drip, Miguel removed the small button from T-Bone's reach. He wanted him to be as uncomfortable as possible while he obtained information.

"Uh-uh. No drugs until you answer some questions."

"What the hell, dude? I need my morphine."

"And you'll get it, but not until you tell me what you were doing at Ray's."

"Fuck you! Get me an attorney."

Miguel dug his fingers into T-Bone's wound and placed his hand over T-Bone's mouth, muffling his screams. He then removed his fingers from T-Bone's shoulder but kept his hand over T-Bone's mouth. "You don't make demands on me, muthafucka."

T-Bone tried to push the man away, but the pain was excruciating, so he just lay there, incapacitated.

Miguel repeated his torture tactics and dug his fingers into T-Bone's shoulder again. T-Bone tried to yell for help, but the agent still had T-Bone's mouth covered.

"You ready to tell me what I wanna know? Or do we continue down this painful road? Now, when I remove my hand, you're gonna answer my questions."

T-Bone closed his eyes and nodded. Miguel removed his fingers from T-Bone's wound and pushed the morphine button back to T-Bone.

"Okay, let's try this again. What were you doing at the bar?"

T-Bone pressed the button to his morphine drip, helping him ease the terrible pain. He took a few deep breaths before answering. "You didn't tell me what your name was."

"That's not important. Answer the question."

"I was conducting some business and things got out of hand."

"What kind of business?"

"Real estate."

"T-Bone, you gonna drag this shit out?"

"Okay."

"Were you trying to buy some real estate, or trying to sell some real estate?"

"Neither."

"Explain to me what the hell real estate has to do with anything. Tell me now, or I'll make sure you'll need double the morphine."

T-Bone tried to raise his hand, but his shoulder hurt too much, so he could only move for a little bit. "All right! All right! Damn. Those dudes were representing a guy I was doing business with. Dude was responsible for buying up property from local business owners."

"How did you get involved with this guy?"

"A sweet little birdie told me about some dudes beating up her people and demanding hush money from them. She asked me to have a convo with them. I realized how lucrative their business was, and I decided to get in the game. You know. Get rid of the competition. So, I beat up a few people to make it legit and went straight to the commander in charge to get my paper. However, the commander sent his bullshit representatives. When my terms weren't met, that's when all hell broke loose."

"What's the little birdie's name?"

T-Bone stayed silent.

"What little birdie? What's her name?" Miguel observed T-Bone's reluctance and reached for his shoulder.

"Benita. That's her name. Benita," T-Bone said in a hurry.

"She put this in motion?"

"Nah. Yeah. Never would have known what was going on if she didn't say somethin'."

"How'd she end up at the bar?"

"Meeting that dumbass bartender. She was at the wrong place at the wrong time."

Miguel continued to interrogate T-Bone until he was satisfied he understood Benita's involvement—or lack thereof. But what concerned him was Benita's request to get T-Bone to find those missing Brooklyn thugs.

"One last question. What's the name of the man who set you up?"

"Benjamin Mahoney. He runs Gold Starr."

"Gold Starr?"

"Yeah, found out it's a part of Johnson Holdings and Madd Dogg Records."

"What did you just say?"

"You heard me. Carl Holiday fucking Johnson owns the fucking company. That muthafucka needs to go down."

This was the break Miguel had been looking for—one more step linking Carl Johnson to illegal activities. He just wished it had been with someone other than this parasite. Miguel couldn't believe his luck, and in an instant, he was about to make a deal with the devil.

"Mr. T-Bone, we seem to have the same goals. I think we can come to a mutual understanding. Interested?"

"I've never shied away from a deal. Whatchu offering?"

The last forty-eight hours had been grueling for Benita, and she was exhausted. She'd had a hard time sleeping because of the throbbing ache coming from her hand. She had almost forgotten the glass that had lodged in her palm until her grandmother made note of it. As soon as Benita walked into the house, her grandmother had made her take a long, hot bath and soak her hand and body in Epsom salts. As she eased her body in the tub, she closed her eyes and thought about Joe being in the hospital and her being interrogated for hours by the police.

If it weren't for her grandmother calling Mr. Matthews, she'd probably still be telling her story to the detective. She thought about all those times she had warned her brother, Wes, to stay clear of trouble. And now, due to unforeseen and uncontrollable circumstances, she'd almost gotten herself killed.

She mostly thought about Joe and how he was in the hospital, trying to pull through from a bullet lodged near his heart. He was fighting for his life while she was safe at home with her family. If only she hadn't involved him in the T-Bone situation, he wouldn't have asked her to meet him early at the bar, and she wouldn't have had to kill someone. When she saw the gun pointed at her, her natural instinct was to pull the trigger without any hesitation. She never suspected she had it in herself to kill someone—no matter how bad the situation.

Her hand throbbed, and as she looked at the small gash covering her palm, she started crying uncontrollably. How did she get into so much trouble? All she had wanted was to stop some bad men from beating up her cousin. But now she found herself in big trouble. She wasn't sure what would happen next, but for now, she closed her eyes, wishing everything was nothing more than a dream.

Chapter 21

After a week of restless nights, Benita woke early and went for a long run through the neighborhood to clear her head. All she wanted to do was get her life back to normal.

She took a long shower, wrapped herself in her favorite towel, and then put on her comfy pink Juicy Couture pull-over hoodie and matching velour pants.

Sitting on her bed, she grabbed her phone when it started vibrating. She didn't recognize the number, but she answered anyway.

"Benita? This is Betty Yuille, Joe's aunt. Just wanted you to know Joe's gonna be okay. He got moved out of the ICU this morning, and now he's on the regular floor."

"That's great, Mrs. Yuille. I'm so happy to hear the news. I called the hospital, but they wouldn't give me any information. Thank you so much for calling me."

"You're welcome, baby. Joe told me to call you. He knew you were worried sick about him."

"Joe's a good man. I'm so sorry about what happened."

"Oh, it wasn't your fault, baby. Sometimes things just happen. I'm just happy my nephew is gonna pull through. It's a shame he spent four years fighting in Afghanistan and came back perfectly safe, and then he gets shot in his own back yard."

"Let me know if you need anything. Anything. I'm there for Joe."

Benita hung up, and once again, her eyes filled with tears that began streaming down her face. She had spent a lot of time crying lately. She thought about calling Nikki but decided against it. T-Bone was Nikki's brother, and no matter what, she would take his side. Blood was always thicker than water.

Grace knocked on the door. "Benita, there are two detectives here to speak to you."

"Did they say what they wanted?"

"No, sweetie. Just told me they wanted to ask you a few questions about what happened at the bar."

Benita walked into the living room, where the detectives were waiting. Her grandmother stood beside her as the men introduced themselves.

"Ms. Jenkins, I'm Detective Harrison Green, and this is Detective Lewis Walker. We need a few minutes of your time."

Benita sat on the couch next to her grandmother. She looked over at the detectives and was immediately annoyed that they were there to ask more questions about the shooting. If Benita could have disappeared from this place, she would have.

"What's this about, detectives? Why you harassing my granddaughter?" Grace asked.

"Grams, it's okay. Let them speak."

Detective Green slid over mug shots of Terrell and Hakeem. "Do you know either of these men?"

Benita picked up the photographs and recognized them as the same two guys she had gotten into a fight with on Livingston Avenue weeks ago. "I don't know them personally, but I may have seen them around."

"Oh, really? We hear you have done more than just 'see them around,'" Detective Green responded.

Grace started to get angry and interrupted the questioning. "What in the world are you implying, detective?"

"Grams, calm down."

"I'm not going to calm down until I get some answers. They can't just come up in our house and start asking you questions about some local hoodlums. What do you want, detectives?"

"Mrs. Jenkins, it seems your granddaughter may be involved in a conspiracy to commit murder."

"What? I never asked anybody to kill anybody. I swear."

"Well, we understand you asked Mr. Ted Taylor to have a talk with these two men and to 'take care of them.' Do you remember having a conversation with him about these two men?"

"Listen, I don't know what Ted told you, but I didn't tell him to 'take care of' anybody."

"Well, Ms. Jenkins, these two men have disappeared, and we fear they were, in fact, handled by Ted 'T-Bone' Taylor. He told us you were the mastermind behind this disappearance."

"I don't know anything about any disappearance. I had nothing to do with what Ted may have done to those two men."

She looked at her grandmother with desperation. "Grams, I had nothing to do with this—nothing."

Detective Walker pulled out handcuffs. "Benita Jenkins, you're under arrest for conspiracy to commit murder."

Chapter 22

Benita had been in jail for the past four months, awaiting trial for conspiracy to commit murder. Her attorney, Thomas Matthews, was filing motions to have the case against her dismissed, but twice the paperwork was misplaced, and motion dates kept getting postponed. He met with Assistant DA Albert Harris, a fiery prosecutor known for his fierce victim advocacy, but Harris had no intention of making a deal. He thought Benita Renee Jenkins was the aggressor, not the victim, and she was going to pay for her role in plotting to kill the men who had allegedly caused harm to her cousin.

Restless, she got up and walked over to her small metal desk, where she kept a calendar. She looked at the circled date. The jiu-jitsu competition was happening in Ohio. She thought about how she had blown off Sensei Leroy because of her busy schedule, but now she wished she were competing. Instead, she was stuck in a six-by-six jail cell.

Kimberly had come to visit a few weeks ago and told her she was moving to California for a job. They also talked about the jiu-jitsu competition and her participation, but when Kimberly asked Benita if she had heard from Nikki, she almost started crying. Benita hadn't heard from her best friend since T-Bone was shot and turned state's evidence against Benita. She was angry about how this career criminal could somehow walk away while she was looking at a lengthy sentence for a crime she hadn't committed. This, thanks to T-Bone's "confession" as to her participation in the disappearance of Hakeem and Terrell. What did he gain from setting her up for this? Who had put him up to it? How did the pieces fit?

Benita shook off her anger and started stretching. She wasn't the fashionista she once was. She couldn't wear makeup, and her hair was a mess. She missed her hairpieces and her wigs, but she wasn't allowed to have them. At least she could work on her fitness regimen.

Benita completed 500 sit-ups, 50 dips, push-ups, and 100 kicks and squats.

Just as she was finishing her last squat, Officer Julia Kain walked up to the cell.

"Morning, Benita. I see we're keeping ourselves busy."

Benita was greeted with a huge smile, but she had a hard time returning it. She had never met anyone who loved her job as much as Officer Kain loved hers. Although Benita appreciated her sincerity, she still didn't allow herself to get too close. She kept to herself and observed her surroundings. Growing up in Brooklyn, alienation was a necessary evil to protect oneself from the shady characters in the hood. Her grandmother had always told her that not everyone was trustworthy; it took time for them to prove themselves. Officer Kain was no exception.

"Someone's here to see you."

"Is it my attorney?"

"Nope. Somebody new on the roster."

"I can't go out looking like this. I'm not presentable. I look like holy hell."

"Sorry, Benita. There's nothing I can do about that."

Benita looked in the small mirror near her cot and stroked her hair back. She lightly tapped her cheeks to bring some kind of life back to her face, then rubbed underneath her eyes. There was not much she could do without her hair weaves and makeup. She turned around and walked toward the open cell door.

Officer Kain escorted Benita to the interview room and locked the door behind her. Benita turned around when she heard a deep voice calling her name, and she was completely shocked to see a familiar face.

"Hello, Benita. Have a seat."

She sat across from the handsome stranger she had met once before. "It's you. The guy from the club. What are you doing here?"

Miguel rubbed his goatee before he answered. He'd been keeping tabs on her and doing his own investigation while she sat in jail, awaiting her trial date. His heart skipped a beat when he saw her. He felt bad Benita was in jail, but it was a necessary evil to convince her to join DTCU and forget about her old life.

"I heard about your hard times, and I thought I could help."

Benita seemed surprised. "Why'd you want to help me?"

Miguel stood up and walked over to a small window facing the prison courtyard. With his back to Benita, he said in a deep, monotone voice, "What if I told you there's a way for you to get out of here?"

"Who the hell are you?"

"My name is Agent Miguel Perkins, and I work for a special task force committed to bringing down the worst criminals you could imagine. We've been watching you, and we want you to join the task force."

"We? We who?"

Miguel walked over to Benita's chair and placed his hand on her shoulder. "DTCU needs you."

Benita looked down at her shoulder and then back at Miguel. She pushed his hand away. "Listen, Mr. Agent Man. I don't like people touching me without my permission. Is this some kind of joke? DTCU? Why haven't I heard of this organization?"

"Because it's a secret organization. Do you wanna get out of this conspiracy mess? Or do you wanna stay in here for, let's say, twenty years?"

She looked defeated, and she clasped her hands. "I don't understand any of this. Somehow, I'm accused of plotting two murders that I had nothing to do with. But the real culprit, T-Bone, can say whatever he wants, and people believe him. I'm the victim here."

Miguel sat next to her. Although she looked a mess in her prison garb, not at all glamorous like when he'd first met her, she was still a beautiful woman. He'd hoped she would be free on bail, but her family couldn't come up with the money. Then, the Johnson case had stalled when another informant changed his mind about testifying against Johnson. So, Miguel had a renewed sense of urgency to get her out of this hellhole and train her. She was the right person to infiltrate Johnson's camp, and Miguel needed her immediately. He just had to convince her to work for him.

"Sometimes circumstances lead us down unexpected paths. In your case, by trying to help your cousin get out of a bind, you caused bigger problems for yourself. One simple choice can affect your entire future."

"So, what are my options? Stay in jail or join some secret organization?"

"The sooner you agree, the sooner you can get out of here and start a brand-new life."

"What do I have to give up in return for this brand-new life?"

Miguel smiled. "Good question. I knew I was right about you—always thinking. The bottom line is, your old life will cease to exist. It's going to be hard to just have you walk out of here without coming up with a cover story. There'll be some sort of 'accident,' causing your"—he used air quotes to emphasize the last word—"*death*."

"What? Wait a minute. You gonna kill me off? Are you serious?"

Miguel stared at Benita without blinking. "As a heart attack."

"What kind of life would I have if I can't share it with my family?" Benita asked quietly.

"Freedom, Benita. What kind of life would you have after serving twenty-five-to-life in jail? I know you want better for yourself. Working for DTCU, you can be free to do important things. Change is hard, but I guarantee your life would be exciting. Traveling around the world and creating a life your family would be proud of. Why don't you think about it for a few days?"

Miguel touched Benita's arm and smiled. He left the room, leaving her to envision a new future.

Benita went back to her cell and lay down on her small cot, wiping away the tears streaming down her face. She pulled her legs close to her chest and rocked back and forth until she calmed down. There was a good chance she would go to trial and be found guilty. How would she survive life in the prison system day in and day out? Things would never be the same. But was she strong enough to let her old life go? The one thing she knew for sure was she would not rest until she found out why T-Bone had set her up and who was behind the weekly shakedown.

The thought of putting her family through so much hurt was unbearable. It was as if someone had slapped her in the face—and kept slapping. Her grandmother and little brother meant everything to her. How could she just walk away and act like she was dead?

After tossing and turning for what seemed like hours, she drifted off to a restless sleep.

Chapter 23

Benita walked into the visiting area where Grace, Wes, and Deon were waiting. She dreaded these Sunday dinners because it made her depressed to see her family trying to keep up the happy routine. She had tried to discourage her grandmother from coming to prison every Sunday, but Grace wouldn't take no for an answer.

Today was a special day because it was Benita's birthday. Grace had cooked an incredible spread, including fried chicken, potato salad, green beans, black-eyed peas, glazed ham, turnip greens, sweet potato pie, and peach cobbler. She even made Benita's favorite drink, strawberry Kool-Aid. Grace wanted Benita to have a wonderful celebration with the family.

Benita had a hard time hiding her sadness, and Grace noticed. "What's on your mind?"

"Grams, I'm so sorry for all the problems I've caused."

"Baby, you don't have nothin' to be sorry about. We need to focus on getting you out of here."

Benita gave Grace another hug. Benita looked over at her brother and cousin, who had visited her often during the last four months. Deon had gotten back on his feet and was paying for the attorney. He felt guilty for Benita being in jail. If she hadn't tried to help him, she would be home sleeping in her own bed.

Wes's friend Martin had gotten him a job working for rapper Bobby G. He hoped to eventually get a job working at Madd Dogg Records, Carl Johnson's label, but for now, the pay was good, and he was helping his grandmother as much as he could.

Grace consoled her granddaughter. "Ah, baby, it's gonna be all right. We're gonna get you out of here. You just keep on believing, my love. Hold tight. It's gonna be all right."

Benita held on to her grandmother for dear life. She didn't want to let her go. It was then that she shed her last tears.

"It's gonna be okay, baby, let it out," Grace consoled.

"I love you, Grams. I love all of you. Whatever happens, never forget I love you."

Benita was watching television in the recreation room while braiding her friend Juanita's hair.

"Owww, chica. You're pulling too hard."

"Sorry, Nita."

"What's wrong with you? What you thinking about?"

"I just got a lot on my mind."

Two troublemakers, Marie and Big Girl, walked up to Benita and Juanita. Marie had been in jail for about two months, but she and her sidekick had gained the reputation of being the resident bullies. For some reason, Benita had been the target of Marie's obsession. They tried to bully her as much as they could.

However, Benita wasn't afraid of them and would use her skills to defend herself if necessary. Sensei Leroy had taught her to remain calm, meditate, and be prepared in times of danger.

Benita stayed clear of any trouble while she was in jail. She did her work obligations and kept to herself. The one friend she had made in the joint was Juanita, and they protected each other.

Marie reached to touch Juanita's hair, but Juanita slapped her hand away.

"Juanita, nice hair. Benita, you think you can do my hair? Rumor has it you're some kind of hairdresser."

Benita rolled her eyes at Marie and continued doing Juanita's hair.

Big Girl took a step forward and stood face-to-face with Benita. "Bitch, Marie asked you a question," she barked.

Benita moved past Big Girl and stepped in front of Marie. "The answer is no. No, I can't do anything with your hair. In fact, I'm not at all interested in doing your hair. Now, if you don't mind, beat it."

As Benita walked back behind Juanita's chair, Marie started laughing. She turned to Big Girl and said, "Do you believe this broad? She got some balls on her, don't she? Well, I think it's time I taught her a lesson."

Benita raised her voice about two octaves. "Damn it, Marie. What the hell is your problem?"

"You're my problem."

Juanita stood up between them. "Marie, you heard Benita. Keep it movin'. Nobody wants any trouble with you and your bodyguard, Big Girl."

"Who you calling Big Girl?"

"You, bitch."

Benita didn't want to start a fight. She tried to defuse the situation before things got out of hand. "Marie, we don't want any trouble. Let's just squash it, all right?"

Marie moved in on Benita. She pushed two fingers into her chest. "You don't tell me what the fuck to do. I tell you. Understand?"

Big Girl pushed Juanita down to the ground, and Benita helped Juanita to her feet. "Juanita, you okay, girl?"

"Oh, yeah. I'm about to kick this bitch's ass."

Big Girl jumped toward them, and Benita elbowed her in the chin. She fell hard to the floor. Juanita tried to kick Big Girl in the side, but Big Girl grabbed Juanita's leg, causing her to fall. They started scuffling on the ground.

Marie moved in on Benita with a small knife, who stuck out her leg and tripped Marie, causing her to lose her balance and fall on her back. Benita stepped on Marie's right hand and removed the knife. She then moved her foot and pressed it against Marie's chest.

While Benita was standing over Marie, four guards broke up the fight, apprehended the four women, and carried them off to the lock-up.

Benita was placed in a small, windowless cell, where she remained for twenty-four hours. Although she hadn't started the fight, she got the same punishment as the others. She had discovered early that women in jail had no rights. Most of the time, the guards turned their backs on fights, but it was when things got out of hand that they stepped in to deal with the problem. Everyone involved had to deal with the same consequences.

Benita had tried to keep a low profile while she waited for her trial, but that day's fight was inevitable. Marie had taken things too far when she pulled a knife on her, and Benita had to defend herself, even if meant ending up in isolation. She sat on the floor with her legs crossed and began meditating. She thought about her meeting with

Miguel. She didn't trust him, but she also wanted out of this place.

Miguel was coming to visit her the next day, and she was ready to give him an answer. She spent the remainder of her time visualizing being on the outside with her family and friends. She'd had enough of the current situation and was ready to break free, even if meant sleeping with the enemy.

Chapter 24

Miguel was waiting in the interrogation room when Benita arrived, escorted by another female guard. She plopped down in the chair beside him, crossed her arms, and closed her eyes. She was exhausted after spending the last twenty-four hours in isolation and not getting much sleep.

Tapping his pen on the table, he was the first to speak. "Rough night?"

Benita said, "Don't take this the wrong way, but fuck off."

Miguel gave Benita a slight smile. He was glad she had gotten tired of this place. He had seen the video and enjoyed how she defended herself. But in prison, it didn't matter; everyone paid for their actions.

"Have you made up your mind?"

Benita opened her eyes, uncrossed her arms, and placed her elbows on the table, glaring at Miguel. "When I first saw you, I thought you were the finest man I had ever seen. Tall, nice body, and your swag made my heart skip a beat. And those lips. Oh, those lips. I just wanted to grab your face and kiss those luscious lips. But today, I just wanna punch those lips."

"I'm sorry you feel that way."

Benita rolled her eyes. "Whatever, man. Save your comments for somebody else. What I wanna know is, what kind of organization would keep their agents from their family and friends?"

"An organization that prides itself on keeping everyone safe. This is a dangerous place to work, and we want to protect you and the people closest to you. We recommend our recruits start with a clean slate."

"Recommend? So not everyone's cut off from family? Agent Perkins, things are not adding up for me. My dream wasn't to work for such a heartless organization. This is not what I envisioned for my life."

"Your circumstance is quite different from other recruits'. You don't have a choice. Unless you want to do time, you'll come work for me."

"If I accept your offer, what will you tell my family?"

"You died."

"Oh, hell nah. I refuse to let you put my family through any kind of pain. Are you insane, or are you just crazy?"

"What would you like me to tell them, Benita?"

"You're the smart man with all the answers. Figure it out."

"Fine, a better story."

"How long have you been stalking me? It's just a little too convenient that you're reaching out to me now."

"Benita, you have two options. You can either stay in this hellhole, or you can work for DTCU. Which one would you prefer?"

"Will you be training me? Protecting me? Or will you pass me on to someone else?"

Miguel took a deep breath and felt more at ease. "With the help of others, I'll personally teach you everything I know."

"Listen, I'm not finished. I have a few demands."

"Okay, what are they?" Miguel asked.

"I want three hundred thousand dollars set aside for my family—and a lifetime of free cable. It shouldn't be too difficult for you to do. I mean, you do work for DTCU, don't you?"

"Three hundred thousand and free cable? Not sure about that."

"You came to me, remember? Not the other way around. If you want me to play ball with you, then you need to agree to my demands. I'll join your secret organization, but I need my terms met. Now, why don't you go back and work it out? The ball's in your court now, Agent Perkins."

Benita stood up from the table and walked over to the locked door. She banged hard and yelled for the guard to take her back to her cell. If the organization had this much power, then this was the best way for her to get out of jail. She would do whatever she had to do to make sure she remained an asset, and she would also use DTCU to find out why T-Bone had set her up.

The guard unlocked the metal door, and Benita left without turning around to say good-bye to Miguel. She didn't trust him. He was hiding something from her; she could feel it. But in the meantime, she would use him to her advantage.

Miguel was surprised by Benita's behavior. He thought she'd hit rock bottom and would accept his offer. He'd waited to approach her when he figured she was hanging on for dear life, but she had proven to be tougher than he thought and had come back to him with an offer of her own.

He hated to have to go to his boss and explain her requests. Mr. B. always needed a lot of convincing, no matter what the circumstances. But Miguel had learned a long time ago to always go to his boss with indisputable ammunition that he couldn't discredit or blow off.

He couldn't stop thinking about her. He gathered his thoughts, packed up his briefcase, and headed out the door. He had to come up with an ironclad case before meeting with his boss. Benita would be an amazing asset to the organization as well as for him.

Chapter 25

Miguel stood outside Bolden's office, gearing up for another pow-wow with his temperamental boss. He needed a sign-off on Benita, and he wasn't leaving until he got it. He brought Rodriguez and Stratsburg to back up his case.

"You guys ready?" Miguel asked.

Both nodded.

Miguel, Rodriguez, and Stratsburg walked into Bolden's office and sat in the three empty chairs facing Bolden's desk. Miguel handed Bolden a one-page document.

Bolden glanced it over and looked up, clearly quite angry. "Perkins, what the hell is this?"

"Mr. B, this is the key to solidifying the deal with Benita."

The executive director slammed his fist on his desk. "I'm sick of hearing about this woman. Either she wants to be part of this damned organization or she doesn't. She sounds too much like a loose cannon. That's how she landed in jail in the first place. For God's sake, Perkins, she's a damn criminal. How dare she ask for anything other than getting out of that rat hole? But no, she has the nerve to ask for some bullshit before agreeing to work here. We're not a bank, Perkins. We bring down crime lords and gang members."

Stratsburg interjected. "We do business with criminals all the time, sir."

Bolden was steaming from Stratsburg's comment. "Shut your trap, will ya?"

Miguel replied, "Benita is the key to bringing down Carl Johnson. She's from the streets and can infiltrate where we can't. We've had several inside people who couldn't get close to him. We need her, sir. You were the one who told me to close this case. Well, we keep hitting roadblocks time and time again. It's time we do something different. Benita can do it. She's got the right attitude and the appeal to bring this guy down."

Stratsburg couldn't help himself. He commented again. "She's Delilah, and Johnson's Samson. And a hothead—like Perkins."

Miguel cut Stratsburg off before he said something to ruin his chances of getting a sign-off. "What he's trying to say is she's strong-willed, smart, and can hold her own. She's ready to get out of jail and work for DTCU." He placed his hand on Stratsburg's shoulder to quiet him down. "Director, we can't close this case without her."

Bolden turned to Rodriguez to get her opinion. "What do you think about this woman?"

"Sir, I spent a few hours with her where she works. She made her living as a hairstylist, and a damn good one, I may add, but from my observations, she's a hard worker, focused, and tough. She told me she wanted to eventually work in law enforcement, which is not a stretch for what we do. I have to agree with Perkins. With the right training, she could become an amazing agent. I believe she'll serve as a great asset."

Bolden picked up the paper again and was about to veto Miguel's request when Stratsburg pulled out a DVD.

"Sir, Benita's a little rough around the edges—well, a lot rough—but the girl knows how to kick ass and defend herself. Let me show you something." Stratsburg queued up the DVD of Benita fighting two inmates. "Look how smoothly she knocked down those two women and took away the knife."

Miguel winked at Stratsburg and then turned to Bolden. "Sir, she's in a bad predicament and, even in her worst times, she didn't crack under pressure. She's learned to adapt to her surroundings. She's our secret weapon."

Bolden relented. "All right. Perkins, I'll give you what you need to close the deal with this woman. But I'm warning you now—any slipups with this girl, it's your ass on the line. Do you understand me?"

"Yes, sir. Understood."

Bolden turned to Stratsburg and Rodriguez. "I hope you two hear what I'm saying. I'll also hold both of you accountable if things go wrong. Now, get out of my office and find me three hundred thousand dollars and some damn free cable."

Miguel turned around when Benita entered the interrogation room. He greeted her with a smile. "Good morning. Hope you had a good night's sleep."

Benita wasted no time getting down to business. "Did you work things out? If not, then I'll just go back to my cell."

Miguel reached into his pocket and pulled out an envelope, sliding it across the table. "I think you'll find all your requests have been agreed to by DTCU."

Benita opened the envelope and read the contents. Without saying a word, she folded the letter and placed it back on the table.

Miguel saw the hate in Benita's eyes, and it was the first time he felt bad about it. "We good?"

"Does it matter?"

"That's no way to speak to me, Benita."

"If you think I'm supposed to be happy working for you, then forget it. I'll do my job, but it doesn't mean I'm gonna like it. I care about my family, not about you or this damn group you work for. Do you understand where I'm coming from?"

"Understood. I think we want the same thing."

"You have no idea what I want."

He didn't want to create any more animosity between them, so he decided to wrap things up. "Your grandmother will receive an official letter confirming she won three hundred grand in a contest. She'll also receive a separate letter about her free lifetime cable. Any questions?"

"How am I getting out of here?"

Miguel shifted his body to a more comfortable position. "We're still working out the details."

"You gonna keep your end of the deal, right? You won't tell my family I died?"

"Yes, I'll keep my word. But it's gonna be tricky devising the perfect plan."

"Isn't that what you do? Figure things out?" Benita walked over to the locked door and banged on it.

The guard opened the door and escorted Benita out of the room, leaving Miguel dumbfounded by Benita's attitude toward him. Maybe he was getting more than he bargained for, but it was too late to turn back now. She was to be his greatest challenge, and he'd have to turn things around for both their sakes.

Chapter 26

It was three o'clock in the morning, and Benita lay fully dressed under the light blanket on her cot. She would be free from her hellhole any minute now. It had been two weeks since she'd seen Perkins, but one of the guards had told her to be ready to go tonight. How many times had she envisioned walking out of this damn place? Now the time had finally come.

Two guards unlocked the door, and Benita followed them out. Benita looked around at the other inmates still sleeping. The guards walked her to the east wing of the building, which was off-limits to the inmates unless visiting the warden. Was he part of the plan? As they passed his office, she noticed Miguel speaking to the warden through the window. She felt a little less nervous when she first saw him, but just when their eyes met, Miguel turned away from her and continued his conversation with Warden Christopher Stevenson. Benita bit her lip, thinking about how betrayed she felt by Perkins's actions.

As Stevenson watched Benita and two guards walk past him, he thought about the details of Benita's "escape." He'd been working with DTCU for the past few years, but he resented being forced to comply with the organization's every need. He never thought he would end up shuffling agents in and out of prison, but he had no choice but to follow the agency's requests if he wanted to keep his job.

Three years before, Stevenson was eating alone at his favorite restaurant when a beautiful young woman named Luciana approached him. He wasn't a bad-looking guy, but he lacked the charisma to attract anyone gorgeous. But this particular night, it was as if the heavens had opened up its gates and sent him an angel.

Two hours later, he was back at her duplex apartment in Cobble Hill, Brooklyn, and sitting on her burgundy suede couch, drinking expensive champagne and eating chocolate-covered strawberries. After his second glass of wine, the room began spinning, and he passed out.

Twenty-four hours later, Stevenson woke up in his own bed, wearing nothing but his underwear and black socks. He struggled to get up and made his way to the bathroom, took off the remainder of his clothes, and took a long, hot shower. Later, he walked into his living room, where he found a large manila envelope with his name on it. Inside, he found photos of himself with a chubby stripper. He threw down the photos and plopped on the couch.

He had just been appointed to be Brooklyn's newest warden at the Metropolitan Detention Center, or the MDC. Run by the Bureau of Prisons for the feds, this nine-floor, two-sided jail held about three thousand prisoners in various stages of the criminal justice system process. If these photos got out, his career would be over.

His cell phone rang from a private number.

A deep voice greeted him. "Either cooperate with DTCU or you will lose your job. What's it going to be, warden?"

Stevenson had no other choice but to give in to the blackmail.

Three years later, he was being used by DTCU to stage fights, conduct illegal searches, and "lose" important paperwork. He felt bad for Benita because she had no idea what she was getting herself into. Once you got pulled into working for DTCU, it was impossible to get out.

He watched the agents take Benita out the back door to an unmarked white van. "We done for tonight?" Stevenson asked Perkins.

Perkins turned around from the window. "Yes, for tonight. I'll be in touch."

Stevenson hated Perkins. Karma always had a way of coming back around, and if anyone deserved to pay for his sins, it was Perkins.

Chapter 27

A blindfold was removed before Benita was escorted into a sterile white room located inside DTCU's headquarters. The first person she saw was Miguel, and her eyes turned cold as ice.

"Welcome. I hope your trip was pleasant," Miguel commented.

Benita jumped up from her chair and tried to grab Miguel's neck, but the guards stopped her.

"Take your hands off me, you pricks." Benita jerked her arms away and looked at Miguel with disdain. "Good trip? Are you kidding? I've been riding around all night with the nastiest and rudest people I've ever met. And you sit over there responsible for my bad trip. I hate you right now. I didn't think I could hate someone as much as I hate you, but I do."

Bolden, Stratsburg, and Rodriguez walked into the room where Miguel, Benita, and the guards were waiting.

Bolden held out his hand to give Benita a handshake. "Hello, Ms. Jenkins. I'm Executive Director Jeremiah Bolden. I'm in charge of DTCU's operations and recruitment. I've heard a lot about you. Glad you agreed to join our establishment."

"Really? 'Cause I never heard squat about you."

Bolden laughed at Benita as if she'd told a joke. "Agent Perkins, you never told me Ms. Jenkins was so

funny. Why don't we all sit down and have a little chat."
One of the guards slid Benita's chair closer. She did a
poor job hiding her anger, and now she had regrets about
joining this group. Her life had been in complete chaos
since being thrown in jail. She was second-guessing
herself. How could she be sure she'd made the right
decision to work for DTCU?

At first, she hadn't recognized Rodriguez as the
woman who had come into her salon.

"Oh my God. Luciana? You're an agent too? Wait. You
were spying on me?"

"I was on assignment, but I loved what you did with
my hair. Much appreciated."

"For real? Ain't this some shit. You can't trust anybody
nowadays." Benita looked around at a stark-white, windowless room. The two guards were standing by the door,
and she was surrounded by a group of people who didn't
show an ounce of compassion. She no longer wanted to
be there.

Looking over at Miguel, she wanted to punch him
in his fucking face. "This is bullshit. Send me back. I'd
rather spend the next twenty-five years in prison than sit
here looking at you stone-faced bastards."

Bolden laughed again, making everyone in the room
nervous. "Perkins, she's funny and feisty. Would you like
to address Ms. Jenkins's request?"

"Perkins," she snapped, "you're an asshole. I don't
want to hear anything you've got to say."

Bolden motioned for Benita to remain silent, and she
did what she was told. "I understand you're a little irritated right now. You're tired and had a rough night. But
don't let this experience cloud your judgment. You're
embarking on an amazing journey, and it will change
your life forever."

"Man, are you kidding me? A little irritated? I got a whole boatload of irritation. You could have brought me here yourself. Instead, you sent the most heartless assholes on the planet to drag me here. You told me I could be an invaluable asset to the organization, but I'm nothing but a prisoner beholden to DTCU. I'm sitting in this ugly-ass white room with a bunch of stiff-ass people who don't give a damn about my well-being. I'm just another damn quota for you to fill. Send me back, asshole. Now!"

Miguel was sick of Benita's bitching in front of his boss and coworkers. "You know what, Benita? You're one of the most ungrateful people I've ever met. All I've done was help you reach your full potential."

"Who the hell asked for your help? I don't even know you."

"Well, if you want to go back to prison, then fine."

"I don't ever wanna see your triflin' ass again."

"Fine."

"Fine!"

Bolden couldn't stand the bickering between Miguel and Benita. "Would you two knock it off? What are you two, some old married couple? If I wanted to hear this, I'd call one of my ex-wives. Ms. Jenkins, you're not a prisoner. You're a recruit with special circumstances. Mr. Perkins has convinced me you'd be an important asset to the agency. Now, we could send you back to prison, but you'd be giving up an incredible opportunity to do some good work for your country. Plus, with your temper, I can envision you letting off some steam and kicking some criminals' asses."

Bolden's voice softened. "I promise you'll be treated like everyone else is treated around here. Give it time."

"Let me ask you something, Mr. Bolden. If you were thrown in jail for a crime you didn't commit, approached by a complete stranger to accept an offer keeping you away from your family, and then forced to sneak out in the middle of the night wearing ugly-ass clothes, would you want to be cooperative?"

"Make no mistake. We didn't put a gun in your hand and pull the trigger. Nor did we convince you to get in bed with some bad guys and end up in jail. You did that by yourself. Now, listen to what I'm saying, young lady. Either you learn to play nice, or you go back to jail. Rodriguez, why don't you take Ms. Jenkins to her quarters? I'm sure she'd like to get some rest."

"Yes, sir. Come on, Benita. Let's go." Luciana pressed a huge silver button, opening the door to a long corridor.

Benita, too tired and weak to confront Bolden, followed Luciana to her room.

Bolden started laughing and pointed his finger at his subordinate. "Well, Perkins, she just might be one of the toughest recruits you've ever worked with. Feisty, I tell ya. Feisty!"

Bolden got up from his chair and headed out the door. He turned around and looked back at Perkins. "Try to handle her, will you?"

Bolden disappeared, leaving Perkins and Stratsburg alone to think about the morning's events.

Benita attempted to wash away her troubles from the past six months. She had apparently left one jail cell for another. But at least this one had its own bathroom.

Her bra, panties, socks, T-shirt, jogging suit, and white sneakers were laid out on her bed, freshly laundered.

She picked up a small photo, which she'd hidden in her bra, of her grandmother and brother. Tears ran down her face, but she wiped them away with the back of her hand. She placed the picture under the mattress. She didn't know what to think about DTCU and the people working there. If she were to survive this place, she'd have to play their game—and she planned on being the best player they'd ever seen. She climbed into bed, closed her eyes, and drifted off to sleep, dreaming about how she would one day reunite with her family.

Chapter 28

Agent Samantha DeVreau sat behind her mahogany desk, reading a file on her latest charge, Benita Renee Jenkins. She studied the photo of the attractive young woman and closed the folder, tapping her perfectly manicured red fingernails on the desk, thinking about the right approach to take with this girl.

Benita was hostile toward the agents and the team. She was a challenge, but no one could blame her. She'd been pulled out of her normal life and thrown to the wolves. She had been treated more like a pawn than a person. It was Samantha's job to make her feel human again.

She walked over to the window. A small bird bounced around the sill. She placed her long fingers outside. "Hey, there. I have my own little 'birdie' to deal with. How am I going to get her to see her full potential?"

Samantha had been working for DTCU for the past ten years as a criminal psychologist. She was responsible for training the worst of the worst and turning them into loyal fighting machines for DTCU. Before DTCU, she had served on an international task force geared toward turning terrorists into allies for the United States. She was one of the top experts in her field and specialized in post-traumatic stress disorder cases, where she worked specifically with ex-military who were suffering from the disorder.

One Saturday night, while attending a fundraiser for one of DC's most prominent politicians, she was introduced to military man Jeremiah Nathan Bolden. He was handsome, and Samantha approached him like a sleek black cat checking out her potential prey. They spent the entire night talking about current events and the state of affairs. She invited him back to her apartment for a nightcap. The connection was strong, and they couldn't deny it.

She'd found herself being pulled toward this handsome stranger, and whatever Samantha wanted, she got. Her confidence was overwhelming for the average person, but she had met her match with Jeremiah. They had a passionate affair while he was married. He was private and kept a lot of secrets from her, especially his involvement in the Delta Forces.

When she asked him if he was in Delta Force, he would neither confirm nor deny. These soldiers worked for whoever needed them—the Army, the FBI, or the CIA. They were professional soldiers following their own rules and doing whatever was needed to complete their missions.

As much as Samantha respected Jeremiah's commitment to the military, she was never really able to feel the love he claimed he felt for her. He had many demons buried deep inside him, and Samantha knew all too well from her patients that once a person locked away painful experiences, he could never fully recover. Many times, when she and Jeremiah were together, she didn't feel he was totally there with her. Even when she tried to talk to him about it, he would shut her off or bark at her to stop analyzing him. He was who he was, and if she didn't like it, she could end it.

She truly loved him, but he could never love her the way she needed to be loved. She needed to be with a man who could share his deepest feelings, and Jeremiah had been trained a long time ago to bury the compassionate side of himself. He was a trained assassin who'd learned to play the role, nothing more and nothing less. A year after their first encounter, Samantha ended the relationship in order to save herself from many nights of pain and aggravation.

She was surprised when he called her two years later to come work for him at DTCU. He told her it was imperative that she join the organization because she needed someone she could trust. Ten years later, they were still working together. Even with their share of ups and downs, even when another man came between them, they always kept things in perspective regarding work.

Samantha was excited to be working with this lady from Brooklyn. She sat again and reached for her Dior eyeglasses to reread the file. This young woman intrigued her. There was something that reminded her of herself when she started in the field. Jenkins was outspoken, disciplined, and had a bad attitude. Samantha was looking forward to meeting her.

Bolden knocked on her door. In all the years she'd known him, he'd never come to her office without an invitation. Whenever they were alone together, his hard exterior melted, and he became this soft shell of a man. It was endearing, and she couldn't help but hold a special place in her heart for him.

"May I come in?" He sat in one of the plush burgundy armless chairs across from her.

She removed her glasses and smiled at him.

"I just met the new recruit. She's stubborn. Strong. Defiant. I like her. Reminds me of someone we both know," Jeremiah said.

"Really?" Rubbing her hand over her long ponytail, she gave her ex-lover a stern look.

"She's busting at the seams. Antsy and irritable. She doesn't want to be here."

She shrugged. "Not surprising. Everyone tries to escape from somewhere."

"Well, let's hope you can rein her in. But I don't have to tell you this, do I?"

"I wish there was more in this file to work with. She seemed like a normal girl. She worked full time, went to school, studied martial arts, and hung out with her friends. But then she ended up with the wrong crowd. She claims she had nothing to do with the conspiracy charge. Hmmm."

"I want to make sure Perkins takes full responsibility for her. He brought her here and knows he has to work to make sure everything goes off without a hitch."

Samantha nodded. "Got it. Perkins's ass is on the line."

"Good luck with her. You'll need it." Bolden left Samantha's office, leaving her to study Benita's file on her laptop.

Samantha entered Benita's room and greeted her with a huge smile. "Hey, Benita. I'm Agent Samantha DeVreau. How are you enjoying your stay?"

Benita sat on her bed with her legs crossed and eyes closed. She'd been meditating for what seemed like hours and didn't feel like answering any questions from this DeVreau woman.

Samantha sat in a plush chair and crossed her legs. She opened her file and began reading out loud. "So, you grew up in Brooklyn. Your mother died of cancer when you were fourteen, and you never knew your gangbanger father."

Benita continued to meditate in silence.

"You lived with your grandmother and younger brother. You worked for your cousin, Deon, at his hair salon. But you got yourself in some trouble when you tried to help him deal with a certain situation." She took a deep breath and looked over at Benita, who hadn't moved. "Benita, you're gonna have to talk to me sometime."

Benita opened her eyes, uncrossed her legs, and placed her feet on the floor. She stood up, stretched her body, and then poured herself a glass of water. She turned toward Samantha and took her time drinking her water. "White."

Samantha stared inquisitively. "Excuse me?"

"White. Everything in here is white. White walls. White floors. White sheets. White. White. White. Why white?"

DeVreau raised her eyebrow and cocked her head to one side. "Why not white?"

"Come on, lady. Don't try to play me. I may not be a psychiatrist, but I've taken a few psych classes. And I know when I'm being analyzed and tricked into talking."

"You think I'm trying to trick you?"

"C'mon. I'm not stupid. Listen, how about some color in here? Like a splash of red? Or gold? This place needs some pizzazz."

"Hmmmm . . . how about a disco ball too?"

Benita laughed. "That would be dope. Then I could get my dance on."

"Ms. Jenkins, the first thing you'll need to learn is that we follow certain protocols here. You're being trained to be an agent, and there's a level of professionalism we all must follow. Your attitude will have to change if you're planning on being successful at DTCU."

"Do I have a choice?"

Samantha stood up and placed a large manual on Benita's desk. "Why don't you get started reading this? We'll pick up tomorrow. We have a lot of work to do to get you up to speed."

"What kind of work?"

"Anger management, for one. If you want to survive here, you'll have to control your temper. Rest up. See you later."

Samantha walked out of the room, leaving Benita to stew.

"Damn," Benita muttered. "Everybody needs an ass whooping around here."

Chapter 29

It was six in the morning when Benita woke. Opening her eyes, she threw back the covers and placed her feet on the plush carpet. She stretched out her tight muscles and took a long, hot shower.

She looked in the mirror and barely recognized her own face. The last four months had been hell. The stress had done a number on her skin, and she looked as if she'd aged five years in less than half of one. She used to wake up every morning with a beauty routine and left her house feeling like a million bucks. Nowadays, she felt old and worn out.

She walked out of the bathroom to find a clear wrapped package on her bed. It contained a royal-blue jumpsuit with a gold *DTCU* stitched on the right hip, a white T-shirt, and white-and-blue sneakers. She ripped open the attached envelope and read the letter:

Welcome to our team. Today is the first day of the rest of your life. Once you're dressed and had breakfast, we'll discuss next steps. Samantha.

Benita reread the note and placed it on her small desk. She finished dressing and sat on the bed, tying her sneakers. She heard the door unlock and saw Miguel standing by the doorway.

"Good morning, Benita. May I come in?"

"Do I have a choice?"

Miguel smirked. "You absolutely have a choice." He paused for a moment. "Look, I wanted to apologize for how I behaved yesterday. You're right. I should have driven you here myself."

"Whatever. It doesn't matter. I'm here now, right?"

He sat on a small chair, clasped his hands, and leaned forward. "I don't think you realize how special you are. I've never seen a woman who handles herself the way you do. You have a sharp tongue and a sharp kick to match. I'll never forget how you kicked those two guys' asses in Brooklyn."

"How'd you know about . . . Oh, right. You know everything, don't you?"

"I was watching those clowns, and you happened to be there at the wrong time and the wrong place. But you handled yourself like a true warrior. You were so, so raw."

"Raw?"

He stood next to Benita. "Yeah. Raw."

Benita's heart began to beat a little faster when he stood next to her. She hated that he had invaded her space and she liked it.

"Benita, you can become one damn good agent if we work together. All you have to do is let yourself go and let your true talents shine."

A chill raced across her body. This handsome asshole had an uncanny ability to make her forget her troubles and digging deep into her soul. "I don't know if I have what it takes. What if I fail?"

"I have faith in you. You've made it this far. You can go as far as you wanna go."

"Will you be there for me?"

He touched Benita's face and looked into her almond-shaped eyes. "I'll always be there. No matter what. You're ready to take this organization by storm."

Benita wanted to believe him but still didn't trust him. "Well, I hope you don't change too much about me. I like who I am. I wanna shine."

They had come to an understanding, but neither would admit having feelings for the other. For now, they just worked on building the kind of trust needed to move things to the next level.

Chapter 30

Agent Evan Green had just finished a five-mile run in the woods behind DTCU's main building and was dripping with sweat. He walked over to the water dispenser and drank down two cups, then bent over to touch the tips of his shoes and stretch out his back. Green had started DTCU's training program two weeks ago and had never experienced so much pain and soreness. Other recruits in the group were in tiptop shape and were running circles around him, but he was determined to finish at the top of his class.

Everyone was required to run five miles a day, and whoever came in last had to run another five miles. Evan finished last every day during the first week. But by the beginning of the second week, he had picked up speed and moved up in the ranks. He continued running on his days off to build up his endurance and make Mr. B. proud.

Evan remembered when he first started working at the agency. He used to push his heavy metal cart through a set of double doors down the hallway toward the south wing of the building. Each morning began the same way: with him starting at six and prioritizing his appointed mail delivery schedule. It was a labor-intensive job, but Evan was glad to be off the streets and in a stable work environment.

As he walked past an open area filled with rows of cubicles, Evan maneuvered between people down the aisles and the small walkway leading to his mail route. Today seemed extra busy, and workers were a little more spastic than usual. However, they seemed oblivious to news reports flashing on various flat-screen TVs mounted on two opposing walls.

Dropping off and picking up mail, Evan heard a reporter announce the discovery of a dead body in the East River. A photo of a young black male named Malik Williams covered the screen, and Evan shook his head in disgust. He muttered, "Damn shame. Wonder what he did to end up swimmin' with the fishes."

Evan had delivered packages to Bolden for the past two years and looked forward to seeing him every day. He couldn't remember a time the executive director didn't share nuggets of wisdom when Evan stopped by. Mr. B., as he affectionately called him, was confident, professional, and authentic. He respected everyone in the unit, and Evan admired him. Growing up around drug dealers and gangbangers, he was thankful for Mr. B. as his ultimate role model.

One day, Evan stopped in front of Bolden's office and asked him how he'd become top man at DTCU. Bolden looked up from his paperwork and motioned him to come sit. Evan gladly obliged and plopped down in the leather chair across from the director.

"So, Evan, you wanna know how I became the man. Well, I'll tell you. It was through a lot of hard work and dedication. Twenty years as a Green Beret, another five training Green Berets, and ten years recruiting and training agents here at DTCU. What do you wanna do with your life?"

"Mr. B., I wanna make a difference."

Jeremiah leaned back in his chair and looked up at the ceiling. "Okay, you wanna make a difference. But how do you want to make a difference?"

"You're the man, Mr. B. I see how you run things up in this place. You hardcore, and I respect your gangsta. I want to get out of the mailroom and work as an agent to bring down the bad guys. I wanna be like you."

Bolden stared at Evan for a long time before answering. Evan knew Bolden respected his work ethic; he'd told him as much. Evan took his job as a mailroom guy seriously. Bolden encouraged Evan to ask him questions. He clearly liked passing on life lessons to Evan and anyone else who asked. Evan was rough around the edges, but Bolden saw something special in him. He told Evan he hoped he wanted to pursue a real career. In fact, he hoped Evan would seek him out, he said, because he saw real potential in him.

He braced himself before responding. "Are you serious? Or are you just blowing smoke up my ass?"

"I'm for real, Mr. B. I'd never blow smoke up your ass."

Bolden leaned forward and looked Evan in his eyes as if to see if he was telling the truth. "Do you think you have what it takes to become an agent?"

Evan nodded. "Never been so sure in my life."

"Son, let me school you on some things. First, being an agent is more than just being cool and carrying a gun. It's about hard work, long hours, and little pay. Agents get assigned to cases that place them in the middle of nowhere. Our job here at the unit is taking care of garbage no other agencies want to handle. I see a twinkle in your eyes, but I'm here to tell you the finish line will be the hardest thing you've ever done. It's a tough business, and if you choose to join the training program, you get no breaks. Understand?"

Evan nodded emphatically.

Bolden opened his desk drawer and handed Evan a manila envelope. "There's a new training class in three months. If you're serious about becoming an agent, fill out this application and bring it back to me. If not, no hard feelings."

Evan stood up and picked up the envelope Director Bolden had slid over to him, thanking him for his time before walking out. He appreciated his mentor's candor and wasn't wasting this opportunity.

The following week, Evan handed Bolden a completed application.

"You sure you want to do this?"

"Yes, sir."

"Okay, Evan, I believe you. Now comes the hard part." He looked over the application, signed the back of it, and handed it back. "Take this downstairs to Agent Gerty, and he'll set up some initial interviews."

Evan had looked at the signed application and walked out of Bolden's office with a new level of confidence. He planned on taking full advantage of this opportunity and would not let Mr. B. down. Evan would prove he was serious and worth it.

And now, thanks to his mentor, Evan was a part of something big, and he was grateful for his achievement. As he finished drinking his second cup of water, the young man noticed a beautiful young woman enter the exercise room with Perkins. Evan hated Perkins because Perkins was an arrogant prick who was only out for himself.

This woman wore the same training gear as his, but he had never seen her before. Perkins barked at her while she stretched before starting a warm-up routine. "Come on, Benita. Show me what you got."

The woman looked up and pointed her middle finger at him. "Man, up yours. You try stretching after riding in a van all night."

"Can't use that as an excuse."

"I'm ready, Mr. Agent Man."

Miguel and Benita circled each other in anticipation of the other's moves. However, Benita was surprised when he blocked her every move.

"Oh, yeah. Take that, girl."

"Please, I've been studying martial arts since I was five years old. You don't scare me." Benita punched Miguel's chest and then kicked him in the stomach. He keeled over long enough for Benita to bring down her guard. He threw out his leg and tripped her, and she ended up on the floor. He pinned her, and the harder she struggled, the longer he kept her down.

"Say uncle."

"Never!" She continued to struggle.

"You need to learn to do what I tell you."

"No, get off me."

"Not till you say the magic word."

Benita looked at Miguel and relaxed her body. "Hmmmm, I never noticed how beautiful your eyes are."

Miguel almost kissed her but was interrupted when Samantha and Evan entered the recreation room.

"I hope we're not interrupting anything," Samantha commented.

Jumping up, Miguel helped Benita to her feet. "No, just getting her up to speed."

"Fantastic. Benita, I want you to meet one of our newest recruits, Evan Green. I found him outside the exercise room, and I thought it would be a perfect opportunity for you to meet someone who's just started the training program."

Benita reached out to shake Evan's hand, but he apparently decided against it. He rubbed his hands on his shorts. "Sorry, my hands are sweaty. Nice to meet you."

Samantha watched Miguel as he eyed the exchange between Benita and Evan. She caught a little twinge in his facial expression even though he tried to remain expressionless.

"Evan, could you please show Benita around the facilities? I'll meet you outside. I need to speak to Agent Perkins for a minute."

"Sure, Agent DeVreau."

He escorted Benita out of the exercise room and made a quick left, leading outside the training facility.

Samantha placed her hands on her hips and looked at Perkins. "Is there something you want to speak to me about?

He walked over to a table, grabbed a towel, and wiped the sweat off his face. "I'm not sure what you mean."

"Oh, I think you do. You wanna talk about what I just walked in on?"

"You didn't walk into anything. Nothing happened."

"Don't play me for a fool, okay? Make sure you keep your distance from her. If I find out you've crossed any lines, I'll have to tell Bolden." She removed her hands from her hips and stormed out of the room, leaving Miguel to brood in silence.

***

Evan and Benita walked through the facility and headed outside to wander the grounds. Benita was surprised to see so much open area filled with trees, large rocks, and a pond. It was absolutely beautiful. As she attempted to step over a protruding rock, she tripped, and Evan grabbed her waist to keep her from falling.

"You okay?"

She smiled at Evan, who all of a sudden looked kind of cute. "Yeah, I guess I'm not used to walking around in the woods. Does Prospect Park in Brooklyn count?"

"You got jokes. I like that. That where you grew up?"

"Oh, it's a long story. Too long to explain." Benita leaned against a large oak tree and picked up a stick. As she started making figure eights with it, she looked up at Evan, who was staring at her. "Where are you from?"

"The Bronx."

Benita sat on the ground and stretched her aching limbs. "Don't take this the wrong way, but you don't look like an agent. I mean, these folks seem to be far removed from the Bronx."

"Yeah. But I've been working here for a while and wanna do something good with my life. Like they do. So, Mr. B.—I mean Executive Director Bolden—took me under his wing. He helped prepare me for the training program."

"Mr. B? Should stand for Mr. Badass," Benita mumbled.

Evan slid down the tree and squatted beside Benita. "How'd you end up here? Really?"

Benita saw Samantha coming out of the double glass doors, walking toward them in her beige Jimmy Choo stilettos, but she stopped at the end of the cement floor.

Samantha motioned Evan and Benita to come forward. Benita chuckled at this graceful and elegant woman who wasn't about to ruin her shoes on some gravel and grass.

"Evan, thank you so much for showing Benita around. It's much appreciated."

"You're welcome, Agent DeVreau. Do you need anything else?"

"No, we're fine. Thank you, Evan."

Evan nodded and left the two ladies alone by the rocks. He looked back at Benita one more time and then disappeared through the glass doors.

Samantha reached into her jacket pocket and pulled out her Dior sunglasses. She perched them on the bridge of her nose. "So, Benita. What do you think so far?"

"The scenery is breathtaking. I'm glad to be outside. Better than those four white walls."

"While you're here, you'll learn more about yourself than you could ever imagine. How do you feel about making a difference?"

"I don't know how I'm supposed to feel. This is all happening so fast. One minute I'm in jail, the next I'm here. I can't talk to my family or my friends. I'm all alone."

"My sweet Benita. You're not alone, my dear. Think of us as your new family. I'll do whatever it takes to make you see that this is going to be a ride worth taking. By the time I'm done with you, your own grandmother won't recognize you. Let's get started. Shall we?"

They headed toward the opposite end of the building, where Benita would begin her intense training. The next few months would be a culture shock for Benita, but Samantha would be there for her every step of the way.

Chapter 31

Carl was standing on the rooftop of a luxury apartment building overlooking the Brooklyn Bridge. He absolutely loved his new digs, mainly because of the access to his private roof deck. As he turned around, Benjamin Mahoney, two of his bodyguards, and Ernest Brown walked toward him. He beamed when he saw his former partner.

"Ernest, I'm glad you could make it."

Ernest snapped, "Like I had a choice. What do you want, Johnson?"

"Benjamin tells me you haven't returned any of his calls."

"I'm not giving up any more of my artists."

"Ernest, we used to have a great working relationship. What's up with all this animosity? Totally unwarranted."

"Really, now. Well, I think when my ex-business partner screws me out of royalties—several times, mind you—I have a right to be angry."

"I think we should just let bygones be bygones."

"I've signed on with another management company, a more reputable and trustworthy one."

"Ernest, man, you should know by now you can't bullshit me. I know you haven't signed any contracts. In fact, I understand you're still reviewing your options."

"How the fuck do you know that?"

"I know everything that happens in this business. Now, what kind of shit is this for you to lie to me? I'm your former business partner. You can trust me."

"Carl, you're scum."

Carl pushed Ernest toward the side of the roof. "Ernest, before you leave this building, you're gonna sign this contract."

Ernest looked at Carl. "Go ahead. Threaten me. Beat me to a pulp. That's what you do, isn't it? Bully people into doing what you want them to do? Well, I'm not scared of you, and I'm not signing any bullshit contract."

Carl kneed Ernest in the groin, causing him to yelp in pain. He then hit him in the side and stomach. He pulled out a picture of Ernest's young daughter and placed it close to Ernest's face. "I'm not fucking around here. I think you may want to reconsider. You have a beautiful little girl. You wouldn't want anything to happen to her, would you?"

"If you ever touch my daughter, I swear to God, you'll regret it."

Carl smirked. "All you have to do is sign this damn contract stating all future clients will be signed to Madd Dogg Records. But for now, I'll be satisfied with D. J. Grill." Carl reached inside his pocket and pulled out the document and a pen. "Sign it, Ernest."

Defeated, he signed the paper.

"I expect to see you and your client in my office tomorrow morning, nine sharp. It was great doing business with you again. You can see yourself out."

Carl, Benjamin, and his bodyguards left Ernest by himself, licking his wounds.

Ernest pulled out his phone and left a message. "Call me when you get a chance. This shit has got to end."

***

Benjamin was standing on the corner of Fifty-Seventh Street and Eleventh Avenue when a black sedan pulled up next to him. He had been hovering under the awning, trying not to get soaked by the current downpour. When he saw the back window slowly roll down, he pulled his trench coat over his Brooks Brothers suit and hurried himself into the back seat.

"What took you so long? I've been waiting outside for the past thirty minutes," Benjamin barked as he looked over at Ernest.

"Traffic," Ernest responded. He directed the driver to drive toward the Henry Hudson Expressway and north toward the George Washington Bridge. He glanced over at Benjamin with a disgusted look on his face. "Your boss is getting out of control. I thought you were getting the goods on him."

Benjamin shivered as he removed the wet trench coat, trying not to shake the water all over himself and the back seat.

"What the hell do you think I've been trying to do? That man is a vulture. He'll eat you alive if you don't do what he wants."

"I can't be signing over any more of my artists to him. If you can't nail anything on him, I'm going to the feds."

"The man has nine lives. They can't touch him," Benjamin whined.

"Listen, at least they can get him on extortion charges."

"With his high-priced attorneys, he'll be out of jail in a day, and guess what? Your body will be splattered against the closest concrete."

Ernest looked at Benjamin in disbelief. He thought his friend wanted to bring Carl down as much as he did, especially since Carl made it a habit to threaten Benjamin every chance he got.

"Bennie, talk to me. What's going on? Why you stalling on this?"

"I'm not stalling. I'm just saying I need a little more time to find something we can use."

"Well, whatever it is, you'd better find it fast because if I have to give up any more artists, I'll be out of business."

Benjamin turned his head toward the rainy Manhattan streets. The car was on the Henry Hudson. They were headed out of the city for a quick dinner to freely discuss the Carl situation. However, Benjamin was stalling Ernest as long as he could because he had another plan in mind. It was time for Benjamin to leave New York before Carl found out he was embezzling from some of his businesses. If Carl found out he and Ernest were working together to bring him down, he would torture them until they wished they were dead.

The rain continued to pour. A black SUV had been following Benjamin and Ernest's sedan since leaving Brooklyn. Michael Foreman, one of Carl's employees, was the driver of the SUV. He looked over at the camera that was propped up on the passenger's seat, then turned toward the highway to make sure not to lose sight of the car during the bad weather conditions. No matter where the car was headed, he was sure to follow.

Chapter 32

The last time Grace saw Benita at the prison, she wasn't acting like herself. She was depressed, clinging to her grandmother the entire visit. She found it strange Benita wasn't eating her favorite foods or enjoying her weekly visits from her family. When Grace pressed her granddaughter to share what was going on, Benita assured her everything was okay and not to worry. However, that was three months ago, and Benita had since "disappeared" from prison. Grace believed Benita had been taken against her will because there was no way she could escape on her own from such a well-guarded penitentiary.

Grace remembered when she first got a call from the prison to discuss Benita's unfortunate situation.

"Mrs. Jenkins, this is Warden Stevenson. I'm calling about your granddaughter, Benita Jenkins."

"Has something happened to her?"

"She's disappeared."

"Disappeared? What do you mean she's disappeared?"

"It's come to my attention that Benita has had several run-ins with members of a gang called the She-Devil Crew, and there is a hit out on her. We had to take extra precautions to protect your granddaughter—but now she's no longer in her holding cell."

"Where is she? Tell me right now. What have you done with my granddaughter?"

"Ms. Jenkins, you need to calm down."

"Calm down? You call me to tell me my grandbaby is missing, and you want me to calm down? I want some answers, and I want them now."

"I can only tell you we are currently investigating her disappearance. This case has been turned over to another agency that's better equipped to handle these sensitive matters."

"What agency? This doesn't make sense. What kind of cover-up are you trying to pull? Where is my grandbaby?"

"Ms. Jenkins, all I can tell you is that someone will be contacting you shortly."

"Wait a minute. Wait one damn minute! Who's going to be contacting me?"

Grace was dumbfounded when the warden suddenly hung up without further explaining Benita's disappearance. She immediately called her lawyer and friend, Thomas, to find out if he had heard anything about Benita's disappearance.

"Thomas? There is something shady going on at that prison. Where's my Benita?"

Grace wasn't waiting for someone to contact her. She sprang into action and made phone call after phone call to the governor's office, the mayor's office, the police commissioner's office, and even to FBI headquarters. She contacted every media outlet, but no one would pick up her story.

A week later, she got a knock on the door from two big, burly guys wearing black suits and designer sunglasses.

"I'm Agent Barry Malone, and this is my partner, Agent Ricky Torres. We're from DTCU. We're here to discuss updates regarding your granddaughter, Benita Jenkins. May we come in?"

"Not until I see some ID."

Malone pulled out his badge and handed it to Grace. After scrutinizing the documentation, she reluctantly stepped aside and let the two men in, escorting them to her living room. She sat and started sipping her tea and nibbling on ginger snaps. She stared at the two large men, who sat quietly while she ate her snacks.

"So, if you're here to talk about Benita, spill it."

Two men looked at each other without answering.

"What have you done with my grandbaby?"

Wes was sitting beside his grandmother, and he touched Grace's arm. "Calm down, Grandma. Don't let these clowns get you upset. They're not worth it."

"These folks know what happened to your sister, and they don't want to tell us anything. I see two bureaucratic weasels trying to sweep things under the rug. It's been three months, and these people finally appear out of thin air. What is this DTCU agency? Why haven't I ever heard of you?"

Agent Malone replied, "Mrs. Jenkins, Warden Stevenson discussed with you the danger your grand-daughter is in. She's under our protection. But you can't go around accusing the state prison system of unsubstantiated conspiracy theories."

Wes yelled at the agents, "This makes no sense. How are you here sitting in our house, telling my grandmother not to accuse the state of abducting my sister? We wanna know who you really work for and why you got my sister."

The agent looked at Wes and continued in a monotone voice. "You must be the brother."

"You think? Didn't I just say she was my sister? Damn, you sure are smart. Grams, I don't know about you, but these fools are hedging. Something happened in jail, and they're covering it up. For all we know, Benita has been shuttled off to another country, being somebody's sex slave."

"I think you've been watching too many movies, young man."

"Maybe I have been watching too many movies, but I don't see you trying to answer my questions."

Agent Malone took off his sunglasses and responded to Wes as diplomatically as possible. "As we told your grandmother, we work for the Domestic Terrorism Crime Unit. We were contacted by the DA's office to investigate a dangerous female gang that seems to be funneling drugs and trafficking females through the prison system."

"See, Grams? I told ya. Benita's been turned into a prostitute for a huge Columbian drug cartel."

Agent Torres slammed his fist on the table, almost spilling Grace's tea. "Man, what is wrong with you? Are you and your grandmother crazy? Nobody's turned your sister into a prostitute."

Agent Malone, Grace, and Wes looked on in silence at Torres, who had been quiet during most of the exchange. He regained his composure and let Agent Malone continue his explanation.

"As I was saying, Benita witnessed something she wasn't supposed to see while in prison, and that put her life in danger. For the best interest of our investigation, we thought it was best to remove her from that situation."

"Where is she now?" Grace calmly asked.

"We're not at liberty to say."

Wes stood up and yelled at the stoic men. "You dumb asses! For the best interest? What about our interest? Tell us where my sister is."

Grace pulled Wes back to the couch. "I think it's time for you two gentlemen to leave my house."

"One last thing, Mrs. Jenkins. We would appreciate it if you stopped contacting media outlets. You're just putting Benita in more danger."

"Good-bye, Mr. Malone." Grace shut the door and walked back to the living room, where Wes was pacing back and forth.

"Grams, do you believe these clowns? Why won't they tell us where Benita is?"

"Praise Jesus! We got somebody's attention." Grace hugged her only grandson and kissed him on his forehead. "Baby, I refuse to leave your sister's life in the hands of some agency claiming they're protecting her whereabouts. Don't worry, Gram's got a plan."

Grace picked up the phone and made a call to someone she had sworn never to speak to again. She needed his help, and he owed her.

It had been five years since Leroy last laid eyes on Grace Jenkins. At one of his open houses, he'd spotted her with a young woman who was there to sign up for one of his classes. Grace had crossed her arms, giving him one of the meanest looks he'd ever seen.

He introduced himself. "Hello, I'm Leroy Jones. Welcome to my school." He shook the young lady's hand and reached for Grace's, but she dismissed him and never uncrossed her arms.

"Grams, why are you being so rude? Hi, I'm Benita Jenkins. This is my grandmother, Grace Jenkins."

"Nice to meet you, Benita. Mrs. Jenkins."

"Benita, why don't you go and look around the facility? I'd like to speak to Mr. Jones for a bit."

Benita was reluctant to leave her grandmother alone. For some reason, the instructor had rubbed her the wrong way, and there was no telling what her grandmother would say to him. "Okay, Grams, but behave." Benita walked away and joined other students who were thinking about signing up.

"So, now you're Leroy Jones?"

"I think you've mistaken me for someone else."

"Don't you dare try bullshitting me. I know who you are. In case you didn't know, Margarie Jenkins was my daughter, and she told me everything about you. I never forget a face—and yours? You haven't changed a bit after twenty years. Still got those big ole ears and lanky walk."

Twenty-five years ago, Leroy was working undercover for the FBI when he was transferred into a task force formed to bring down drug dealers in Brooklyn. He met Margarie Jenkins, who happened to be one of the most beautiful women he had ever laid eyes on. They fell in love, and Leroy shared his secret life with her. He promised that after his assignment, they would be together. But things went wrong, and he had to abort his assignment to keep from getting killed. He was sent to another country to get him off the grid. In the process, he left Margarie behind, but he never forgot her. He had many regrets about not coming back for her.

By the time he came back to Brooklyn, Margarie had married her ex-boyfriend. Leroy decided it was better to stay out of her life, but he kept tabs on her even after he started working for DTCU. He gave up everything for his job, even a life of happiness with his one true love. He'd let her slip through his fingers, and he was heartbroken when she died of cancer. He had asked for her forgiveness, but she refused. Losing the love of his life was his greatest loss.

Leroy was surprised when he heard Benita had disappeared. Grace called to seek his help to find her granddaughter, but he wasn't sure what he could do. He headed for the bathroom and took a long, hot shower to ease his anxieties. Grace's call had shaken him to the core, especially when she mentioned a visit from DTCU. His entire body tensed, and he remembered his meeting with Agent Perkins months ago. How had Benita gotten involved with his former employer?

Later, he pulled out an old Rolodex of telephone numbers from the top shelf of his closet. He texted an old buddy who was still at the agency: Got a call from a woman wanting to know about her granddaughter, Benita Jenkins. What's the story?

He received a text message back from an unlisted number: The girl is now working for DTCU. Not sure on what assignment. My orders were to calm the grandmother down. bm.

Leroy deleted the message. As an ex-agent, he couldn't reveal sources or share secrets with civilians. But this was Benita's grandmother, and she was making noise at anyone who would listen. He had to think long and hard about how to help her. Benita must have made the decision to work for DTCU, and if this was the case, there was nothing he could do about it. Once a person was in, he or she was in for life.

Chapter 33

In three months, Benita had been thrown into a whole new world of training she had never experienced before. Every day began at five a.m., when she ran ten miles, followed by hundreds of push-ups, pull-ups, and sit-ups. She then moved on to training in mental interrogation. She was placed in a windowless eight-by-eight room for twenty-four hours to build her mental stamina.

She had worked with military experts in weaponry, teaching her to assemble guns and rifles, making small bombs out of baking powder and small wires, and learning how to spot and plant surveillance bugs. She worked with a computer hacker named Huey Graham, who taught her how to break into restricted sites to access classified documents.

During her physical training, Samantha taught Benita how to move with grace and sophistication and develop the ability to use her femininity to manipulate men. Benita had always been direct in her approach, but Samantha taught her to be a better listener and not so quick to fly off the handle. She needed to learn to be mysterious and calm instead of confrontational and stubborn, which would help her go a long way.

Samantha said a woman's mind and body were the two things she needed most to survive any attack in this business. She had the power to seduce, manipulate, and bring a man to his knees. A woman with the right training could make any man fall for her, and all it took was a touch, a breath, or even a smile.

Benita was in awe of Samantha, one of the most beautiful women she had ever met, and one of the smartest. She was full of life and tough as nails, but she exuded the true essence of being the perfect woman.

Samantha gave Benita a complete physical makeover. Benita's weave and bright nails were gone. Now she sported a spiky pixie cut that flattered her face and short, manicured fingernails. Her biggest lesson learned? Real women didn't have to flaunt; they just had to be.

Samantha had a saying: "If you want to be taken seriously as an agent, it's time to shed your old habits."

After a long day of training, Benita thought about her family and what they must be going through. But more importantly, she thought about Joe. He had crept into her mind like a thief in the night, and she wanted to know how he was doing, so she recruited her new hacker friend Huey Graham to do a little digging on Joe's status. She rested easy when she found out he was recovering from his shooting. She wanted to tell him how sorry she was, but she couldn't. Her heart ached, but she buried her feelings.

Although she was growing into a new person, she would always be a "do or die" Bed-Stuy girl, a "round the way girl with an overhaul." She chuckled as she sipped on her lemongrass mint tea, remembering the good times she'd had with her family. No matter what she'd promised Miguel, she wouldn't give up on seeing them.

***

Grace looked at Leroy's trophies and photos of him and his students. How could this be the same man she'd met twenty-five years ago? She was never fond of him, but he was a little better than her daughter's ex-husband, Terrence. Margarie always did have a soft spot for the shady characters from the neighborhood, and Leroy was no exception. Margarie used to talk about a young man who had just moved into the area, and soon Grace's daughter started spending less time with her boyfriend and more time with Leroy. Grace tried to warn her daughter not to cause a rift between the two men, but Margarie wouldn't listen. She was in love and didn't care what Terrence thought. Then, all of a sudden, Leroy left town.

Not only had he abandoned the woman he loved, but he also left behind a beautiful daughter. But he never came back for her or his beautiful girl. Margarie never got over the loss of her true love. She ended up marrying Terrence, but when Benita was six and Wes was one, Terrence went to jail for selling cocaine. Grace stepped in and took care of her daughter and grandbabies.

Grace frowned when she saw Leroy approaching her.

"Mrs. Jenkins, I see you made it."

She folded her arms and gave Leroy a once over. "I never thought I'd ever say another word to you. But sometimes desperate times call for desperate measures."

"Understood."

"I've hated you for the past twenty-three years. You left my daughter and never came back. Do you know how hard it was for her?"

"I loved your daughter, but she refused to speak to me."

"What did you expect her to do? Wait for you forever?"

"Of course not. I never meant to hurt her. If I could take it all back, I would."

"Well, you can do the right thing about Benita."

"I don't know what I can do."

"Don't play games with me. Margarie told me all about you working undercover for the FBI. And you left Brooklyn because your life was in danger. I know you got connections, Leroy. I need for you to find out about this DTCU agency and why they got your daughter."

"What are you talking about? My daughter? Benita's my daughter?" Leroy's strong legs buckled underneath him, almost causing him to collapse to the floor. He made his way to the couch and tried to catch his breath. "I always wondered, but I just assumed . . . Why didn't she tell me? Margarie looked me dead in my face and told me she didn't love me anymore. She said she'd moved on and was happy with Terrence. I didn't want to cause trouble, so I let her be."

"She couldn't trust you. What would it have been like for Benita to know her father would be in and out of her life? Margarie did what she had to do to protect her heart. But now you know you have a daughter, and she needs her daddy. For the past five years, you've taken her under your wing. You've taught her how to be a world-class athlete and a better person. Well, she needs you now more than ever. Make some calls, Leroy."

Later that day, Grace opened the door and saw a film crew and a well-dressed man holding a microphone standing outside.

"Mrs. Grace Jenkins? I'm from Publishers Clearing House. You've just won three hundred thousand dollars! How do you feel?"

"Lawd Jesus! Wes? Wes? We just won three hundred thousand dollars! I can't believe it. Wes?"

Wes ran to the door. "Grams, what's going on?"

The man holding a microphone smiled at the camera and then turned to Grace and Wes. "Your grandma just won three hundred thousand dollars from Publishers Clearing House. How do you feel?"

Wes and Grace sported grins that split their faces. They were handed a giant-sized check with Grace's name on it, and they held it while the camera crew filmed them.

"Oh my Lawd, thank you, Jesus! Thank you, thank you, thank you!"

Chapter 34

Miguel and Benita sat down for dinner at Di Marra's Ristorante, one of the best Italian restaurants in Philadelphia. Di Marra's was known for its multifaceted home-style dishes using beef, chicken, fish, veal, and homemade pasta.

This was the first time Benita had been out of the compound since arriving at DTCU. She had been pushed to the brink, and it was a miracle she had survived her rigorous training. Now she was out to dinner with Miguel, enjoying an incredible meal with her dreamboat boss.

"Thank you for bringing me here. If I had to eat another meal in the cafeteria, I think I'd have gone crazy," Benita cooed.

"You've worked hard the last few months, and I thought it was time for a celebratory meal."

A young waiter walked over to the table, holding a pitcher of tap water and a bottle of sparkling water in each hand. "Good evening. Welcome to Di Marra's. Would you like sparkling water or tap?"

Miguel said, "Sparkling, and could you bring us a bottle of your best champagne? We're celebrating tonight."

The waiter poured sparkling water in their glasses. "Wonderful, I'll be right back with your champagne. Would you like any appetizers?"

"Yes, we'd like some bruschetta, arancini, and the artichoke and basil pesto bread rounds."

"All righty, I'll give you a few minutes to look over the menu." He relayed the night's specials and then added, "I'll be right back with your appetizers."

Benita was impressed with Miguel's knowledge of the menu. She wondered how many times he had been there before and if he had brought any other women. She was curious but didn't dare ask. He'd barked at her many times that his personal life was off-limits. She didn't want him to shut her down because of her questions.

"Great choices—they sound delicious. So . . . can I ask you something, Miguel?"

He popped a few olives in his mouth. "It depends. Go ahead, ask."

"Okay. What made you decide to work for DTCU?"

He sipped his water. "When I was just graduating college, I applied to the FBI, but after scoring so high on the entrance exam, I was approached by someone at DTCU. He told me I could do a better job working there."

"Have you ever regretted your decision?"

"Nope. I enjoy what I do. It's a lot of hard work, but the accomplishment you feel by completing an assignment is overwhelming. A natural high you can't get anywhere else. But why don't we just enjoy our meal and not talk about work right now?"

Two waiters brought over the appetizers and champagne. They spent the rest of the night enjoying delicious food and great bubbly. For the first time in a long time, Benita was happy and enjoying herself without a care in the world.

Miguel paid the check, and they walked to the black SUV with tinted windows parked across the street. Benita was laughing and holding on to his arm. He opened the door for her, and she climbed into the passenger seat. She was talking nonstop as Miguel drove for about thirty minutes in the opposite direction of the headquarters.

"Ahhhhhh, Miguel, where are we going?"

"It's a surprise."

Benita looked at Miguel, and a devious smile slid across her face. "Really? A surprise? What kind of surprise?"

"You have to wait and see."

Benita arched her back and playfully stretched out her neck. "Come on, Miguel. Give me a little hint."

Miguel didn't speak until he stopped across the street in front of a restaurant called Paulio's in Trenton, New Jersey.

Benita was confused. "What are we doing here?"

"It's your first assignment. Surprise!"

"You're joking, right?"

"When do I ever joke?"

"You have got to be one of the biggest assholes on the planet. I let my guard down and pow! You shoot me in the freakin' heart. I'm not looking at any folders tonight. I'm off the clock, dude. Off the clock!"

Miguel was still holding the folder in Benita's direction, and Benita relented. She took the folder and opened it, reviewing the contents. "Wow, look at these men. They're huge. Like, really huge. Like baby whales."

"Okay, Benita, I get it. They're big."

"Wait a minute. What am I supposed to be doing with fatso and fatso?"

"I need to see how you handle yourself."

"What the hell does that mean? Handle myself? Damn, Miguel. What kind of sick person are you? Does this shit turn you on?"

"Are you finished? I need to see how prepared you are for the real world. At any given time, shit could go down. Are you up for whatever? Even after having a great meal?"

"Whatever, man. Let's just get on with it. What am I supposed to do? I wanna get out of here, do my thing, and get back to DTCU and go to bed. It's not like I don't have to get up early in the morning to run another twenty miles."

"You see the man on the left? He owns the restaurant across the street. I want you to go in there and take him out."

Benita looked at Miguel in horror. "Hold on. Just one minute. Are you saying you want me to walk in there and kill the man? Why would I do that?"

"He runs a human trafficking and drug ring. We've been hired to eliminate him."

"Then you need to do it yourself because I'm not. And you can't make me."

"Oh, I beg to differ. I'm your commanding officer, and you do what I say. It's part of your job to follow all rules, and this is a direct order. You see the van across the street? There are men in the van who are ready to kill you if you don't carry out your assignment."

"You can't be serious."

"As a heart attack. Now, if you want to see another day, you'll take this gun and shoot Mr. Fatso." He pulled out a 9 mm Glock and tried to hand it to her.

"Man, you can go to hell. I'm not shooting anybody."

"Maybe I didn't make myself clear. You don't have an option. It's kill or be killed. Now, go in there and handle your assignment. Eliminate the target."

Benita crossed her arms and turned her head toward the van. She then looked back at Miguel. Fuming, she took the gun from his hand and opened the door. "I hate you so much right now. All I wanna do right now is beat your ass to within an inch of your life. Maybe I should just shoot you and get it over with."

"You can shoot me later. Now, go."

Benita looked at the two scary-looking guys who were watching them from across the street. She stayed put, closing the door and looking past the men toward the restaurant. "Okay, Miguel. There are some things you need to clarify for me. Since I have to go in there and off somebody, where the hell is my escape route?"

"Excuse me?"

She flipped through the folder and didn't see any documents besides the photos of the two men. "Hello? Where are the blueprints for the restaurant? You seriously don't think that I'm going to walk in, shoot somebody, and then just walk out?"

Miguel smirked at Benita and handed her another document of the restaurant's floor plan. She glared at him and jerked the document out of his hand.

"That's the front of the building."

"I can read a floor plan, Agent Perkins. What? I'm not supposed to know how to read a damn plan? I did go through a whole lot of training."

"Never said that."

"Then why you always testing me?"

"Because that's what a boss does."

"Whatever." Benita reviewed the document and looked back at the restaurant. There were two exits she could use to escape. One was through the front door, and one was through the kitchen in the back. There was also a basement that seemed to be off the kitchen as well, but no other exits.

After reviewing the file for about five minutes, she handed it back to Miguel. "Which one am I offing?"

"Neither. You're gonna kill the boss-man, Carmine Tucci." He pulled out his iPad and pulled up another photo. "He's sitting at the head of the table, wearing a baby-blue button-down."

"What? You are making my head hurt, Miguel. You show me photos of the big dudes, but they're not the ones I'm supposed to kill. I'm supposed to kill another guy as he feeds his fat face with pasta. Is your job just to irk the shit out of me? 'Cause I'm irked."

Benita frowned when she saw the photo of Carmine. He was bigger than his associates and had huge craters on his face. "Damn, he's ugly. I need to get me a piece of that."

"He's responsible for shipping drugs inside the stomachs of live puppies. Once they're shipped, he kills them to remove the drugs from their guts."

"Did you say puppies? Bastard!" Benita felt sick to her stomach. She didn't want to kill again. The first time she had killed was out of necessity, a life or death situation. This time, it was part of her job to permanently eliminate the bad guy. What happened to just arresting criminals and throwing them in jail?

She suddenly had to puke. Benita opened the door to the vehicle and made it to the back of the car, where she vomited so much that her stomach quivered.

Miguel got out of the car and handed Benita a bottle of water. "Here, drink this."

Benita took the bottle, guzzling the water and then taking another swig to rinse her mouth out. Miguel handed her a tissue. She was so angry she couldn't say another word to him. All she could do was to glare at him. Miguel had tricked her into believing he was there to show her a good time that night, but his agenda was different, as usual. He'd set her up again.

Opening the back door, she dropped the empty bottle and tissue paper on the floor. She walked around to the passenger side and picked up the gun and her purse, placing the gun inside her bag. She closed her eyes and thought about her family. What would they think about her becoming an assassin? Could she really do this? Could she simply walk into the restaurant and take someone out?

Her breathing became heavy, and she held on to her stomach with her empty hand. She looked down at her bag and then looked across the street. The van was no longer parked, and the men were gone.

Miguel handed Benita a small earpiece. "Put this in your ear."

"What for? Are you going to save me if all goes wrong?"

"Yes. You can let me know if you need assistance."

She took it out of his hand and placed it in her right ear. "Anything else?"

"You can do this."

Benita walked into the restaurant. She opened the door and heard music that sounded like it belonged in the *Godfather* movies. *What the hell?* she thought. The restaurant wasn't anything like she was expecting. It was old and dingy. The red vinyl seat covers on the bar stools were cracked and ripped, and the cruddy walls needed a serious paint job. Black and white pictures of men she didn't recognize covered the faded wallpaper.

"Damn, this place sucks," she muttered.

She looked around while holding on to her purse for dear life. There were about five people scattered throughout the restaurant, and it looked like the place was about to close down for the night. She walked over to the bartender and sat on one of the weathered bar stools.

"Hello there, little lady. What're you having?"

"I'll take a Jack straight up."

"Rocks?"

She nodded, and he added ice cubes to a glass. He reached for the bottle of Jack Daniel's and poured Benita half a glass.

"No, make it a double."

He continued pouring until the glass was almost filled. "You must have a death wish."

"Oh, you have no idea." Benita guzzled the drink in one fell swoop. She felt the warm sensation move from her throat down to her stomach. She knew she shouldn't be drinking, but she needed to calm her nerves. "Whoooo. That hit the spot."

The bartender laughed as he removed the glass and took out two clean ones from under the bar. "That's what I hear. How about one more?"

Benita and the bartender took another shot of Jack, and this time, her mouth began to pucker. "Wowwww! How much do I owe you?"

"On the house, lovely girl." He winked at her and touched her hand. "Would you like another drink?"

"Ah, no. I'm good." She placed a generous tip on the bar. "But I'd love to know where the ladies' room is."

He pointed to the back of the restaurant. "Pass the fellas at the table to your left."

"Thank you." Benita took her time standing. She moved past three men having dinner at a table located in the middle of the room. Carmine, her target, was sitting with his back to the bar. She made a mental note of his location as she found the restroom, but she was really looking for the kitchen and found it through a set of swinging doors. She peeked inside to confirm the location of the door leading to the outside of the restaurant, and she noticed a door leading to the basement. She made a mental note and backtracked to the bathroom. She took a few minutes to relieve herself and splash water on her face.

Grabbing her bag, she headed out the door. She slowly walked toward the table, but at the last second changed her mind and headed toward the front door. As she passed the three men, she heard one of them ask why "the bitch" was there.

Benita stopped dead in her tracks, did an about-face, and sat across from the criminals. Crossing her legs, she started giggling, disarming the men. "Well, hello, gentlemen. Hope you all are enjoying your meal."

Benita looked over at Carmine and pointed her finger at him. "Wait, you're Carmine Tucci, the owner of this fine place. I heard all about it and had to visit."

Without looking up from their meals, Carmine spoke between bites. "That's me. Ain't it past your bedtime, little lady?"

Carmine and his comrades started laughing. Benita looked around and saw two bodyguards sitting at the bar with their backs toward Carmine's table. She started giggling again and smiled at the men. She looked behind her and knew she had a clear path to the back of the restaurant.

Benita pulled out the gun and pointed it at Carmine.

"What the hell are you doing?"

"I need you to come with me."

"What? I ain't going nowhere with you."

"If you want to live, then you will get your fat ass up and walk out the door with me."

"Little girl, I think you betta put that toy down and walk away."

"Man, don't make me hurt you."

Carmine raised his hands, and his two bodyguards stood up and drew their guns in Benita's direction.

"Kill the bitch!"

"Oh, shit!" Benita yelled.

She dropped the gun and picked up two of the plates from the table. She threw them like Frisbees at the two goons hurtling toward her. She slowed them for a few seconds and then grabbed the table, pushing it on top of Carmine and the three men, causing their chairs to move backward.

She took off toward the back of the restaurant, missing bullets ricocheting off the walls. When she reached the back door and headed out, she saw two more men running inside. She slammed the door on one of the men and ran down to the basement.

Her heart was pumping pure adrenaline. She hid behind stacked boxes of wine and searched for any kind of weapons she could use against the guys coming after her. She picked up a broom handle and waited for her chance to attack.

As one of the bodyguards came around the boxes, Benita hit him in the leg with the broomstick and knocked the gun out of his hand. She then swung the broom handle across his face, knocking him out. She pulled the unconscious man out of the way and kept an eye out for the other guy searching for her.

She tiptoed to the other side of the basement and hid behind a large beam blocking the stairwell. A bright light shone in her face, and she used the broom handle to bust the bulb. As the second guy moved down the stairs, Benita picked up a bottle of wine and hit him over the head, knocking him to the floor. When he tried to get up, she kicked him with her high heel, making sure he was down for the count.

She grabbed his gun and went back upstairs. She stayed close to the floor in the kitchen and crawled toward the wall. When she got close to the swinging doors, two more bodyguards came running through the kitchen. When one goon ran out the back and the other one went downstairs, Benita took off her shoes and ran as fast as she could, shutting both doors and deadbolting them.

She caught her breath and closed her eyes. Without all the commotion, she remembered the earpiece in her right ear.

"Miguel, I swear to God. I hope you can hear me, 'cause if I get out of here alive, I'm gonna kick your Dominican ass."

She peeked through the circular window and saw the coast was clear. She cocked her gun and pointed it in front of her. When she saw Carmine talking to the two fat men who were sitting at the table, she caught him off-guard and pointed the gun at his head. However, she still had to deal with another bodyguard pointing a gun directly at her.

"Damn, where did you come from? Lookie here, fat man. It's been a helluva night, and I wanna get outta here.

Call your goon off, or I'll shoot your fat ass for real this time." She shoved the gun against his head. "And trust me, there won't be any hesitation. It'll be your extra-fat brains oozing out."

Carmine yelled. "Vinnie, put down the weapon. Let this young lady pass."

But Vinnie still pointed the gun at Benita.

"Did you hear what the man said? Put down your weapon or he's toast," Benita said.

Vinnie lowered his gun, but Benita kept the gun cocked against Carmine's head as she led him toward the door. "Okay, fat boy. We're almost out of here. Keep walking backward. Miguel, I don't know if you hear me, but I'm about five seconds from walking out of this place. You better have that car ready for me."

As soon as they made it to the door, Benita saw some lights flashing from Miguel's SUV.

"Sorry I gotta do this, but it's either you or me." Benita pulled the trigger and shot Carmine in the back, causing him to fall to the floor. She ran out of the restaurant toward Miguel's SUV and jumped inside as if her life depended on it.

"Hang on." Miguel sped away while Benita turned around to see a group of undercover agents running into the restaurant behind him.

Benita looked over at Miguel with hate. "So, I take it you heard everything?"

Miguel nodded.

"I should kick your ass right now."

He was about to respond, but she put her left hand in his face and shook her head.

"Don't speak to me."

Miguel looked at his rearview mirror and did a quick U-turn back toward the restaurant.

"What the hell? Why are we going back?"

He parked the car and headed toward the restaurant, but then he turned back around, backtracking to the passenger side and opening the door. "Come on. I wanna show you something."

Benita reluctantly got out of the car and walked barefoot into the restaurant. She saw the men standing around what seemed to be a crime scene. When Benita saw Tucci walking out of the bathroom, her mouth dropped.

"What the hell? I shot you in the back."

He laughed and walked up to Benita. "Yeah, and that hurt, doll. That really hurt."

Tucci and Miguel shook each other's hands and acted like they were old friends.

"Agent Jenkins, meet Agent Tucci."

"Nice to meet you. For such a little lady, you sure know how to handle yourself."

"Miguel, you wanna tell me what just happened?" Benita asked.

"This was your first assignment. Congratulations. You made it out alive. But, if it had been a real mission, you may not have been so lucky. We need to work on you following the rules. No more taking things into your own hands."

Benita headed out the door, climbing into the vehicle. She had nothing else to say to Miguel. She desperately wished she could hail a cab and avoid being with him at all, but the compound wasn't exactly on the beaten path.

Miguel followed her outside and watched her from afar. As mad as he knew she was, he was convinced beyond a shadow of a doubt that she was his secret weapon—and he didn't care if she was happy about it or not.

Chapter 35

Jeremiah Bolden walked into JQ's Watering Hole, located on the outskirts of Trenton, New Jersey. He looked around the crowded room and saw Leroy sitting at a small round table, having a drink.

"Kojak."

Leroy looked up at Jeremiah but didn't acknowledge him.

Jeremiah took off his jacket, rolled up his sleeves, and took a seat opposite Leroy. "So, it must be real important for you to call me out here in the middle of the damn night," he said.

Leroy took a swig of his drink and stared back. "I think you know why I called you."

A young waitress dressed in a baby-blue T-shirt and a pair of tight black jeans came over to the table and took a rum and Coke order for Jeremiah and a Johnnie Walker Black for Leroy. She sashayed toward the bar and disappeared into the sea of people.

"I'm busy, Kojak. I'm not sure what you're talking about," Jeremiah said.

"How about we talk about a young lady by the name of Benita Jenkins?"

"You know personnel's classified."

"Bullshit, Jeremiah. You owe me."

"I don't owe you shit."

Jeremiah thought about how tight they had been as they worked together side-by-side for years. But their friendship had ended when Leroy fell in love with Samantha. It was unforgivable, and Jeremiah had forced Leroy to leave the unit. As far as he was concerned, Leroy could go straight to hell.

"Jeremiah, tell me the truth. Why the hell did you recruit her?"

"Perkins found her, and you trained her. A perfect combination I couldn't refuse."

"You never should have done that."

"I'm the executive director. I do what I please. Why do you care about this woman?"

"I know the family, and the grandmother wants answers."

The waitress maneuvered through the crowd and placed the drinks on the table. Jeremiah picked up his drink and took a long swig. He reached in his side pocket and handed her two twenty-dollar bills. "Keep the change."

The young lady smiled and walked back through the crowd. Jeremiah took a sip and enjoyed the strong and lingering taste coating his throat. "Well, she's fine. Case closed."

"The case is not closed, Jeremiah. The family deserves to know what's going on."

"The family knows what the family needs to know. It's none of your concern, Kojak. Why don't you go on back to your little school and teach your little kids? That's where you feel more comfortable."

Leroy finished his drink and walked out of the bar without saying another word to his former colleague and friend. He had to leave before he did something he'd regret later.

How could he have known Benita would end up working for DTCU? She had no idea just how dangerous that place could be. He needed to make sure he had someone from the inside to watch over his daughter, and he had just the person in mind.

Chapter 36

Miguel pulled up to a gated community in Livingston, New Jersey, and punched in codes to open the locked gate. Benita hadn't spoken a word to him after they left the restaurant. She couldn't believe that after an amazing dinner, he had forced her into trying to kill her target. Little did she know that what she thought was her putting her life on the line was nothing more than an exercise.

She looked at Miguel with total disgust. He was pompous and sneaky. This was the last time she'd let her guard down around him.

Miguel parked in front of a newly constructed apartment complex located at the end of a dead-end street. He unbuckled his seat belt and got out. He headed toward the entrance but realized Benita was still sitting in the car. He backtracked and opened Benita's door.

"Lucy, we're home."

"Fuck you and your Lucy. Why are we here? What? Another damn surprise?"

"Something like that." Miguel chuckled at Benita and shook his head. He was trying to lighten the mood, but it was in vain.

Benita jumped out of the SUV and looked around her unfamiliar surroundings. "Where the hell are we, Miguel?"

"Just follow me, Ms. Jenkins. No more jobs tonight."

Miguel punched in another code, buzzing them into the building. Unlike the rooms at DTCU, the walls were painted an eggshell color with chocolate trim. Beige carpet covered the floors in the large lobby and hallways. They walked past a security guard, who ignored them as he finished up paperwork. He pressed the up button, and the doors opened. Miguel and Benita got on the elevator and rode it to the tenth floor.

Miguel looked over at Benita and tried to deal with the silence, but after a while, it began to bother him. "Don't you want to know why we're here?"

They got off the elevator and walked to apartment 10B. He pulled out a set of keys and opened the door.

Benita's apparent anger softened, and she looked nervous. "Wait a minute, playa. What the hell are you doing? You almost got me killed, and now you think I'm putting out in your love nest?"

Miguel stepped aside to let Benita walk in before him. "Not my love nest. It's your love nest. I mean your new apartment."

Had Benita just woken from a bad dream? She couldn't believe how beautiful the apartment was. The open kitchen overlooked a large living room that was furnished with a white leather couch, two small mahogany leather chairs, a glass coffee table, a medium-sized flat-screen television, and a white rug.

"This is mine?"

"Yup, all yours."

She moved past Miguel toward the bedroom. She flipped on the light to find a queen-sized bed with an ivory-colored headboard, a lavender comforter set, and a birch dresser and bookshelf. The room had one large bay window overlooking a small pond surrounded by lots of trees.

She turned around. "It's gorgeous, Miguel. I don't know what to say."

He walked to the bay window and looked out at the view. "You've worked hard, and no matter what's been thrown at you, you shine like a true star. Tonight was a little over the top, but I hope the apartment makes up for my poor judgment. You've earned the right to live on your own."

"Oh, Miguel. Thank you. You know, it hasn't been easy working with you—I mean, you can be a downright asshole. I can't tell you the number of times I just wanted to wring your neck and squeeze you till you couldn't breathe anymore."

Benita jumped on the bed, making angel wings with her arms and legs. She felt the softness of the down comforter and closed her eyes.

He looked at her and smiled, then placed a set of keys and a new cell phone on the dresser. "These are yours."

She sat up on the bed and perked up when she noticed pictures of her grandmother, brother, and cousin strategically placed on the top of the dresser. Benita moved toward a blinking light that caught her attention located above her closet doors.

"Ah, a surveillance camera. Why am I not surprised?"

"It's temporary. We want to make sure you're safe."

"Right. Safe, huh."

"There's one more thing I'd like to show you. Follow me, please."

"What now?" Benita followed Miguel down to the garage, where a black convertible Mustang GT was parked in spot 10B.

"For real, Miguel? This is my ride?"

"Technically, it belongs to DTCU, but it's yours to drive."

Miguel pulled out a set of keys from his pocket to hand to Benita, but she didn't take them. She stood there in silence.

"What's wrong? You don't like the car?"

"Why are you doing all this?"

"What do you mean, why? You earned it."

"No. There's something you're not telling me. This can't be this easy. You taking me out to dinner, bringing me to this place, telling me I'm free to drive this fancy car. Something just doesn't feel right."

"I know it's hard for you to trust any of this, but it's real, Benita. You've given up a lot for the unit, and now it's time you're rewarded. Nothing more, nothing less."

Miguel dangled the keys, and Benita snatched them. She opened the driver's side door and sat inside, inhaling the new-leather smell. She'd never owned such a luxurious car or lived in a classy apartment building before. Her life used to be modest, but now all that had changed.

Benita rubbed her hands across the steering wheel, thinking about what all this meant for her. No matter what kind of toys the organization threw her way, she still wasn't free. This put her further under the thumb of this organization. She had a bigger debt to pay.

"Well, it's been a long night. I think it's time for me to head home," Miguel said.

At first, Benita didn't hear him because her thoughts were miles away, but when he said it again, she got out of the car and set the alarm.

The two agents took the elevator back to the first floor, and Miguel said good night. "Oh, by the way, you're being inducted as a full-time agent. Be at headquarters by seven a.m. The directions are already set in the GPS. Don't be late."

Benita rode to the tenth floor and went back to her new apartment. Walking around the rooms, she checked for bugs around the furniture and light fixtures and on the portable phones strategically located in different rooms. "I found you," she said, commenting on her success in finding three cameras in the living room, hallway, and bedroom. Benita made a mental note to be careful when she entered and left the apartment. Not sure how long she would be watched by Big Brother, she didn't want to give them any reason to mistrust her.

Twenty minutes later, Benita went to the kitchen and found some herbal tea in one of the cabinets and heated up some water in a kettle. She brewed the tea and made her way over to the new leather couch, relaxed, and closed her eyes.

She thought about her family and how much she missed them. Although she promised Miguel she would have no contact with them, she didn't plan on keeping that promise.

Chapter 37

Raven arrived at Carl Johnson's ten-thousand-square-foot, three-story loft around two in the morning. She had taken a cab there so he wouldn't make her leave. She heard the music from two blocks away. He was probably hosting a listening party for some of his artists, and it could possibly go on all night.

As Raven made her way through the small crowd, she saw a number of people smoking weed, drinking, and snorting cocaine. Carl, who was dressed in an Italian silk shirt and jeans, was off in the corner, speaking to Bobby G, who was repeatedly turning his white baseball cap from front to back on his head.

"Carl. Look who's here. One of the finest bitches in Brooklyn."

Carl walked over to Raven, grabbing her ass and pulling her close.

She pushed away. "Stop it, Carl. You're drunk."

Benjamin, who had walked out of the bathroom, saw Raven and couldn't keep his eyes off her. He acted more like a shy kid than a business advisor.

Raven noticed Benjamin and wiggled her way out of Carl's grasp. "Hey, Benjamin. I'm surprised you're hanging out with these losers. I thought you had more class."

Embarrassed, all he could do was blush. "Hello, Raven. It's good to see you."

Bobby G laughed. "Look at that clown, turning red and shit. This ain't no place for you, white boy. Right, Holiday?"

Carl grabbed Raven's waist, but she pulled away from him again and fixed her outfit. "Dammit, Carl. Stop. You're like a dog in heat. You know I don't like you grabbing all over me like that."

"You should be happy somebody wanna touch your uptight ass."

When a slow reggae song started blasting from the oversized speakers, Carl walked over to a young hottie. "Let's dance, baby."

This only infuriated Raven. She yelled at Carl, "What the fuck are you doing?"

Carl babbled under his breath, "Girl, you can take that attitude outta here."

When Carl pulled the young lady closer and rubbed his pelvis against hers, Raven ran over and slapped him across the face. He returned a backhanded slap across her face.

She started punching and kicking him. "You fucking asshole. I'll kill your ass! I'll kill you!"

Carl's bodyguard, Big Boy, picked up Raven by one arm and moved his body between the two fighting maniacs. She was trying to get away from his grip, but she was no match for the humungous creature. "Raven! You know the rules. You need to chill."

"Fuck you, Big Boy. Carl, I swear, I'm tired of your shit. Tired!"

"Then fucking leave. I didn't even invite you here."

"Oh, it's like that? It's like that? You don't even want me here? Well, fine. I don't have to be here. I'm out. Big Boy, let me go. I'm done with this piece of shit. I'm outta here. I swear to you, Big Boy, you will regret it if you don't let me go right now."

Big Boy had known Carl ever since they were kids, when he used to terrorize him and his sister in the neighborhood. One day, Carl clocked him on the nose. After that, he stayed clear of the little guy and became the laughingstock of the neighborhood. Years later, Big Boy was working as a bouncer for one of the hottest clubs in Manhattan, and Carl and his entourage walked in and headed for the VIP section. Ironically, it was Carl who reached out to Big Boy. At first, Big Boy was skeptical, especially considering their history, but after Carl offered a huge salary to keep the undesirables away, Big Boy jumped at the chance, and he'd been working for Carl ever since.

Although Big Boy was more than six feet three inches and two hundred sixty pounds of pure muscle, he still was afraid of what Carl would do to him if Raven caused another scene. The last time Big Boy was supposed to keep the peace, Raven had broken a plate over Carl's head. The party ended, and Carl had to get five stitches. Carl promised to cut Big Boy into several pieces if he ever allowed that broad to hurt him again. From that point on, Big Boy had paid closer attention to Raven's every move.

"Boss? You good?"

"Yeah, let her go. Raven, you gotta get out of here before you get yourself hurt."

Big Boy let go of Raven but stayed between the two of them.

Raven calmly spoke over Big Boy's shoulder. "I need a ride home."

"Benjamin was just leaving. Drop her off, please."

Big Boy gently nudged Raven by the elbow to leave. She stood for a few more seconds, glaring at Carl, but then she relented, storming out the door with Benjamin following.

Carl plopped down on his leather couch. He put his hand to his forehead and closed his eyes for a few seconds. "Big Boy, I just don't trust that broad. She's always up to no good. Make sure you have somebody follow her home. I wouldn't be surprised if she found a way to get back at me, even if it's with that lame-ass white boy."

"Done, Holiday."

Bobby G took a swig from his bottle of beer. "Yo, man. She cray-cray. Bet she's the shit in the bedroom, though. All those crazy-ass bitches are crazy passionate."

Carl looked up at Bobby G and threw an empty glass in his direction, but Bobby G moved out of the way before it shattered on the floor. "You shut the fuck up. Don't talk about my lady like that."

"Damn, playa. I didn't know it was like that. Fuck, I'm gone too."

"Get the fuck out. All you muthafuckas get out. Now!" He sneered at the thought of someone else touching Raven. She was crazy, but she was his crazy. Fucking Raven.

Benjamin looked over at Raven, who was biting her bottom lip, trying to hold back tears.

"I know you're wondering how in the world Carl and I got together in the first place, right?" she asked.

"I wasn't thinking anything, Raven. People get together for many different reasons. I'm more surprised by the way he treats you. Nobody deserves to be disrespected."

"Really? Because he treats you like you're his lapdog. And how are you cool with that?"

"Well, I guess none of us should be disrespected."

Raven looked out the passenger window. She started crying and wiped the tears from her eyes.

They remained silent for forty-five minutes while he drove up the FDR Drive to Raven's building on 124th Street and Fifth Avenue. He shut off the engine and turned toward the beautiful lady.

"We're here."

"Yes, we are. Thanks for dropping me off, Benjamin. Really appreciate it."

"Oh, no problem. It was on my way home."

"I think it was a little past your home. Don't you live in Little Italy?"

Benjamin chuckled and rubbed his ear, which he did when he was nervous. "Maybe a little, but it was no problem."

"Damn, I wish you weren't so damn nice. You're too nice to be working for Carl. He's a real piece of work. A bona fide prick."

Raven opened the car door but stopped herself from getting out when she noticed Benjamin had opened his door. "No, you don't have to get out. I'm good." Just before she got out of the car, she kissed him on the lips. "Thanks again."

"You're welcome."

Raven got out of the car and slammed the car door. She ran toward her building and disappeared inside.

Benjamin glanced at a pair of headlights flashing behind him, and when he looked in his rearview mirror, he noticed a black SUV. He became nauseous when he realized he was being followed. It was time for him to make his exit strategy sooner than planned.

Chapter 38

After attending the official graduation ceremony, Benita followed the other graduates into a large conference room where the wait staff was serving hors d'oeuvres and champagne. Standing close to the back of the room, she listened to Executive Director Bolden give brief comments to the agents.

He finished his speech with, "Congratulations to the entire graduating class. You're all champions. Cheers!"

Evan walked over to Benita and Luciana.

"Way to go, Agent Green. You even got a shout out from the boss man," Benita said.

Evan flashed his beautiful white teeth. "Congrats to you too. Maybe we should go out and celebrate."

Benita looked over at Luciana, but she offered no help. Benita said, "We might be able to arrange that. You know what, Evan? Would you mind getting Luciana and me something to drink?"

"Sure." Evan walked over to the bar to get two glasses of wine.

Luciana teased Benita. "Hmmm . . . he likes you."

"Oh, puhleez. We're both newly appointed agents. We bonded."

"Who did you bond with?" Miguel asked, joining them.

"Well, hello, Agent Perkins. Fancy meeting you here," Benita replied.

"We need to go over some rules going forward. Meet me in ten? Thanks." He walked away.

"What's up his ass?" Benita asked. "There's never any consistency with him. He either shows a little bit of feeling, or he's as cold as they come."

"Let's just say that's why he's great at his job. In this line of business, your emotions are a liability. You've got to be able to shut them off," Luciana said.

Benita crossed her arms and started in Miguel's direction. "Huh. I hope I never get to that point where I hate being around my own self."

Benita walked into her apartment, exhausted. She kicked off her shoes and plopped down on her couch. She had just finished a two-hour pow-wow with Miguel, who grilled her on the dos and don'ts of being an agent. He reiterated the importance of her staying off the grid because he didn't want anyone to see her out. After a while, Benita could only tune his voice out. She picked up a few words relating to abusing privileges or losing her apartment, but she didn't really care to listen to him anymore. She nodded in agreement and thought about how she was going to celebrate her accomplishments that night.

She pulled out her cell from her bag and made a call. "Hey, Luciana, you still down to hang tonight? I'll pick you up at ten. Lata."

Benita and Luciana arrived at Indi Blue, one of the hottest and most exclusive clubs in Philadelphia. Thanks to Huey, her DTCU hacker friend, the ladies hit club Indi

Blue and walked to the front of the line, gave a secret password, and were escorted to the VIP section.

Benita and Luciana were dressed in sexy little black dresses and über-high stilettos. They sipped Bellinis and danced to Beyoncé, Lady Gaga, and Nicki Minaj. Every man in the club was checking them out.

Slurring, Luciana yelled in Benita's ear, "How is it you're not drunk?"

"Please, I'm from Brooklyn. We know how to handle our liquor." She switched gears. "Girl, why'd you become an agent?"

"My dad was a cop. My brother was a cop. My uncle was a cop. I wanted to be more than a cop. After getting the top score, Miguel approached me. He asked if I wanted to make a real difference, and I jumped at the chance."

"Even if it meant doing unethical things?"

"If it meant taking down the bad guys, then hell yeah. I'd do it every time."

"Shit. I never thought I'd become this sexy super-agent bringing down bad guys. All I was doing was living my life. I was working as a hairdresser, going to school, and hanging out."

Luciana started laughing. "Us sexy girls got to stick together."

"Right!"

They downed their drinks and continued dancing.

"By the way, Benita, rumor has it Perkins has big plans for you. Are you ready for your first real assignment?"

"Puhleez, I'm ready for whatever that fool throws my way. I've been meaning to ask you. What's up with you and geek boy?"

"Who, Huey? Nothing."

"Come on, Luciana. I may not have known you two for a long time, but I got eyes, and I've seen how he looks at you. He wants you, girl. You just gotta give him a little bone so he can fetch."

"I don't know. He's shy. I think he's in love with his computer. It's his girlfriend. Plus, I don't have time for a relationship. This job will suck all the energy out of you."

"I don't plan on letting this job take over my life. I plan to work hard, play hard, and love hard. Oh, it's my song! Come on, Luciana. Let's get our dance on."

Benita and Luciana danced the night away. They had to enjoy every moment because in the blink of an eye, a job could come knocking. Benita didn't notice Miguel watching her from the balcony. He had installed a GPS system in her car and phone and had the ability to track her whereabouts at all times.

Since she was no longer under the thumb of DTCU, she had the freedom to come and go as she pleased. Miguel didn't fully trust Benita to keep a low profile and stay out of trouble, but who could blame her? Benita was a beautiful young woman who had been confined to a short prison stint and watched closely at the unit.

After meeting with Benita earlier that day, something in her eye screamed rebellion. So, he went home and activated the tracking system on Benita's phone. A few hours later, he saw her on the move and followed her to Indi Blue. He wanted to know what she was doing at all times. As hard as it was, he couldn't stop his heart from falling in love with her. He wanted her, no matter how wrong it was.

Chapter 39

Benita woke in a cold sweat after having a recurring dream of attending Grace's funeral. She stood over the casket, and Grace opened her eyes and said, "Benita, Wes is in trouble. You need to help him."

Benita sat up in bed and started crying, unable to control her emotions. It had been close to a year since she had seen her family, and she missed them.

After a long, hot shower, she looked in her closet and pulled out a short, black wig in the shape of a bob with bangs. She put on dark-blue jeans, a camel tank-top, black boots, and a black leather jacket. It was five a.m. when she jumped into her sports car and drove east on Interstate 78 headed toward New York City.

She crossed the Holland Tunnel and drove east on Canal Street toward the Manhattan Bridge. It was about 6:30 a.m. when she made it to downtown Brooklyn. She drove to her grandmother's house in Bedford Stuyvesant and parked a block down the street. Benita knew her grandmother always looked out her kitchen window, and she didn't want to be recognized.

She sat in the car, thinking about what her next move would be. A homeless man walked up to the car and tapped on the glass. Benita cracked the window.

"Hey, classy girl. This ride is tight."

"Beat it."

"You remind me of a movie star or something. You sure is fine."

Benita opened the window and handed the homeless man a twenty-dollar bill. "Look, make yourself useful and watch my car. Okay?"

"Damn, girl. What else you got up in your bag?"

"Man, get the hell out of here. Take your money and stop talking."

The homeless man took the money and was about to say something else, but Benita glared at him, and he stepped back.

Benita held on to her steering wheel. She could hear Miguel's voice in the back of her mind, warning her to stay clear of her family. Biting her bottom lip, Benita opened the car door and walked toward her grandmother's house.

She was about to cross the street when she saw a limousine pull up. Her brother got out, and she watched it drive away. A Madd Dogg symbol was on the license plate. Wes ran up the stairs and went inside the house.

Benita noticed the curtains move. She knew her grandmother was watching, and Benita didn't want to risk being seen. She got back in her car and drove away.

Grace had indeed looked out the window and saw a young woman who looked a lot like her granddaughter. This young woman was about to cross the street but clearly changed her mind.

Grace removed her hand from the curtain and sat at the kitchen table. She didn't know what to believe anymore. She saw her granddaughter everywhere. But Grace hoped one day she would see Benita for real before she left this world.

Chapter 40

Miguel passed a large packet of information labeled *Confidential* to Benita. "Agent Jenkins, this is your first official assignment."

Benita opened the folder and saw an old mug shot of Holiday Johnson. "Carl Johnson is my first assignment? What's he done?"

"He's been involved in many illegal activities, including extortion, intimidation, tax evasion, fraud, and has been linked to several murders. He's cheated his artists out of millions; however, we've had a hard time proving it. A few grand jury probes went nowhere."

Benita flipped through the notes and news clippings. "An ex-gangbanger turned music mogul. You don't get to that level without stomping on a bunch of thugs' necks. Or pulling out a gun and pistol-whipping whoever gets in his path. No matter what the story, the bottom line is people keep their mouths shut. Snitching is a no-no."

Miguel was impressed by Benita's street smarts. For someone who had lived a pretty sheltered life, she was knowledgeable about the people around her. "Well, it's a good thing we have you to infiltrate Carl's world and find us the evidence we need to bring him down."

"Me? You expect me to walk into this business and make him give up the goods? Wow. That's a tall order, Miguel."

"One I know you can fill. I know you can go in there and work your charms."

"You want me to smoke him?"

Miguel smirked. "Not if you can help it. Graham's working on setting up your cover, creating a passport, driver's license, credit cards, et cetera. You've spent the last year in Paris working for a fashion boutique. Samantha will create a new look and help you prepare to make sure your cover is believable."

"How much time do I have to prepare?" Benita asked.

"Two weeks. The sooner, the better."

After the meeting, Benita went to Huey's office. He was quite stylishly dressed for a geeky guy in a blue plaid shirt with extra-skinny jeans and navy-blue Converse sneakers. He sat behind four computer monitors strategically located side by side on his desk.

Without looking up from typing a hundred words a minute, he shook his head no. "Whatever it is, I don't have time. There's a missing agent in Compton I need to find."

"Huh, but aren't you supposed to be working on setting up my cover?"

"Yes, I am, but just not at this particular moment. I'm busy. Can you come back?"

"Sure, I can come back, but you gotta promise you'll help me out with something after you're done with this crisis."

"Sure. Whatever."

"Thank you, Huey." She was about to walk out, but he stopped her.

"Benita, what do you need?"

"I need to know if my brother, Wes, is working for Madd Dogg Records. Can you help me?"

"That information is off-limits. I'd need a sign-off from your boss. I could get into some serious trouble if I access that information without him knowing it."

"Huey, I would never want you to do anything to jeopardize your job. But wouldn't you need to update files pertaining to the Johnson case anyway? How's that breaching anything? I'm sure he'll understand you're just looking to be thorough and pull Johnson's employee records. I mean, when was the last time you updated your files? Just think about it. If you still can't do it, I'll understand."

Huey sighed. "Listen, I'll talk to Perkins and see what kind of information he needs for this case. And then I'll slip a few extra jobs in and troll around to see if your brother is working for Johnson's company. Okay?"

"Thank you. Okay, I'll get out of your way. Find that agent." Benita exited his office, leaving him to his current assignment.

When she looked back, he was typing uncontrollably, as if his life depended on it.

Benita approached the door to her apartment, and Miguel was standing there. "What are you doing here?" she asked.

He walked past her and entered her apartment. "We need to talk."

"Well, come on in. But can't this wait till tomorrow? I'm tired and hungry, and I've been working with Samantha all day to get my cover straight. All I wanna do is take a long shower, eat something, and go to bed."

"No, this can't wait."

"What now?"

"What's going on with you and Graham?"

Benita looked at him strangely. "What are you talking about? We're colleagues."

"I know you asked him to do something for you on company time, and that's against policy."

Benita became angry about Miguel's confrontation, but she was angrier that Huey had told him about her request.

"Listen, Miguel. I didn't mean to get Huey in trouble. I just asked him for a simple request."

"He's not supposed to be using his computer to put you on VIP lists."

"Oh, the VIP list at Indi Blue? You came over to talk to me about that? You're straight-up nuts. What I do with my free time is my business."

"What you do is my business. I don't want you to go back to jail because you can't follow policy."

"What? Are you threatening me now? If I don't follow your every damn rule, you'll ship me back to jail? Well, do what you gotta do, because I'm not working every waking minute of the day with no fun. No way. Maybe if your ass loosened up a bit, you'd understand life is more than DTCU."

"Fine. If you don't want my advice, you're on your own," Miguel screamed back at her.

"You don't give advice, Miguel. You bark at me. Give all kinds of orders. Why do you care if I go to a party? It's none of your business. Stop riding me like I'm a damned child, Miguel."

"Then stop acting like one."

"Get the hell out of my apartment."

Miguel sat on Benita's couch and leaned forward with his hands clasped. He noticed the anger on her face. "The first time I saw you, I knew you'd be a kick-ass agent."

"You've told me a hundred times. I get it. You feel responsible for me, but you don't have the right to control my every move. Let me live, will ya?"

"I'm sorry. I just want to make sure you're okay. I know you didn't become an agent on your own. I just want to be there for you."

Benita took a deep breath and sat beside him. Her anger had subsided, but now she was feeling compassion for her crazy boss. She touched his hands. "I'll be fine. I promise I won't compromise my identity or an important assignment. Okay? Feel better?"

"I do care about you, Benita. I may have a funny way of showing it, but I do care."

"Sure you do."

Miguel kissed her on the lips. Benita was surprised by his actions and sat there speechless and motionless.

He was about to kiss her again, but she stopped him. "I think you should leave."

"Benita, I'm sorry." He slowly made his way to the door and left in silence.

Chapter 41

Ernest Brown was annoyed that his old friend Benjamin had provided no help in bringing Carl down. He sat on the couch in his apartment on 110th Street, talking to Agent Alex Stratsburg about Carl Johnson.

Ernest had been receiving threats from people in Carl's circle. A week ago, he was walking out of his office building, and someone shoved a gun in his back. He was thrown to the ground and told not to look at his assailant. A large envelope landed beside him.

"Carl says he's watching you. No matter what you got planned, stop it, or you gonna regret crossing him. Got it?" Then the man just walked away.

That was when Ernest contacted the FBI. A few days later, Agent Stratsburg was at his apartment, interviewing him about the alleged assault and threat.

Alex had been working with Perkins for more than two years, investigating Johnson to bring the man to justice. Perkins had received a call from his counterpart at the FBI. He assigned the call to Alex, who set up an appointment to interview Ernest.

"What was in the envelope?" Alex asked.

Ernest got up and left the room. A few minutes later, he returned with three black-and-white photos and a torn-open envelope. He handed everything to Alex, who looked at photos of Ernest and another man having dinner at a restaurant.

"What's the significance of these pictures?" Alex asked.

"The guy in the photo is Benjamin Mahoney. He works for Carl, and he's been helping me get the goods on him."

"What kind of goods?"

"Carl wants exclusive rights to my artists. When I wouldn't sign with him, he threatened to hurt my daughter. He forced my hand, Agent Stratsburg. I had to make a deal with the devil, and my artist DJ Grill got caught in the crossfire."

"This isn't going to be enough. We need proof he threatened you and your daughter. Do you have any witnesses I can speak to?"

"You can speak to Benjamin. He can verify it."

Before Alex could ask any more questions, the doorbell rang, and Ernest excused himself. Then, Alex heard yelling coming from the hallway, followed by what sounded like a gunshot and then a thud. He jumped up from his chair and pulled out his gun. As soon as he turned in the direction of the doorway, a piercing pain erupted in his shoulder. He looked down at his shirt and saw blood. The last thing he saw was a man pointing a gun to his head.

Before Alex could pull the trigger, he was shot in the middle of his forehead, dead before he hit the floor. His gun landed next to his body. The assailant grabbed Alex's iPad, smartphone, and the pictures from the table. The killer walked out the door, leaving two dead bodies behind.

Miguel was with Luciana in Morristown, New Jersey, going through old files related to the Johnson case when he received a call from a detective friend at the NYPD.

"Miguel, it's Henry. I think you need to come to New York ASAP. There's been an incident involving your guy Alex Stratsburg."

Upon arriving at the address of the victim, Ernest Brown, on 110th Street in Manhattan, Miguel and Luciana were stopped by two police officers standing by the building's entrance. Yellow police tape blocked the entrance, and residents were left to wonder who'd been hurt.

The two DTCU agents flashed their badges, and the policemen allowed them to enter. When they walked on to the scene, there were two crime scene investigators taking photographs and carefully collecting and logging evidence, while a third was dusting for fingerprints throughout the apartment. The coroner worked diligently to verify the identity of victims Ernest Brown and Alex Stratsburg and collected pertinent evidence before the bodies could be bagged and eventually removed from the apartment.

Detective Phillips greeted Miguel and Luciana and escorted them to the living room, where Stratsburg's body was lying in a pool of blood. Miguel bent down to get a better look. "What happened?"

"The first victim, Ernest Brown, was found near the door. From what we've determined, he opened the door and was shot at close range in the chest. The perp then walked to the living room, where he fired two shots into Strasburg—one in the shoulder and one in the head. But your guy got off at least one round."

Luciana stared down at Stratsburg and bit her bottom lip. "I was supposed to come with him."

Miguel looked at her and stopped her from going down a bad road. "And if you'd been here with him, you may be dead too." He turned back to Detective Phillips. "Any idea who may have done this?"

"I was hoping you could tell me. I mean, your guy was here conducting an investigation. Why was he here?"

"Unfortunately, I can't comment on any open cases DTCU is working on, but if we find this not to be the case, I'll provide you with updates."

"Of course. I know the drill. Well, do what you gotta do. You know where to find me." Phillips left the room, leaving them some time alone with their deceased agent.

Miguel bent down and checked Stratsburg's pants pockets, frantically searching for a phone. He turned to Rodriguez. "Do you see his phone? We need to find it. Alex texted me earlier. Maybe he had some information pointing to his killer. Check around the couch."

Rodriguez searched the perimeter of Stratsburg's body, including the couch. "I don't see it. Maybe one of the investigators logged it as evidence. I'll go find someone. If not, call Huey. See if he can track it." She stepped out of the room to find the investigator, while Miguel remained with Stratsburg's body, vowing to make the person pay for killing his fellow agent.

Chapter 42

Benjamin splashed his face with water and tried to stop shaking. He'd gone to Ernest's apartment to speak with him about the call Ernest had placed with the FBI. He never expected to see Ernest's dead body lying by the front door.

He had reached over to knock, but when he saw the door ajar, he pushed it open. Benjamin checked Ernest for a pulse, but it was too late. He ran to Ernest's office to see if he could find the photos of him and Ernest having dinner. As he passed the living room, he saw another man lying dead on the floor.

At this point, he felt the need to vomit and ran to the bathroom, where he relieved himself of the bile that had built up in his throat. "Carl did this. I know it," he said to himself. He splashed water on his face and was about to wipe his hands on a towel but stopped and used a paper towel instead. He wiped off the sink, faucets, and toilet then left the bathroom. He did a quick glance to see if he could find the photos, but when he couldn't, he left the apartment, wiping off the front doorknob.

He grabbed a beer from his refrigerator and guzzled it down. He never in a million years thought Carl would kill Ernest, but he knew he had to be next. Carl had never mentioned he was having Ernest followed, but after Ernest called him, freaking out that he'd been attacked by one of Carl's goons, it became clear to Benjamin that Carl meant business.

Back at his apartment, Benjamin sat in front of his computer, pulling up several bank accounts that he'd opened a year ago. He had started moving funds from Carl's business accounts to his own in preparation for his relocation to a small island in the Caribbean. After his botched attempt to pay off T-Bone, he tried to cover his tracks by dissolving the company and setting up a new one. His early retirement was happening sooner than he had anticipated. The accountant knew it was only a matter of time before Carl found out about his deception, and he would end up like his friend Ernest.

"Damn, Ernie. Why did you have to get yourself killed? I gotta get out of here."

Benjamin picked up the phone and called the airline to book the earliest flight out of JFK.

"Yes. One-way ticket to the Cayman Islands. What's your earliest flight? Six a.m.? First class, please. Yes. Carlos Franklin."

After giving the airline representative all his pertinent information, he frantically started going through his closets and drawers in the bedroom and the bathroom, pulling out only the bare essentials. He could buy whatever he needed when he got to his new villa. He then made a beeline to his office, where he opened up a small safe housing several passports, two thumb drives, and important documents related to his properties.

There was one final step necessary before Benjamin could leave the country, and that was to ensure that incriminating files detailing Carl's shady dealings were sent to DTCU. He had always kept them as an insurance policy if Carl ever tried to kill him. He wasn't sure who to send the files to now. Ernest had been the one with a contact at the agency, and that contact had been murdered too. He looked at the thumb drives and decided to wait until he got settled at his new location.

Taking a bottle of Xanax out of the medicine cabinet, he downed two of them with a bottle of water. He needed to be calm and stop himself from having a full-blown anxiety attack. It was only a few hours before he caught his early flight. Benjamin couldn't wait to get as far away from Carl as possible.

Donning a long, honey-blonde wig with bangs, green contacts, and chunky black-rimmed acetate frames, Benita walked into Madd Dogg Records' reception area wearing a white lace top, a short stretch poplin black-and-white full skirt, black tights, and Prada patent-leather pumps. Samantha had taken great care in dressing Benita for the part of Bridgette Toussaint, a young woman who, according to her cover story, had spent the last year working in Paris for a small designer boutique. Huey had worked overtime, creating the appropriate credentials, and Benita took two twelve-hour courses to teach herself French so she could hold a basic conversation.

After Stratsburg's murder, Miguel became hell-bent on getting Benita into Carl's organization as soon as possible. He was convinced that Carl had ordered the hit on Ernest Brown and that Stratsburg had been at the wrong place at the wrong time.

Luciana tracked down Carl's assistant, Sophia Nales, and gave her an offer she couldn't refuse. She told Sophia that her boss was under investigation for criminal activities and that she could be brought up on charges by helping him cover up some of his shady dealings. If she wanted to stay clear of the crossfire, she needed to get out of town fast.

DTCU provided her with a first-class ticket to wherever she wanted to go and wrote a fat check to tide her over for the next six months. The next day, Nales was boarding a plane to the Dominican Republic, where she would spend time with her parents and relatives. She left a message for Carl, telling him she had a family emergency and would let him know when she would be coming back to work.

A young receptionist greeted Benita. "Hello, may I help you?"

"Yes, I'm Bridgette Toussaint, Mr. Johnson's temporary assistant."

Evan had been placed in the company as a mailroom guy and was walking by the reception area to pick up the mail when he saw Benita. He barely recognized her. She winked at him and felt more comfortable knowing he was there to watch her back.

"Please have a seat in the lounge area. Someone will come to get you shortly."

Benita sat on the red leather couch, watching music videos of Bobby G on several large flat-screen televisions. She crossed her legs and bopped her head to the music.

Benjamin presented the latest financial update to his boss, who sat at his desk with folded arms.

"Benjamin, you know what, man? I have to say you're one of the hardest workin' white boys I've ever met. Whatever I need, you always provide it. When things don't seem to go in my favor, you just sit there, quiet as a mouse. Do you even have a backbone, man?"

Benjamin remained silent, even with Carl hurling insults at him.

"I'm just messing with you, Benjamin. You do a great job for me. I think it's time to expand my empire. There are a couple of new artists I want to sign. Now that Brown is dead, he had a whole slew of artists we can round up. What do you think about that?"

Again, Benjamin remained silent.

"It's a sad thing he was murdered. A very sad thing. You know what's even sadder? That he tried to screw me with the FBI. Now, I know you know this because I had you followed. I'm hoping you were trying to convince him to do the right thing."

"Carl, I didn't know he was going to the FBI. I swear."

"I know you didn't. Because if I did think you were trying to do an okey-doke on me, you wouldn't still be breathing."

Carl suddenly became quiet and stared at him. Benjamin felt nervous.

Carl finally spoke. "Okay, I need you to get me those artists. And I don't care how you do it, but see if my attorney, Don Buckley, can make this shit happen. I want them on my books by the end of the quarter."

Carl's phone buzzed. "Yeah. Send her up." He hung up and turned back to Benjamin. "Damn, I had to call this bullshit agency to send me over a new assistant. My old one just picked up and left me in the lurch. Hopefully, this one can answer some phones and write a damn memo. Just need her to handle my business discreetly. You know what I'm saying?"

Benjamin nodded.

Carl laughed and slapped him on the back. "All right, Bennie Ben. Get the hell out of here. And see how I can bring in some new artists."

Benjamin rushed out of Carl's office and bumped into Benita, almost knocking her down. He was planning to be on a plane to the Cayman Islands in fewer than five hours. He had to get home and finish packing before Carl came after him.

As Benita caught a glimpse of him, she noticed how nervous this man was and made a mental note to find out his story at a later time. She knocked on Carl's door, and he yelled for her to come in.

Carl was on a call but stopped mid-sentence when he saw Benita. "Damn, baby. You are one beautiful woman. I must have died and gone to heaven."

"Thank you. I'm Bridgette Toussaint, and I'll be your personal assistant for the next couple of weeks."

"Well, I'm gonna need a lot of personal assisting." He laughed at his own joke, but Benita just smiled.

"Anything I should know before we get started? What do you need?"

"My former assistant screened my calls, set up my appointments, and kept the bad boys away. Think you can handle it?"

Benita gave Carl one of her devious smiles and walked out the door without answering. When she turned back, his eyes were following her ass. Hook, line, and sinker. It would only be a matter of time before she had him eating out of her hand.

Benita arrived at six thirty the next morning to set up surveillance at the office. Still wearing her disguise, she changed into a dark-colored wig and a royal blue blazer with a matching short pleated skirt, a ruffled white silk top, and matching royal blue and black polka-dot platform high heels. She still wore thick-rimmed glasses, making her feel comfortable that no one would recognize her.

The night before, Benita met with Huey to discuss how the security system worked at Madd Dogg Records. Huey had hacked into the company's mainframe system to obtain information about where the cameras were positioned in Carl's office and in the assistant's area. The system would reset itself once a day at random times during the middle of the night, but during the reset period, there were eleven minutes needed to rewind the digital tapes. He planned on resetting the system at 6:54 a.m., giving Benita until 7:05 a.m. to comb through Carl's office to search for any important documents and install small bugs in his phone and in key areas.

Benita sat at her desk and booted her computer. She installed a virus that would run along with the security system to provide entry for Huey. The computer genius had written a program that was pretty much undetectable, and it was Benita's job to install the virus on her boss's computer.

She looked at the clock and waited for Huey to text her, giving the go-ahead to enter Carl's office. A minute later, she got a text, and with her phone, a thumb drive, and two bugs in her hand, she walked quickly to Carl's office, unlocking his door.

Moving quickly, Benita flipped through files on his desk and checked the unlocked drawers. She thought it was odd that she didn't see any photos or personal items anywhere in his office, leading her to conclude he was extremely private. She wondered if he was still seeing Raven, or if she had been kicked to the curb. She would ask Carl for a list of people whose calls he wanted her to put through. If Raven was on the list, then she had to be extra careful not to be recognized by the Ice Queen.

She ran her fingers across the top of his bookshelf. After doing a thorough inspection, she found nothing of interest. However, while planting a bug, she felt a hidden compartment underneath the desk. She knocked on the wood, and a small door opened. A key was taped in place. She removed the key from the hidden spot, laid it on the desk, snapped a photo with her phone, and replaced the key.

Benita looked at the clock on Carl's desk: 7:00 a.m. "Damn! Not enough time."

She booted Carl's computer and quickly installed Huey's virus from her thumb drive. Then she shut down the computer and wiped away her fingerprints. She checked the room one more time and walked out, leaving the door ajar. She sat at her desk and placed a bug on her phone and computer. It was 7:05, and she had safely completed her task. Feeling uneasy, Benita walked to the small kitchen to get a cup of tea to settle her queasy stomach.

She was surprised when Carl arrived at 8:00. The evening before, he mentioned he would have a late night attending a few industry parties and didn't think he would be in early. But here he was, dragging himself into the office, wearing sunglasses no less. He acknowledged Benita with a quick wave but headed to his office to prepare for his early conference call.

Benita went to the small kitchen and made Carl some French roast coffee. She walked into his office and placed the cup of coffee on his desk. "Here ya go, Mr. Johnson. I thought you needed a little pick-me-up."

"Thank you, Bridgette. This hits the spot."

"Let me know if you need anything else. I'm only a few feet away."

"Will do. Thanks for the coffee."

"You're welcome." Benita sashayed out of the office, knowing Carl was following her every move. She couldn't wait until the assignment was over. With all the intel she knew about him, he made her sick to her stomach.

As Carl watched "Bridgette" walk out of his office, he planned on sleeping with her. He thought about his hands caressing her beautiful brown skin and shapely body. He was happy she was working for him.

He took another sip of coffee and prepared for his early meeting. An hour later, Carl came to his door and watched Benita as she sorted through the stack of mail on her desk.

"Bridgette, I know it's last minute, but how would you like to go with me to the Hip-Hop Music Awards tonight?"

"Really? There's no one else you wanted to invite? Like a girlfriend?"

Carl chuckled and looked at her with a devious smile. "Ah, you care about a girlfriend, huh?"

"Ah, yeah. I am not really interested in stepping on anybody's toes."

"Well, there's no one. I promise. What do you say? Should be fun."

"I'm sure it will be a blast. But, Carl, I don't have anything to wear."

He handed her his American Express black card. "Then why don't you take the rest of the day off and go buy yourself something hot? There's an apartment on the fifth floor. You can change there. I'll have a limo here to pick you up at six. Cool?"

Benita took the card and walked out of his office. She grabbed her designer bag and headed out the door with the Amex card in hand.

Chapter 43

Benita crossed the street and headed north on Broadway to a local print shop. Walking to the back of the store where agents Perkins, Rodriguez, and Santos were waiting, she sat at a small table to discuss updates on Carl's case. They had a plan to install surveillance cameras in Carl's penthouse in the Tribeca area in Manhattan.

"Santos, how much time do you need to install the equipment?" Miguel asked.

Santos pulled up the floor plans on his iPad and quickly analyzed the document. "We first have to survey the apartment to see what kind of security system he has now."

Huey chimed in on speaker. "He uses Safe Guard Security System, same company he uses at Madd Dogg Records. It resets at two a.m., but I can run a program causing it to loop for an hour, tops."

Santos continued with his updates. "His house staff leaves around eleven every night, so I'll have my techs there by eleven-thirty. We'll get in and out."

Benita wasn't sure how long the event lasted, but she knew there was also an after-party. "But what if he wants to leave early? I know there's an after-party, but he was out late the previous night. He may get tired and wanna leave and go back to his apartment."

"Well, Benita, it's your job to keep him out as long as you can," Miguel replied.

Luciana commented. "Why not have Benita get invited back to Carl's apartment? She can drug him, and we set up surveillance equipment as well as do a sweep of the apartment to find key evidence to support our case. It's a win-win situation."

Benita smiled at Luciana. "That's an excellent idea. I can tell him I'm tired and suggest we go back to his crib for a nightcap."

Miguel was not amenable to the idea. "I don't like it. It's too risky."

"Too risky? What the hell are you talking about, Miguel? Isn't this whole damn undercover thing risky? What difference does it make if it's day or night?" Benita questioned. "I'm a trained operative, and I can handle this guy. Trust me. I'm doing it. I'll get him alone and drug his ass."

Luciana handed Benita a small silver compact. "You see the side of this mirror? Use this"—she opened a tiny compartment—"to put into his champagne. It'll knock him out for at least five or six hours. This way, he'll be incapacitated, the techs can install the equipment, and we can look for important documents."

Benita smiled. "I'll bet you knocked out a bunch of dudes on this stuff, huh?"

Luciana grinned. "Maybe one or two."

Santos handed Benita a small pendant. "This has a hidden microphone chip. Put it somewhere on your outfit. We'll be able to track your whereabouts and hear your conversation with Carl just in case something goes wrong."

"So, while I'm drugging this guy, where will the team be situated?" Benita asked.

Miguel asked Huey to speak on their potential stake-out. "Huey, do we still have access to the apartment building across the street from Carl's penthouse?"

"Well, that's hard to say. I mean, I was able to secure a few apartments on the top floor, but not all of them. There are a few people who just don't want to leave the building. You know what I'm saying? Especially this little old lady who carries her dog in a baby stroller. Who carries an animal in a baby stroller?"

Miguel suddenly became frustrated by Huey's ranting. "Graham, do we have a place to set up our stakeout or not?"

"That's what I was trying to tell you. We do have an apartment that's perfect for surveillance. But there's one problem."

"Which is?"

"It's not in the building we occupy. It's down the street."

Miguel sighed. "Not across the street? But down the street from the building that's across the street? Well, did you check to see if there was an apartment available in Johnson's building?"

There was silence on the other end of the speaker-phone.

"Well?"

"Actually, I never checked."

Miguel was about to lose his cool with Huey, but Luciana interjected. "Huey, could you check right now? Maybe there's an empty apartment in the building."

"Sure. Hold on a sec." A few seconds later, Huey came back on the phone. "Yup, we're in luck. I found one. There's a vacant apartment one floor below Carl Johnson's."

"Great, thank you, Huey," Luciana replied and turned back to Miguel. "So, we don't have a problem anymore. It's a quick setup."

Miguel reluctantly answered his charge. "Not so fast, Rodriguez. Santos still has to get the equipment over to Carl's building. We don't have much time to be moving equipment in."

Santos replied, "We'll be installing four cameras. Not a lot of equipment and very light. The tech guys will be ready to go in a Safe Guard Security System van. I'll make sure the monitors are set up in our stakeout apartment as soon as we're done with our meeting."

Miguel relented. "Okay, it seems we all have our plans. Rodriguez will help Santos set up surveillance. Huey will create a diversion to make sure the security resets, malfunctions whatever works, and Benita will lure Carl back to the apartment and drug him."

Benita placed the pendant and mirror in her bag. "Okay, well, I'm off. Got a little bit of shopping to do."

Miguel stopped Benita before she got up from her chair. "Watch your back."

Benita glared at Miguel. "Don't you worry. I got this."

Benita curled up on Carl's couch and watched him grab two empty glasses and a bottle of champagne from his modern stainless-steel kitchen. She had shined earlier in a cute little hot-pink micro-mini dress she'd picked up at Saks Fifth Avenue. They left the party and came back to Carl's apartment for a nightcap.

Carl had been smitten all night and couldn't keep his eyes or hands off her. What she wanted to do was kick him in the groin every time he touched her, but she suggested they leave the after-party early and head back to his place.

Carl handed Benita a glass of champagne. "Here ya go. So, Bridgette, how'd you end up in New York? Weren't you living in Paris working for some punk-ass fashion designer?"

"I was born in New York, but I've lived all over. After college, I got a fashion internship in Paris and loved it. But I wanted to be back in the States, so here I am. What about you? What's your story?"

Carl leaned back on his couch and caressed the inside of Benita's thigh. "Born and bred in Brooklyn. Ex-gangbanger. Got involved with music. Started producing and built my empire. Damn, girl, you are straight-up fine."

"Thank you."

"It's hard to find good quality women nowadays. The chicken head bitches are taking over."

It took everything Benita had not to throw her glass of champagne in this asshole's face. She took a sip to stop from slapping him. "Why do men love to call women bitches?"

"Because most are bitches."

"Carl, it's an awful word to call a woman. You're calling a woman a female dog. We're not dogs. I don't call men pigs, even though most of them are. We live in a society where people disrespect each other. It's a vicious cycle. We need to stop hurting each other."

"Smart and beautiful. I like those qualities." Carl leaned over to kiss Benita, but she stopped him.

"What are you doing?"

"Ah, trying to kiss you."

"How about we have some more champagne?"

"Huh. Okay, sure."

"I'll get it. You just relax, Carl. I'll be right back." Benita walked to the kitchen and reached into the side pocket of her dress and pulled out the mirror. She opened the hidden compartment and poured the white substance into his glass. She then poured champagne into both glasses and walked back into the room.

She sat down and handed Carl his glass. "Here ya go, sweetie."

"Thank you." After finishing his champagne, he grabbed her by the waist and attempted to kiss her, but he tipped over into her lap.

"Carl? Carl?" She took the opportunity to slap him, but he didn't wake up. She pushed him off her lap and stood up, then walked to the door while speaking into the microphone.

"He's out like a light. Come on in."

Perkins, Santos, and Rodriguez had been listening from an empty apartment just below Carl's. A few minutes later, five techs came in to set up surveillance equipment throughout the apartment. Miguel and the team followed behind and soon started rummaging through Carl's documents.

Miguel and Benita went to the back room to look through his closets and search for hidden compartments. While they searched through Carl's drawers, Miguel let it slip how annoyed he was with Benita.

"Did he kiss you?"

She stopped in her tracks. "Miguel, stop. Just stop."

Luciana walked into the bedroom and observed the intense moment. "Am I interrupting?"

"No. What is it?" Perkins asked.

"We found some ledgers in his office safe."

"Great. Make photocopies and put everything back where you found it. Can you check on the installs? Benita, get your stuff. I don't want you here when he wakes up."

Benita shook her head. "No, I can't leave. We need to get him to bed, clean up the living room, wash out those glasses, and leave him a note, letting him know I had a great time. He needs to believe something happened. I'll be fine. Don't worry about me, Miguel. I've got this."

"Fine. Luciana, take care of the ledgers. I'll talk to Carlos and see how much time he needs. Benita, why don't you go handle Carl."

"Whatever you say, boss." Benita walked out of the room with Luciana, leaving Miguel alone in the bedroom.

Chapter 44

Rapper Bobby G and Martin, Benita's former jiu-jitsu classmate, were smoking weed and playing video games when the doorbell rang. Martin answered, and Wes walked in with a bag of groceries and headed into the kitchen. Martin followed Wes and grabbed the chips and two beers.

"Thanks, buddy. You're doing a great job. Much appreciated."

Wes hated being Bobby G's errand boy, but he'd promised Benita to stay off the streets. Wes loved rap music and thought working for a well-known rapper would help him move up the ranks in the record industry, but all this job did for him was have him run around the city, picking up frivolous stuff for the rapper.

After putting the groceries away, Wes sat in the armless chair across from Bobby G and Martin. Bobby G sat back on the couch and took a huge hit off his blunt.

"Wes, man, you need to try this shit right here."

Wes shook his head. "Man, my grandma would kill me if I came home high."

Bobby G passed the blunt over to Martin, who took a long drag.

"You know what? It's time I start my own record label," Bobby G said.

Martin took another hit before handing it back to Bobby G. "You know Carl ain't gonna let you go do your own thing. He owns you, man. Will kill you first."

"Shit, he don't know who I am. All the shit I got on him? He won't be a problem."

Wes watched Bobby G and Martin continue getting high. "You got it like that, G?" he asked.

"Believe dat, Wes. Damn, Martin, save me some chips. Pass them over to me."

Wes hated Bobby G and thought he was nothing more than a bullshitter. He let him talk until he passed out. Wes would continue to work for this clown until he got another job and got paid more money. As crazy as Bobby G was, the money was right, and Wes had no intention of walking away just yet.

Agent Barry Malone had just gotten his routine breakfast—a glass of orange juice, two egg-and-cheese biscuits, and a bowl of oatmeal—at the Westside Diner while waiting for his old friend "Kojak" to arrive. It had been more than five years since he'd seen Leroy, and he was surprised when he received a text from him, asking for information about a new recruit. He knew it must have been important, because Leroy only reached out when it was absolutely imperative.

Months went by, and then Leroy called Barry on his private line and asked to meet. Leroy didn't sound like himself, and that bothered Barry. He and Leroy had known each other for more than twenty-five years, ever since they started their careers together at the FBI. While Leroy was doing undercover work in Brooklyn, Barry was working behind the scenes, gathering intelligence on the Brooklyn drug dealers. It was Barry who discovered that Leroy's cover had been blown and he was in danger of being killed, so he got Leroy reassigned out of the country until things blew over.

Years later, they both made the leap to work for DTCU. Barry knew about the relationship between Samantha and Leroy. He also knew how it had ultimately broken up the friendship between Leroy and Bolden. Soon after the breakup, a heartbroken Leroy informed Barry he was leaving DTCU for good.

"I hope you don't mind I ordered already."

Leroy smiled and shook his head. "Of course not. I know you gotta have your breakfast or there would be hell to pay."

"You know me so well," Barry responded after taking a bite of his biscuit.

A middle-aged waitress with dark-brown curly hair came over and took Leroy's order of coffee and a bowl of fruit.

"It's been a long time. Lookin' good. Still doing all that Bruce Lee shit?" Barry asked.

"Of course. What else would I be doing?"

"I don't know, still working at the DTCU?" He chuckled.

"Oh, no. I'll leave that to you. I thought you would have moved to your vacation home in Florida by now."

Barry took a sip of his OJ and another bite of his biscuit. "Thought about it, but I got a few good years left. Not ready to waste it on the beach and easy life. Kojak, why did you want to meet? What's going on?"

After he got his coffee, Leroy sipped the steaming liquid. "Remember our first case in Brooklyn?"

"How could I forget? You almost got yourself killed. Had to pull you out."

"Yeah, well, that's not all that happened." Leroy slid a picture of Benita over to him. "She's my daughter."

Malone picked up the photo and looked at it. "What, your daughter? Agent Jenkins is your daughter? What the fuck, man? How'd she end up at DTCU?"

"I think Bolden found out about her and convinced her to join."

"Come on, Kojak. You think Bolden would do something like that? I know he can be a dick, but why would he come after her after all these years?"

"Why did I get a visit from his lackey, Perkins? He came to my school and asked questions about her. At the time, I didn't put it all together, until Benita ended up in jail and then was miraculously thrown into a 'make-believe' safe house. I need for you to tell me if she's working on something that could put her in serious danger."

"Leroy, you know I can't tell you anything about other agents."

"Barry, we've worked on hundreds of cases. You and me. Made from the same cloth. I've always had your back, and you had mine. I need you to help me protect my daughter. Tell me where she is and if her life is in danger."

After a few moments, Barry closed his eyes, took a deep breath, and rubbed his forehead. "Okay. What do you wanna know?"

Chapter 45

Carl had been in a deep sleep and woke up groggy. He forced himself out of bed and made his way to the front door.

"How the hell did I get in bed?" he mumbled as he opened the door.

Big Boy took up the entryway.

"What the hell, dude? Why you ringing the doorbell like you've lost your damn mind?"

"Your attorney, Don Buckley, has been trying to reach you all morning. He got some information on your boy Benjamin."

Carl walked into the kitchen and made himself some coffee. He was having a hard time shaking his unsteadiness. "What kind of information?"

"He didn't say, but he told me to find you because he got some information on that little white boy Mahoney. He's up to no good."

"Fuck! Listen, go find that muthafucka and bring him by the office. I need to get out of here. I'll deal with him later."

Big Boy left, and Carl fumed about another man trying to take advantage of him. He went to his master bathroom and splashed water on his face. Looking in the mirror, he tried to focus on the previous night's events. His head was spinning. He'd had a few drinks at the after-party and then two glasses of champagne when he got home, but then everything went black. He had no idea how he ended up in his bed, but he figured Bridgette had somehow dragged him from the couch.

He walked back to his bedroom and saw a note on his side table. It said: *Carl, I had a great time last night. One minute we were talking, the next you were out. I guess I was too powerful for you. I'll see you at work. xoxo. B.*

After a quick shower, he called his attorney, who informed him his number two had been setting up overseas dummy accounts and moving money from Carl's accounts to his own. Fuming, he headed out of the apartment to go to the office. He slammed the door behind him and stopped dead in his tracks. Had he heard voices last night, or had he been dreaming? He wasn't sure, but he had to remain focused on his busy day. One thing that had been moved up on the list was finding Benjamin and stomping on his face.

Benita opened an encrypted e-mail from Huey on her smartphone. As she read it, she became extremely upset by the contents.

Benita, the man you asked about? About two years ago, Carl Johnson's business manager, Benjamin Mahoney, set up Gold Starr Corporation for him. Mahoney was responsible for buying new real estate properties in Brooklyn for Johnson and had set up several bank accounts, making himself the authorized signer. I hacked into Mahoney's personal accounts, and it seems he has been moving money from Madd Dogg Records into his own. I also found a list of businesses Gold Starr Corporation was targeting, and Deon's Hair Salon was one of them. Miguel and Luciana are headed over to Mahoney's apartment to track him down.

"Son of a bitch!" Benita yelled, then e-mailed Huey back: Thanks for the intel. She made her way to the stairwell to make a call on her cell, leaving a voice mail.

"Miguel, call me when you get this. I want to talk to you about Benjamin Mahoney. I know he's somehow involved in the attack on my cousin."

As she finished her message, her phone beeped. It was Miguel.

"When were you going to tell me about Mahoney?" she snapped.

"As soon as I tracked him down. We went to his apartment, but things were in shambles. It looks like he skipped town."

"I would too if I was stealing money from my psychotic boss."

"Well, according to our surveillance from his apartment this morning, Carl spoke to his attorney about Mahoney. He's looking for him too."

"We can't just let him get away."

"We'll find him. Why don't you go back to your desk and wait for Carl."

"Okay. Keep me posted when you find this clown. I'd like to have a crack at him."

"Talk to you later, Benita."

As Benita made her way back to her desk, she bumped into Bobby G, who had just gotten off the elevator.

"Damn, girl. You are one of the finest secretaries I've ever seen. I'm Bobby G."

"Nice to meet you, Bobby G. Mr. Johnson isn't in yet. You're welcome to wait."

"He's not here? Huh. I think I'll wait." He winked at Benita and sat on one of the couches on the other side of the room.

Benita checked Carl's calendar to see who he was meeting with that morning. She hadn't heard from him at all yet and wondered if he was still passed out.

The phone rang on Carl's private line, and Benita picked up. "Mr. Johnson's office."

"Hey, Bridgette, it's Carl."

"Hi. I was wondering if I had to send out a search party to find you."

"I ain't gonna lie. It was a rough morning. Did I get any calls?"

"No calls, but you have a visitor. Mr. Bobby G is waiting to see you."

"Tell him I'll be there in about twenty minutes."

"No problem. See you soon, Mr. Johnson." Benita hung up and turned to Bobby G, who was watching his latest video on the flat-screen TV. "Excuse me, Mr. G? Mr. Johnson said he would be here in twenty minutes."

"Thanks, beautiful."

Bobby G annoyed Benita, and she didn't really know why. Maybe because he was trying to chitchat with her, and she hated chitchat.

Twenty minutes later, Carl walked off the elevator and passed by Bobby G as he headed toward his office. Bobby G stood up and followed Carl.

Benita opened her bag and flipped on a listening device. She placed the small plug in her ear. She turned toward her computer and began reading e-mails sent to Carl from various departments. While she did this, she listened to the conversation between Carl and Bobby G.

Carl sat behind his desk and barked at his artist, "What do you want, G? I've got shit to do before the end of the day."

"I wanted to talk to you about my new record label."

"There's nothing to talk about. Once you've completed your five albums, then we can discuss your record label."

"Carl, I want my own artists, and it's time you took me seriously."

"Not a good time. Money's tight. I can't commit to setting you up."

"How in the hell is money tight? All the money I've made you from my albums should have kept you straight. Hell, I bring in more money than any other artist on your roster."

"And you're one of the most expensive. You've racked up a lot of bills, according to my accountants."

"Fuck you, muthafucka. It's about time I get mine."

Carl jumped up like a panther attacking his prey. He grabbed Bobby G by his collar and started shaking him. "You don't ever talk to me like that, muthafucka. I'll cut out your fucking tongue and feed it to the dogs. You betta show some respect when you're in my office. Now, get the hell out."

"What you gonna do? Kill me and throw me in the East River like you did Malik?"

Carl let Bobby G go and pointed at the closed door. "Get the fuck outta my office."

Bobby G gave Carl a hard look. "Carl, I'm telling you this now. I want my damn record label. I don't care what the hell you gotta do to make it happen, but if you don't do what you promised, you'll regret fucking with me."

"You threatening me?"

"It's no threat, playa."

"G, if I go down, you go down. You don't want any-body to find out you were responsible for luring your friend Malik to my warehouse, do you? I mean, you knew he was stealing from me, and you were ultimately responsible for his death. You're just as responsible as I am. Now, get the hell out."

Benita was shocked to hear Carl implicate Bobby G in an unsolved murder. Although it was hearsay, it gave DTCU some incriminating information linked to Carl.

Benita pulled out her smartphone and texted Miguel: **Murder connection. Body found in East River. Malik. No last name. Johnson and his artist Bobby G.**

She put her phone away when Bobby G stormed out.

Carl buzzed for Benita to come to his office. She put her phone back in her bag and walked inside.

"You need something?"

"Yeah. Go downstairs and buy me some Red Bull. My refrigerator is empty. I thought I told you to keep it stocked."

"I'm sorry, Carl. I'll go get you some right now."

She went to the little deli half a block from the build-ing and picked up a dozen Red Bulls. As she walked back to the office, she saw Bobby G pushing someone to the ground. He climbed into his limo, leaving the kid stranded on the street.

Benita hurried to help the young man, who was hold-ing his side. She was shocked to see it was her brother.

Even with her disguise, Wes recognized his long-lost sister. "Benita?"

Chapter 46

Benita dropped off the energy drinks for Carl, finished up her work for the day, and went to Tompkins Square Park to meet Wes. They used to go there when they were younger to talk about things they couldn't talk to adults about, like the death of their mom. Wes paced back and forth, furious with Benita for assuming another identity.

"What the hell, Benita? You've been fine all this time? Grams has been going crazy trying to find out what happened to you, and you working at Madd Dogg Records? How could you do this to us? How could you do this to Grams?"

"I've wanted to reach out to you guys for a long time, but I couldn't contact you. Your lives would've been in danger. I mean, I shouldn't be meeting with you now."

"What kind of shit have you gotten yourself into?"

"When I was in prison, a man working for a secret organization recruited me to help bring down criminals. I was looking at twenty-five to life, Wes. I had a choice to make: to either take my chances at trial or do something with my life. So, I chose to live."

"But Mr. Matthews said they didn't have a case against you."

"Trust me, Wes. If somebody wants to set you up for a crime you didn't commit, there ain't a damn thing you can do about it. Look, I'm sorry, but I wouldn't have made it in prison for the rest of my life."

"Grams said you'd been abducted. Yo, you gotta let me tell Grams. Let's call her right now."

He pulled out his cell phone, but Benita took it from him. "No, Wes. If DTCU finds out I've had contact with my family, they'd do something to you guys. I'm serious. I can't put your lives in danger. I'm on a strict leash, and they're tugging at me. Plus, you know how Grams is—she can't keep quiet."

Wes chuckled. "I know."

"You gotta promise me you won't say anything."

"Fine, I won't tell her."

"Or anybody else. No one can know."

"Okay."

"Promise me, Wes."

"I swear I won't say anything."

"Thank you. Now, how'd you get involved with Bobby G? He's bad news."

"Tell me about it. Martin got me a job running errands for G. But he's a nightmare. He's smoking weed, playing video games, or threatening somebody. Wait, are you investigating him?"

Benita decided to come clean with her brother. "Yes, him and his boss."

"No wonder Bobby G is always talking about black-mailing Carl. He knows some things guaranteeing him his own record label."

Benita's heart began beating fast. All of a sudden, she felt scared for Wes. "What did he say about Carl? What do you know?"

"Nothing. Just kept talking shit."

"Wes, you need to stay away from Bobby G. Do you understand? Some shit's about to go down, and I don't want you anywhere near him."

"You don't understand. I can't just disappear like you did. I live in this neighborhood, and I'm part of G's crew. Whatever he wants, he gets."

"Okay, but you have to promise to keep a low profile. Don't talk to anyone, even Martin, about Bobby G. It's important."

"Okay, but how do I get in touch with you if something happens?"

Benita wrote a number on a business card and handed it to him. "This is my private number, and it's untraceable. If you need to reach me, just leave a message, and I'll get back to you as soon as I can."

Wes took the number and pushed the card into his jeans pocket. "Was it all worth it? The pain you caused?"

"Little brother, I'd make the choice all day long to protect my family. And right now, this is the one way I know how to do it." Benita hugged her brother and held him close. "Whatever you gotta do, stay clear of Bobby G. Get out of here. I can't risk the chance of somebody seeing us together."

Wes hurried off. She pulled out her phone and dialed Miguel's number, leaving him another voice mail. "I left you a message earlier. We need to pick up Bobby G right away. He's got the goods on Carl."

Two hours later, Bobby G was banging on the glass windows in DTCU's interrogation room in New Jersey. "Don't you know I'm the legendary Bobby G? I got rights. You can't keep me here. I want my attorney."

Solomon "The Fixer" Raines walked into the room while Miguel and Benita watched on the other side of the mirror.

"Okay, who in the world is this man?" Benita asked.

"The Fixer. One of the best interrogators I've ever met. He can close any assignment, no matter how big or small," Miguel responded.

Solomon sat across from Bobby G and propped his size-twelve oxford dress shoes on the table. "What up, man?" he growled.

"What up? Who the hell are you?"

Solomon spoke in a calm, deep voice. "People call me The Fixer."

Bobby G snickered and crossed his arms. "Well, you might wanna start by fixing your clothes, playa."

Miguel braced himself for what would happen next. "Oh, shit. Did I also mention he's a little crazy?"

Solomon jumped over the table and grabbed Bobby G by his collar, knocking him over the side of his chair. "I tried being nice to your dumb ass, but you trying my patience, playa! You feel me, little man?"

With a long stare, Solomon suddenly released the rapper and helped him back into his chair. "Now that we got the introductions out of the way, why don't you tell me all about your relationship with Carl Johnson and what you know about a murder victim found in the fucking East River."

"Other than he manages my music career, I don't know what else to tell you."

The Fixer shook his head in major disappointment. "Bobby G, man, look. I know you know about a murder happening last year. If not, then you are one of the stupidest clowns I've ever met. Don't act like you're innocent up in here."

"I think I'll speak to my attorney now."

"Man, where you are, you don't have any rights. Oh yeah, you got the right to get your head bashed in if you don't start talking. Boy, I'll pull off your fingernails one by one. Then I'll pull off your toenails. Then I'll get to those pearly whites. Now, if I have to ask you one more time, you won't need an attorney. You'll need a freakin' plastic surgeon."

"You can't do this to me. I got rights!"

"Muthafucka, you ain't got no rights up in here. We're not the police, muthafucka. We're you're worst nightmare. Now, I'm gonna ask you one more time nicely. Tell me what the fuck I wanna know."

"A'ight! A'ight! I told Carl's main man Benjamin that Malik was stealing records from him and selling them on the streets. The next thing I know, Malik is dead."

"That's all you know? That's it?"

"Yeah, that's it. I swear."

"And you didn't have anything to do with your buddy getting killed?"

"No! I didn't know Carl was going to have him killed."

"You sure about that?"

"Yeah. I'm sure."

"Bobby G, I don't believe you, 'cause according to my sources, Carl plans on implicating you as the killer. Why is that?" There was silence in the room. Then Solomon yelled in Bobby G's face, "Why, Bobby?"

"Carl called me and told me Malik was dead."

"Now, was that hard? So now you're going to do your civic duty and help us bring Mr. Johnson down."

Benita watched in complete amazement. Solomon reminded her of a homeless man people ignored on the streets until he went buck wild. He could hustle anyone to get what he wanted. "Wow, he's crazy."

Miguel nodded. "I couldn't agree more."

The next morning, Carl was already in the office by the time Benita arrived. She heard him yelling behind closed doors. She booted her computer, pulled out her listening device, and placed the earplug in her ear.

"Big Boy, how difficult is it to find a skinny-ass white dude? Find that muthafucka before I blow up by a hundred. I'm serious! Nobody—not Mahoney, not G—will mess with my paper and get away with it. Yeah. Call me back." Carl slammed down the phone, and the room went silent.

Carl made several more phone calls, and Benita continued listening. She was hoping he would find Mahoney, and if given the chance, she would confront him. Carl wasn't the only one who had to pay for his crimes, and if she had anything to do with it, Mahoney would pay for his as well.

She heard Carl say, "Yeah, I'm coming to Mexico by the end of the week. I can't leave until I take care of some unfinished business. I'll have the product as long as you got the money. Yeah, my attorney will have the paperwork by the end of the day."

Benita texted Huey a lengthy message about Carl and the trip he planned on making at the end of the week.

Carl's line was blinking, and Benita picked up the phone. "Carl Johnson's office."

"Tell Carl it's Raven."

Benita paused for a few seconds. She hadn't heard her nasally voice in more than a year and hoped the mean girl hadn't recognized hers.

"Hello? Is anybody there?"

Benita answered, "Hold, please." She remembered just why she hated this girl and rolled her eyes at the phone. She buzzed Carl, letting him know Raven was on the phone.

Carl picked up the call. Benita listened to Raven yelling and screaming at him, and she actually felt sorry for him. He couldn't get a word in. Finally, he yelled back at her, "Go fuck yourself!"

Good for you, Carl, for taking up for yourself, Benita thought. No one should have to endure Raven's rants and accusations. She was a crazy broad and got everything she deserved.

Carl got off the phone with Raven and then picked up another call from Bobby G. "You again? What is it this time?"

"I got a call from the feds about you, and unless you want me to talk to them, you'll meet me in Prospect Park in an hour."

Carl hung up and quickly headed toward the elevator. When Benita asked him if he was leaving for the day, he mumbled, "Yeah, I'm gone for the day. Feel free to leave early."

Benita texted Miguel, letting him know Carl had left for his meeting with Bobby G and that she would meet him at the park. She forwarded Carl's voice mail to DTCU's answering system account that was set up to track all phone calls coming in and out of Madd Dogg Records. She then used the stairs because she didn't want anyone to know she had left.

Bobby G was nervous as Carl walked up to him wearing a long overcoat, a dark-brown sweater, and dark jeans. Bobby's nervousness increased by a hundred when he noticed the sour look on Carl's face. He seemed pissed to be there, and Bobby just wanted to get this meeting over with.

"Make this quick, G. I've got a lot on my plate right now, and I don't have time for any more of your bullshit."

"I . . . I want my own record label."

Carl grabbed Bobby G by his collar and pushed him to the ground. "What the fuck is wrong with you? The weed has gone to your brain. I'm done with your monkey ass. You hear me? Done."

"I got a visit from the feds today. Unless you want me to talk to them about you, I suggest we work things out."

"Really? And just what do they wanna talk to your ass about?"

"Malik. They wanted to talk to me about Malik."

Carl reached in his jacket pocket and pulled out a gun and pointed it at Bobby G. "Muthafucka, I should put a bullet in your fucking ass." He hit Bobby G across the face with the butt of the gun, knocking him to the ground, then kicked him a few times in the stomach.

Bobby G begged Carl to stop. "Chill, man!"

"G, I don't have a problem blowing your head off right now in this damn park. You're one of the most unappreciative muthafuckas I know. I pulled your triflin' ass out of the gutter. I cleaned you up, and this is how you repay me? You are one disrespectful and disloyal beyotch."

Carl kicked Bobby G two more times, still pointing the gun at his head. "Don't you know I can make a helluva lot more money on your ass dead than I can alive?"

Bobby G tried to convince Carl he was still loyal. "Carl, I'm sorry, man. You're right. You have been there for me. I was wrong to think I could ask anything else from you. Please, man. Don't kill me. Don't kill me!"

Carl looked around the area. A handful of people were strolling through the neighboring trees. He put his gun away and answered his vibrating phone. "Hello. Bridgette. He called? Great. I've been trying to reach him. Thank you."

He ended the call and bent down to get closer to Bobby G. "Now, I'm gonna tell you this one last time. If you don't keep your fucking mouth shut, I'm gonna blow your ass away. You hear me? Now get up, take your ass to the studio, and make us some more hits."

Carl stood up and disappeared through the wooded area. Bobby G remained still until he was gone.

Miguel and two agents appeared and escorted Bobby G out of the park.

Miguel called Benita. "I need you to head over to DTCU and debrief Luciana and Carlos. Things are going down, and we need to make sure we have everything in place so we can bring Carl down."

Benita got out of the van and jumped into a black car headed back to Manhattan to meet with Rodriguez and Santos at the print shop.

Carl was becoming unhinged and more dangerous than anyone had expected.

Chapter 47

Agent Evan Green was feeling nauseous after waking from a deep sleep on the floor of Bobby G's apartment. He tried to stand, but his legs gave way, and he fell back to the floor. He and his partner, Agent Tony Lopez, had been escorting Bobby G into the apartment when he felt a sharp pain coming from the back of his head. He heard a struggle but then passed out.

Touching a small bump on the back of his head, he winced from the pain. He called out to Tony, but there was no response. He stumbled to the hallway and saw Tony's body on the floor close to the front door. A large black man was lying near the kitchen. Evan checked both men. Lopez was barely breathing, having been shot in the stomach. The perp lay dead.

Evan called an ambulance service working for DTCU and then called Perkins to report Lopez was down. Evan checked the rest of the apartment to see if Bobby G had been hurt, but he was nowhere to be found.

Miguel and several DTCU agents arrived at Bobby G's apartment in Brooklyn at the same time Detective Phillips arrived. Paramedics were working on Lopez and treating Evan for a possible concussion.

"Perkins, you and me gotta stop meeting like this," Detective Phillips said.

"Yeah, no kidding. The resident has gone missing, and we need to keep a lid on this case for at least twenty-four hours. If word gets out about a shootout at a famous rap artist's apartment, he could get spooked and leave town. As far as we know, he jetted before all hell broke loose."

"Listen, I'll do what I can. My boss already spoke to your boss. You got twenty-four hours to find your witness. After that, you're on your own," Phillips said.

"Thanks. You're a good man."

"Yeah, sometimes I'm not so sure." Detective Phillips walked over to a crime scene investigator who had just arrived. He explained the delicacy of the situation and looked back at Miguel, letting him know he was handling things.

Miguel walked over to Evan. "What the hell happened?"

"I'm not sure, sir. I walked into the apartment and did my routine check while Agent Lopez and Bobby G were standing outside the door. As I came around the corner, I was hit in the back of the head, and then it was lights out. When I woke up, Lopez was lying on the floor with his gun next to him, a dead assailant near the kitchen, and Bobby G gone."

"You two were supposed to take him directly to the safe house, not his apartment."

"Bobby G told us he had evidence linking Carl to his friend's murder here."

"And you believed him?"

"Yes. He said he had a thumb drive containing information about his friend's murder."

"Dammit, Green. How stupid could you be? You disobeyed protocol. Trust me, you're gonna be written up for this. And you'd better hope nothing happens to Bobby G."

Miguel walked over to the dead body, took a picture with his phone, and sent it to Huey. He was pissed off at the turn of events. Miguel was sure Bobby G knew his life was in danger if Carl got hold of him, and he had gone into hiding.

Placing a quick call to Bolden's office, Miguel left an urgent message, asking his boss to call him back. He then called Santos to send out agents to find Bobby G as soon as possible. He was too close to nailing Carl, and Bobby G was the key.

Luciana walked into the computer room, where Benita and Huey were reviewing digital files taken from Carl's apartment. Huey discovered Carl had set up a bootleg DVD business and partnered up with a criminal named Eric Fernandez, the leader of a Mexican drug ring known as the Banderas. This group was currently being investigated by the FBI because of its involvement in domestic terrorism, money laundering, and drug trafficking. They had assassinated several rival gang leaders to keep their high status in the country.

"Benita, we've got big trouble. Bobby G's missing," Luciana said.

"What happened? Evan was supposed to drive directly to the safe house. How did he let him slip through his fingers?"

"Evan and Tony were involved in a shootout at Bobby G's apartment. Evan's fine, but Tony's not so lucky. He was shot and is in surgery right now."

"Who shot him? Bobby G?"

"No, it may have been one of Carl's cronies. One was dead at the scene."

Benita exhaled a sigh of relief. "I'm glad Evan's okay. Bobby G is probably hiding out, hoping things will blow over."

"What if he's left town?"

Benita smirked at Luciana. "Dude ain't going nowhere. He's from Brooklyn. He was raised there, and he'll die there."

Luciana shook her head. "Miguel's on his way back and wants to meet with us to help find Bobby G."

"Excuse us, Huey. I need to speak to Luciana for a minute."

"No, problem," Huey said. "I'll just continue going through these files."

"Thanks, Huey. Luciana, I think I know where Bobby G may go to hide out. There's a little hole in the wall where he's part-owner."

"Great. Let's tell Perkins."

"Sure, after we go find him first."

Luciana protested. "We can't go there without backup. It's against policy."

"All I've heard since joining this organization is that we live dangerous lives and do whatever it takes to bring down the bad guys. Well, I'm here to tell you we need to do what we gotta do. I'm not saying not to call Miguel. I'm saying we call after we get there. We can handle this assignment ourselves. All we gotta do is dress the part and make sure we keep him in our sight. That's it. Are you down or not?" Benita asked.

"I can't agree to this."

"Fine, Luciana. Fine. I'll tell you what. You go ahead and call Miguel because I'm going with or without you. I thought you had my back."

Luciana was torn between being safe and being aggressive in her approach. She made the decision to follow Benita's lead. Benita knew that world better than anyone on her team. "Fine. What do you have in mind?"

Benita smiled and said, "Find the hottest low-end outfit in your closet. We need to bring it down a notch if we want to fit in."

Forty-five minutes later, Benita and Luciana were speeding up Interstate 78 toward Manhattan. They would be in Brooklyn soon enough, and if anyone was going to find Bobby G, it would be them.

The Fire & Ice Lounge was a place that troublemakers frequented. Many people wouldn't set foot in the place, but it had been open for years, and its regulars felt a sense of loyalty. Located on the corner of Atlantic and Grand Avenues, it was the perfect spot for drug dealers and the "ghetto fabulous" to hang out. There was at least one shootout per weekend outside the club in the early hours of the morning. No matter how many times neighbors called the cops, the club always stayed open.

Benita had gone to the lounge twice, and she had vowed never to return. The last time she was there, a fight broke out. She and her two best friends, Nikki and Kimberly, bounced before all hell broke loose. Now she was back, looking for Bobby G. He had come from a life of crime before becoming famous, and his friends, the local drug dealers, would protect him at all costs.

Benita was dressed in a super-skintight black catsuit, a long, flowing black coat, and thigh-high, black stiletto boots. She wore a long, black wig with bangs, and dark sunglasses. Luciana had her hair swept up in a tight bun. She wore a pair of black short shorts, a white bustier, and 5-inch red platform pumps.

They took two empty seats at the half-filled bar and ordered two glasses of Moscato while looking around the crowd for Bobby G.

Luciana whispered in Benita's ear, "How do you know he's here? What if Johnson has him already?"

"Bobby G is always here. This is his haven. Folks will protect him. He feels safe here. Plus, I've been tracking Carl's e-mails and phone calls through my phone. He's still looking for him. But trust me, he'll be sending his dudes here real soon. We need to check VIP."

Two random thugs offered to buy Benita and Luciana drinks, but Benita smiled and told them they were waiting for their men. They shrugged and disappeared into the crowd.

Benita recognized DJ Master Mic's spinning. He had started his career at the Fire & Ice Lounge and would DJ regularly at the club, weaving the most obscure rap songs into a host of nonstop, classic old-school, and underground hip-hop with a bit of the gangster rap.

Benita turned back to the bartender, batting her extra-long eyelashes at him. "Hey, have you seen G tonight?"

The bartender was busy making two different drinks at the same time. "He's in the VIP section at the back of the club."

"Thanks."

As Benita was getting up from her seat, Luciana grabbed her arm, whispering in Benita's ear. "We seriously need to wait for backup."

"We haven't found him yet. Let's just see if he's here."

"Benita, why are you stalling? We gotta let Miguel know what's happening."

"Fine. Send him a text. Better yet, send Santos a text. I don't think I can handle whatever Miguel has to say, because I know he's gonna be mad," Benita said.

Luciana gulped down her drink and laughed at Benita. "Oh, you have no idea how we're about to get our asses served on a platter."

She sent a text to Santos, then looked down at her vibrating phone. "Okay, Santos replied. Said to watch our asses and be prepared to get the wrath from the big man. Uh-oh. Perkins is seriously pissed off."

"We'll deal with him later. As for right now, let's go land us a shark."

Benita and Luciana walked to the back of the club and found Bobby G smoking weed with two drug dealers and groupies.

Benita turned to Luciana and said, "Bingo. He's so stupid to think Carl wouldn't find him here. Not very bright, is he? We gotta get close to make sure he stays safe."

Luciana nodded to the beat of the music and said, "We should wait for backup."

"How many times are you going to say that? How long will backup take?"

Luciana texted Santos again, and he quickly replied. "Thirty minutes."

"That's too long. What if Bobby leaves and we're back to square one?" Benita asked. "Let's just do this. We'll just stay close and blend in with the groupies."

Benita took a step toward the velvet rope, but some-one grabbed her arm. She spun around and looked the man in the eyes. She was shocked to see Leroy standing in front of her. Benita took a step forward, but her former instructor stopped her dead in her tracks. What in the world was he doing here, and why was he blocking her entry to the VIP section?

Miguel and Evan sped down the FDR Drive with red lights flashing on top of their black sedan. Miguel was pissed off that Benita and Luciana had made the decision to search for Bobby G without proper backup.

Benita had made it clear she didn't want him hovering over her, and he had tried to honor her wishes. It had been tough for him because he cared for her, but he didn't know how to express his feelings. After the night he kissed her, Benita had refused to talk to him about his actions and kept things professional. Was she making him pay for being an asshole, or was she being a hotheaded agent trying to prove herself? Miguel planned on having a serious talk with the wonder twins about breaking DTCU's protocol.

"You need to wait for backup," Leroy commanded.

"I'm sorry, I think you've confused me with someone else," Benita replied.

"No confusion, Benita. You need to listen to me."

"Excuse me?"

"Why don't we go over to the bar and talk?" Leroy tried to grab Benita's arm, but she pulled away.

The bodyguard who was standing by the VIP entrance witnessed the exchange and walked over to Benita, Luciana, and Leroy. "I don't think these ladies wanna be bothered by your ass. Mind stepping away from the entryway? You ladies all right?"

Benita stepped away from Leroy and flashed her pearly whites to the bouncer. "We're trying to make our way into the VIP area to meet G, but this man is harassin' us."

"No worries. Follow me." The bouncer escorted the ladies into the VIP section.

Leroy walked toward the bar but kept his eye on the VIP area. If any trouble was going down, he planned on protecting his daughter.

Chapter 48

Carl was seething, and he wasn't going to let Bobby G live. Bobby G had threatened him, and Carl was not going down for the murder of some dumb-ass bootlegger. He would take care of Bobby G and then head to Mexico.

While sitting on the couch with Benita and Luciana, Bobby G took a puff off his gigantic blunt. He was high and acted like he didn't have a care in the world.

Benita spotted her brother walking into the club and heading to the VIP section. "Excuse me a minute. I need to hit the ladies' room," she said. She made a beeline toward the rope and pulled Wes away, dragging him toward the restrooms.

"Wes, what are you doing here?"

"Bobby G called me."

"Didn't I ask you to stay clear of him?"

"He wanted me to bring a thumb drive for him."

"Thumb drive? Did he say what was on it?"

"No. Just told me it was an insurance policy."

"Wes, I need you to hand me the thumb drive."

"I can't, Benita. He'll kill me."

"If you don't, Bobby G and Carl Johnson will get away with murder. Do you want to be an accessory?"

Wes handed Benita the thumb drive. She turned around and saw two heavyset guys harassing Bobby G and Martin in the VIP section. Luciana tried to defuse the situation, but one of the burly guys pushed her down on the couch.

"Wes, get out of here, now!" She ran over to the VIP section, but one of the security guards kept her from entering.

"Look, my girlfriend is in there, and I need to help her."

"Sorry, nobody's entering that area, understand?"

When they turned around, a bottle of champagne came flying at the security guard, thrown by someone in VIP. He touched the back of his head and felt blood oozing from his scalp.

Benita pushed her way to Luciana.

"Man, I ain't going nowhere with you muthafuckas. Get off me," Bobby G yelled.

Two of Bobby G's entourage began throwing punches at the big men dressed in black T-shirts and black pants. It was hard to distinguish whether they were working for the club or someone else.

Bobby G swung at one of the guys but was quickly put in a chokehold. All of a sudden, the club broke into complete chaos. People were pushing and shoving, and many were trying to get out the front door.

When Benita reached Luciana, they tried to grab Bobby G by the arm and get him outside, but they were stopped by two oversized muscle-heads, who pushed them out of the way like they were rag dolls. Bobby G and Martin made their way through the crowd and headed out the back door.

Martin saw Wes trying to maneuver through the crowd and yelled out to him. "Wes! Man, let's go!" He motioned for Wes to escape out the back door.

Against his better judgment, Wes dodged a drink being thrown in his direction and followed Bobby G and Martin outside.

Leroy, who had been watching Benita and her friend from the bar most of the night, witnessed Benita being thrown around. As he tried to make his way over to the VIP section to protect his daughter, he was grabbed from behind. Leroy quickly grabbed the man's wrist, bending it downward, making a quick move to pin the assailant's arm behind his own back. Leroy then kneed the man in the back, causing him to yell out in pain. He pushed him down and maneuvered through the chaotic crowd. He punched another fighter with a right hook and then a swift kick to the leg to knock him down.

Benita looked around for Bobby G and his entourage, but they were gone. "Damn, which way?"

"Through the back door," Luciana said.

"Let's go."

Benita and Luciana headed outside, but they saw two other guards throw Bobby and Martin into the back of an SUV. The license plate read MADDOGG. Benita and Luciana pulled out their guns and shot at the tires, but they were too far away.

Benita turned to Luciana, trying to catch her breath. "Carl's got 'im."

Miguel, Evan, and two other cars full of agents pulled up near the club to find several cop cars blocking the entrance to the Fire & Ice Lounge. Miguel saw Benita and Luciana talking to one of the cops and motioned them over. The ladies approached Miguel and Evan.

Miguel started yelling, "What the hell were you thinking? Both of you ignored protocol. I'm not surprised at you, Benita, but Luciana? You know better. You're supposed to set an example for Benita, not play her silly games!"

Benita had never seen Miguel like this before, and for the first time, she didn't know what to say. She listened to his rant for another five minutes until he calmed down and leaned against the car.

Benita handed Miguel the thumb drive her brother had given her. "Here. Maybe this will make you feel better. I think this is Bobby G's weapon against Carl."

Miguel handed Carlos the thumb drive to scan the incriminating contents onto his laptop.

"Jackpot," Carlos said. "We got evidence. The drive includes information on different companies, including Gold Starr Corporation, and a dummy company used to transfer money to Eric Fernandez and his terrorist group. There's even information linking to the murder of Malik Williams."

Miguel softened. "Nice work. Now all we have to do is find Bobby G to get him back into protective custody before Carl kills him."

"Miguel, I was able to put a small chip in Bobby G's pocket. Unless he pulls out all the loose change, it's still there," Luciana said.

Carlos typed in some codes, and one of the trackers assigned to Luciana began blinking red. "Bingo. It seems Bobby G is in Red Hook."

"Doesn't Carl own some property down there?" Miguel asked.

Carlos continued typing. "Right again, boss. It seems Mr. Johnson may just be keeping our little Bobby G at one of his properties."

Benita began walking away from the group but stopped and looked back at Miguel. "Well, you coming?"

Miguel smiled.

The group left for the warehouse. Benita and Luciana got into Benita's Mustang and sped off.

Leroy waited until all the cars were gone and followed them. Wherever his daughter was going, he was too.

Chapter 49

It was four in the morning when Carl and his cronies arrived at the warehouse with Bobby G, Martin, and Wes, who had been the first person shoved inside the car when they fled the club. Now they were all being forced to the back of the warehouse.

"You threatened me," Carl screamed. He pointed a gun at Bobby G's chest.

"Carl, man, I'm sorry."

"How many times do I have to tell you to shut the fuck up? And you two stupid muthafuckas are gonna die with him just because you were hanging out with this clown. He ain't nothing but a liability. But after tonight, you all will be nothing but a distant memory."

Benita and Luciana parked a block away from Carl's warehouse. They walked down Van Brunt Street toward the side of the building, where they joined Miguel, Carlos, and Evan behind a huge construction truck.

"What the hell kind of warehouse needs so many guards?" Benita asked.

"When you're so paranoid you think everyone's out to get you," Miguel responded as he looked around the perimeter. "Okay, Santos and I will take out the two on the left, and you three handle those on the right. I just heard from the other two groups, and they'll handle the ones on the roof. Go."

One by one, DTCU agents took out the guards. Benita sneaked up behind one and knocked him out with her Glock. Evan punched one in the face and knocked him to the ground. He was out cold. They dragged the limp bodies out of the line of vision and proceeded forward toward the warehouse opening.

One of the agents was able to prop up the warehouse door about two feet, but the door became stuck. Benita and Luciana tried to slide underneath, but they needed a little bit more room to clear the entranceway. They heard Carl yelling at the top of his lungs at his victims.

Inside the warehouse, Carl plopped into the chair in front of Bobby G and leaned forward. "Brooklyn's been good to me. I've made a lotta money here. I bought all kinds of property. I am Brooklyn."

Bobby G sat with his hands tied behind his back. "Man, what the hell are you talking about? If you gonna shoot, just shoot. I'm tired of your damn rambling."

Carl hauled off and hit Bobby G across the face with his gun. Blood trickled down the side of Bobby G's mouth. He turned his head and spit.

"I'm about to close the biggest deal of my life, and you want your own fucking label? You ungrateful son of a bitch!" Carl yelled.

Bobby G was defiant. "Muthafucka, I made you! You hear me? I fuckin' made you!"

Benita, Luciana, and the other agent finally jimmied open the warehouse gate, causing it to rise another foot. Benita slid underneath and hid behind boxes stacked to the ceiling, but the door slipped back down before Luciana could clear the entryway. Benita turned around to see if Luciana was behind her but noticed that she was stuck on the outside of the gate. Benita and Luciana struggled in vain to raise it.

"Let me see if I can find something to prop it up," Benita said, then searched but found nothing.

Luciana turned around to face the agent. "Hey, can you help? We need this gate up ASAP!"

The agent used the crowbar to try to lift the gate. "It won't move."

"Try harder, man!" Luciana snapped.

Benita made a quick decision to leave Luciana. "Listen. I can't wait any longer. My brother needs me."

Luciana called out to Benita. "Hey! You can't go without me. You always gotta have backup."

"Look, my brother's up there, and I couldn't live with myself if something happened to him. I'll be careful."

"Promise me, Benita, that you won't get yourself killed."

"Pinkie swear."

Luciana continued to work with the agent to get the gate unjammed, while Benita headed in the direction of Carl's voice.

Benita moved behind a stack of boxes and peeked around an opening to see Carl holding a gun on Bobby G, Martin, and Wes. Petrified that this crazy man might hurt her brother, Benita kept her wits about her and tried to think of a plan. She looked back to see if Luciana had made it inside, but the gate was still down.

"Damn."

Benita spotted a huge gray electrical box against the wall and quietly made her way over to it.

"You think you made me? No, muthafucka, I made you. I pulled you outta the gutter, cleaned you up, and created

Bobby G. Remember when you begged me to give you a chance? And what did I do? I did it! Gave your sorry ass a chance. You didn't make me. Nah. I should kill you right now."

Just as he aimed the gun at Bobby G's face, Benita killed the lights in the back of the warehouse. It was pitch black.

Benita yelled, "Carl, you need to put down your weapon. Nobody needs to get hurt."

"I know that voice. Oh, shit. Bridgette? What the hell you doing here? Did you just kill the lights?"

"Yes, I killed the lights. Now, come on, Carl. It's over. You're surrounded."

Carl pointed the gun at the open space, ready to pull the trigger. "Unless you want one of these clowns to go down, I suggest you come out in the open."

"I can't do that, Carl. Wouldn't want your finger to slip and shoot me by mistake."

Carl walked over to a huge electrical box and pushed the lever up, restoring the lights in his office. They illuminated against the window, creating a faint glow with shadowy images.

Carl walked back over to his captives and pointed the gun at them. "Girl, now I remember why I like you so much. Listen, I'm about to finish up some loose ends, and then I'm off to Mexico to start a new life. Why don't you come with me?"

"Oh, Carl, that sounds nice, but I think I'm going to have to pass."

"Really? Oh, well. Your loss. Now, Bridgette, if you don't show your pretty little self, I'm gonna have to shoot someone for real. In fact, let's start with Martin."

Benita peeked around the beam and was mortified when she saw Carl shoot Martin in the middle of his forehead. As if in slow motion, his chair fell backward, and he was dead.

Wes screamed, "Benita! He shot Martin! You gotta help me!"

Carl turned to Wes and pointed the gun at him. "So, your name is Benita? It seems this little shit knows you. Am I right? I'm giving you three seconds before I blow him to hell, just like Martin. And I don't give a flying fuck about myself. Everybody's going down in this fucking place. You hear me, Benita? One, two—"

Benita stepped out from behind the group of boxes into one of the aisles and pointed her gun at Carl. "You don't have to kill anyone else."

Carl pointed the gun at her. "Oh, shit! A chick with a gun. I think you need to put that weapon away before you get yourself hurt."

"Only if you put yours down first."

Carl laughed and walked behind Wes, using his gun to stroke Wes's temple. "So, I guess you never worked at a fashion house, huh?"

"You got me. I was frontin'. I have another job, and that's putting away bad guys like you. Did you know you're at the top of my list? Now, we can do this the easy way or the hard way. If I were you, I'd consider putting down your gun."

Parked a block away from the warehouse, Leroy got out of his car and jogged to the back of the warehouse to look for a point of entry. As he touched his Glock that was situated in the back of his waistband, he spotted a guard taking a cigarette break. He sneaked up behind him and placed the thug in a chokehold, rendering him unconscious.

Dragging the man behind a bush, the former agent spotted an unlocked window and propped himself up and slipped through the window, lowering himself to the ground. As Leroy made his way around an aisle of inventory, he saw Carl standing over a young man bleeding out on the concrete floor.

As Benita worked to get Carl to give up his weapon, Leroy crawled his way behind a metal storage unit, which would be the perfect location to take Carl out. Not realizing that one of the guards had spotted him, he quickly turned around and moved out of the way before being attacked. They ended up fighting in the open passageway, providing a clear shot for Carl or one of his other guards to take aim.

Leroy grabbed one of the CDs from an open box and hit him on the side of his head, causing the oversized guard to stumble a bit while holding on to his wound to stop the bleeding. Leroy began punching him in the face.

Leroy was about to pull out his gun when Carl shot him in the stomach, causing him to fall backward into a stack of boxes.

Benita looked in shock and horror when she saw it was her jiu-jitsu instructor who had been shot. "Oh my God, Sensei!"

Running toward Leroy, Benita rolled out of the way to avoid being shot by Carl. She grabbed Leroy, pulling him out of the open area. "Leroy, what the hell are you doing here? You trying to get yourself killed?"

"I'm sorry, Benita. I was only trying to help."

"Yeah, you can make it up to me when we get out of this place."

Two more of Carl's cronies came from out of nowhere and started shooting at Benita and Leroy, who were shielded by the crates.

The gate was finally pried open, and Luciana and the unnamed agent made their way inside the warehouse. When two more guards came around the corner, the agents started firing off rounds, hitting one of the bodyguards in the chest and another in the leg.

Benita shot at Carl, but the bullet came inches from the side of his head. He touched his ears to make sure he hadn't been hit.

Carl pulled Wes by the back of his chair and dragged him behind a large beam. He pointed the gun at Wes's head.

"Carl, it doesn't have to go down like this. You need to put away your weapon," Benita said.

Carl cocked the gun at Wes's head. "Listen, you're right. You got one chance to make this right. Your life for his."

Luciana aimed at one of the bodyguards and yelled to him. "This is Agent Rodriguez. Drop your weapon!"

The bodyguard started shooting at Luciana, but she got off multiple shots and hit him in the shoulder and the chest.

Miguel, Carlos, and Evan hurried inside the warehouse, holding guns. When they heard the bullets flying, they took cover.

Miguel spotted Benita and the wounded Leroy Jones and made his way over to them, while Carlos and Evan went in the opposite direction to help Luciana.

"Kojak? What the hell are you doing here? Benita, you okay?" Miguel asked.

"Kojak? Who's Kojak?" Benita asked.

"A former agent. A legend, in fact," Miguel answered.

"Miguel, we gotta get him out of here before he bleeds to death. Carl has my little brother, and I swear I'll rip his balls off if he hurts him."

"Okay, I'll get him out, but I need you to cover us so we won't get shot."

"I got you. Take care of my Sensei."

"Carl, you are surrounded!" Benita yelled.

Miguel spotted an industrial metal bin on wheels and dragged Leroy to it. Once he got Leroy inside, he announced, "Okay, we're ready."

Benita got in position and started yelling at Carl. "Carl, did you hear me?"

"Loud and clear, sunshine. But I'm not listening to you. I'm Carl Holiday Fucking Johnson. I don't take orders from no one."

Benita turned back around to see Miguel in position. "Okay, let's go!"

She stood behind the metal bin, letting off shots as Miguel pushed the bin out of harm's way to the other side of the pathway. He then signaled for one of the agents to take the bin outside the warehouse. When he turned around, Benita had worked her way closer to where Carl had her brother.

Miguel yelled, "Benita, don't!"

"Carl, you need to let Wes go. We don't want anyone else to get killed. You're surrounded, and all your gunmen are gone. We can make this easy or hard. Your choice."

"You think I'm scared of some damn bitch?"

"You know what? I am sick and tired of you tired-ass men always referring to a woman as a bitch! I mean, do you have any other words in your damn vocabulary?"

"Why would I, when this word fits you perfectly? A damn bitch!"

"Well, my friend, this bitch will kick your ass!"

Bobby G started to plead for his life. "Carl, you need to give up the dream, man. They're not gonna let you get out of here alive. Untie me. Let me go, man."

Carl turned his head toward Bobby G and yelled at the top of his lungs, "Shut the fuck up, Bobby!" He cocked his gun and pressed the barrel against Wes's temple.

"Carl, this is Agent Miguel Perkins. You need to drop your weapon now! This isn't gonna end well. Do you understand?"

"Carl, how about we put down our weapons and handle this like adults, huh? Let me see what you got. Huh? I mean, I'm a bitch, right?" Benita yelled.

"Damn, you're beautiful and stupid at the same time. I have to say, you do have some big-ass balls. Shit, I'm game. You're not the first bitch who ran her mouth like a man. Okay, let's end this bullshit."

He walked around a half wall, pointing the gun at Benita while she pointed her gun at him. As the two fighters cautiously walked toward each other, Carl pushed Bobby G's chair out of the way, knocking him over on his side. He grabbed Wes by the back of his shirt and pulled him toward the light from his office.

"Carl, let him go now!" Benita screamed.

"If you want him, come and get him!"

When the three got inside the office, Carl pressed a red button, locking the door behind Benita.

Miguel and his team began shooting at the large window, but it became clear it was bulletproof.

"Johnson, let Benita go now!" Miguel yelled. He ran toward the wall and started banging on it with his gun. "Let her out!"

Carl laughed and mouthed the words, *Can't hear you!*

"You're one crazy muthafucka. You know that, Carl?" Benita responded.

"Not crazy, just protective of my shit. Plus, I want us to have some privacy. Don't want to be interrupted when I kick your sweet little ass."

They began circling, still pointing their guns at each other.

"Oh, Carl. You just always say the nicest things. Such a gentleman."

"Why don't we do a little dance and put our guns down? No reason to hold on to them, because as soon as one of us shoots, it's just going to ricochet off the walls, and we don't want that, do we?"

Still circling each other, they laid their guns on the floor and kicked them away. After a few minutes, Carl launched at Benita, but she pushed him out of the way. He went crashing into the Plexiglass wall.

Benita turned around and took a combat stance. "Carl, I don't want to hurt you, but if I have to, I will."

"Shut the fuck up, bitch!" He charged again, but this time, she punched him in the face.

Carl shook it off and tried to backhand her, but she stepped out of the way. He fell to his knees.

"Do you know how much I hate that freakin' word?" she said.

Benita was about to kick him, but he grabbed her foot, throwing her to the floor. She rolled out of the way, but he landed a punch on her side. They staggered to their feet, and Carl grabbed Benita's arm before she could react. He lifted her off the floor and threw her against the wall.

She sat up, taking a moment to catch her breath, but Carl was on top of her in a flash. He wrapped his hands around her neck and choked her with as much brute force as he could muster.

Carl whispered in Benita's ear, "My face will be the last thing that you see, bitch."

Just when he thought he had rendered her unconscious, she used both hands to smack Carl against his ears. He yelled out in pain and loosened his grip. She kneed him in this groin and gave him an uppercut to his jaw. He backed up, clutching his pelvis, and she swivel-kicked him in the chin. He fell unconscious to the floor.

Benita collapsed to her knees. She held her neck as she caught her breath. She looked up and saw Miguel leaning against the bulletproof glass. He exhaled a long breath and smiled at her. He placed his head against the wall and gave one pound.

"Benita, open the door, would you?"

Slowly getting on her feet, Benita pressed the button, raising the Plexiglass walls. She hurried over to her brother and threw her arms around his neck.

"Wes, you okay?"

"Damn, Benita. I knew you were a badass, but nothing like what I just saw. You kicked Holiday's ass!" he responded with excitement.

"This bitch is incredible," Bobby G commented.

Benita walked over to Bobby G and elbowed him in the mouth, knocking him out cold. "Didn't I say how much I hate that word?"

Miguel came in and grabbed Benita by her shoulders. "What the hell were you trying to do, give me a heart attack?"

She smiled at him. "Oh, don't get me started, Miguel. Remember when I had to fend for myself with the fat dude in Trenton? I don't wanna hear it from you."

"Hey, can somebody take these losers out of here? We've got to debrief them before we turn them over to the feds."

Luciana ran over to Benita and gave her a big hug. "You okay?"

"Girl, I'm fine. Thanks for having my back. You're the best partner a girl could ever have."

"Just wish my shoe hadn't gotten caught."

"Things happen," Benita said.

"I'll see you outside."

Evan headed over to speak to Benita, but when he saw her hug her brother, he turned around and walked with Luciana out of the warehouse.

"Wes, how the hell did you end up in this mess?" Benita asked.

"I was headed out the back door when the fight broke out, and Bobby G was coming out. That's when Carl's people grabbed all of us. I'm sorry, Benita. I tried to get away. I did."

She hugged her brother one more time before Miguel came over.

"Wes, this is Agent Miguel Perkins. He's the guy who recruited me. Agent Perkins, my brother, Wes."

Miguel extended his hand. "It's nice to meet you, Wes."

"You've turned my sister into some freakin' secret agent or something?"

He smiled and said, "Or something. But to tell you the truth, she just needed an opportunity to shine."

"Well, make sure you keep her safe. She's the only irritating sister I got."

Miguel said, "The police are on the way, and that means the media won't be too far behind. I need all of my agents to clear out before they get here. Don't need you guys exposed to the public."

"Okay. But what about Wes? What's gonna happen to him?"

"He has to be debriefed. I'll make sure he gets home safely."

Wes looked at Benita but didn't know how to say good-bye. "Will I see you again?"

Benita gave her brother a long, loving hug and kissed him on the cheek. "I'll never be far away, little brother."

Chapter 50

Benita, carrying a bouquet of flowers, walked down the long white hallway toward room 702. She reached the door and thought about turning around, but she had to speak to the man who had tried to save her life. She knocked and heard a deep voice inviting her in.

She looked at Leroy, a.k.a. Kojak, who was lying in bed, watching a news conference about Carl and Bobby G. He turned toward the door, and his face lit up the moment he saw his daughter.

"Hey. How are you feeling?" she asked.

Leroy began coughing profusely and drank a few sips of water before answering. "A little bullet can't stop me. I'm Sensei Leroy, at your service."

"You could have gotten yourself killed last night. Why would you put your life in danger for me?"

"There's so much I need to tell you, Benita. I just don't know where to begin."

Benita pulled up the chair beside him and took hold of his hand. "Why don't you start at the beginning?"

Leroy told Benita about the early days at DTCU and how he started working there. His heart was overflowing with love and admiration for the daughter who was following in his footsteps. If it weren't for her grandmother, he would have never known Benita was his flesh and blood.

Benita sat as Leroy continued talking about his love affair with her mother and how he'd never stopped loving her. From the first time Benita met Leroy, he had taken a special interest in her, treating her like a daughter he said he never had. No matter how long it took or how uncomfortable it felt to be speaking to her father, she was there to listen.

Benita checked her mailbox at home and found an envelope. She tore it open, and inside was a folder with *Confidential* stamped across it. She sat on her couch and began to read the contents written in Miguel's handwriting. He had kept a log of every interaction he'd had with her. He had been keeping a file on her from the first time he saw her at the bus stop when she got into the fight with those thugs. She was shocked to read that Miguel had interviewed T-Bone and had encouraged him to say Benita was behind the men getting hurt.

Benita picked up the folder and headed to DTCU to confront Miguel. He had orchestrated this entire plot to recruit her for DTCU. She stormed into his office, holding the file. He was in the middle of typing notes from the Johnson case. Benita dropped it on his desk when he looked up at her.

"You set me up, you son of a bitch. How could you convince T-Bone to lie about me? I spent four months in jail because of you. I should kick your ass right now."

Miguel stood up and walked around his desk. "Benita, I saw the perfect opportunity, and I took it."

She hauled off and slapped him across the face and then pointed her index finger at him. "It wasn't up to you to change the course of my life. I was fine. I was happy.

I loved doing hair. I loved going to school, and I loved my training. I loved hanging out with my friends and my family. But you took all that away. Who do you think you are, God?"

He caressed her face and whispered, "I'm sorry," in her ear.

She stepped away from him. "Don't touch me! You're no better than any of those criminals we're supposed to bring down. You and me? We're done. I'm sorry our paths ever crossed."

"Where are you going?"

She slammed the door behind her, but Miguel followed her into the hallway, yelling at the top of his lungs. "Benita, don't walk away!"

She kept walking down the hall without looking back. When Benita got to Agent DeVreau's office, she stormed inside without knocking.

DeVreau looked up to see an angry Benita ready to explode. "Benita, did we have a meeting today?"

"Were you part of this?"

Samantha took off her glasses and placed them on her desk. She clasped her hands and looked up at Benita.

"You made me trust you, Samantha. You made me believe I could make a difference here. I was set up, thrown in jail, and forced into this new life I'd have never chosen for myself. You're all nothing but manipulators."

"Benita, I know you're angry, and you have every right to be. But don't lose sight of your potential. You weren't recruited the traditional way, but you've proven to us you can handle anything. You're on your way to becoming one of the best damn agents DTCU has ever seen. Do you wanna throw it all away now because of Miguel's choices? He believed in your abilities. You're more than just part of the team. You're family."

"You're not my family."

"None of us are perfect, Benita. My dear, we all make mistakes. Don't lose out on this amazing opportunity to do extraordinary things. We need you. Don't give up on us."

Benita thought about everything she'd gone through in the last forty-eight hours. She'd helped bring down a bad guy who'd tried to kill her and her brother; she'd found out her former instructor wasn't only an ex-DTCU agent but was her father; someone who called himself a friend provided her with information about how she'd actually been "recruited." She had fallen for a man she probably would never be able to trust because he would always have an agenda.

After speaking to Samantha, Benita sat outside a little café near her apartment. She just wanted to enjoy a cup of hot chocolate and decompress from the day's events. Everything was overwhelming.

She also found out her grandmother had known all along that Leroy was her father, and that was why she'd hated him all these years. She smiled when she thought about Grams. She missed her so much. She had always been there for her and Wes.

Benita had witnessed her brother being thrown in the crossfire of danger and wouldn't be able to bear it if anything happened to her family. She made a promise to stay out of her family's life in order to protect them, but she would never be too far away.

Leroy wanted to be in her life, but she wasn't sure how it could work. She was twenty-five years old and had been plunged into a world of unpredictability and danger. How could he be there for her now? She had to think about it, but she thanked him for being honest with her.

Benita was in deep thought when Evan found her at the café. "Would you mind if I joined you?" he asked.

Benita smiled and motioned for him to sit. "Hey."

"Hey, how are you?"

"I've been better. Can I ask you something?"

"Sure."

"Did you send me that file?"

"What file?"

"Okay, forget I asked."

Evan remained silent.

"But if you did send me a file, thank you." Benita winked.

"I don't know what you're talking about."

"No worries. You don't have to fess up, Evan. We're friends. We need to look out for each other, right?"

At least she had one person she could trust.

"Evan, do you like working at DTCU?"

He sat back in his chair and stroked his newly grown goatee. "Yes, I do. When you put in this much effort to make it through the initial training and then are assigned jobs requiring so much commitment and time, it's all worth it. Are you having second thoughts?"

Benita took another sip of hot chocolate and thought about his question. "I don't know if I can answer that."

"You're special, Benita. You're real special. And no one else can say they were handpicked to do this job. We need you at DTCU. I need you at DTCU. Think about all the fun we can have. We can do some serious damage."

"Ah, Evan, you'd miss me if I left?"

He smiled and drank his iced tea in silence.

Benita went home and took a long, hot shower to clear her head and wash away the day's events. She then fell on the bed and slept for a few hours before calling Miguel. She asked him to come over so they could talk. She had a lot to get off her chest.

Twenty minutes later, Miguel showed up. She opened the door but stood in front of him with her hand pressed against his chest. She wasn't ready for him to enter the apartment just yet. She stood there in silence.

"I guess you're not gonna let me in?"

"No, but I have a few things to say to you. First, what you did was wrong. Dead wrong. But I think I understand you saw something in me and had to have me for the job. I know I'm a real asset to the organization."

"Yes, I was trying to tell you."

"Shut it. I'm not finished."

"Sorry. Please proceed."

"Second, you owe me. You need to do whatever needs to be done to make things right. I want you to clear my name. I don't care how you do it, but I need that to happen. I'm not gonna work for any organization holding shit over my head, threatening to send me back to jail every time I do something wrong. Not gonna happen."

"Check. Clear your name. Anything else?"

"Yes. I want a whole new wardrobe and flowers every day until I get sick of seeing them. And I don't want you yelling at me when I don't follow your damned protocol."

Miguel lightly pushed Benita back into her apartment as she continued to give him a list of her demands. He closed the door behind him and kissed her on the lips.

"Did I tell you how amazing you were fighting Carl?"

"Hmmmm. Really? You wanna go there right now? You know I hate you, right?" she asked him.

He smiled and kissed her again, but this time she didn't resist. She may have been angry, but she wasn't crazy.

"Did I ever tell you about the second time I saw you?" Miguel asked.

"The second time?"

"Yeah, I bumped into you at Ray's Place, and you didn't even notice me. You were so focused on getting to T-Bone. I knew then and there that I needed to find out who you were, and I needed a plan to bring you into the fold."

"No matter what the cost."

Miguel stared intensely at Benita. "No matter what the cost. What if I told you that I think I love you?"

"I'm not sure if I would believe you."

Miguel slowly kissed Benita, and she did not resist. It had taken Benita a while to figure out her feelings for Miguel, especially having a love-hate relationship with him, but she knew that she couldn't survive this place without him. She was an agent who was madly in love with her boss. Although it would be against DTCU's policy, she enjoyed living on the edge, no matter how much trouble she could get herself in. She was with the man of her dreams, and nothing was stopping her from being with him. Not even a little reprimand.

Chapter 51

Two months later, Benita drove to Brooklyn to visit her old neighborhood. It was late when she parked her car two blocks away from her grandmother's house, remaining inconspicuous so she wouldn't be recognized. Opening up her laptop, Benita viewed a live stream of her family's living room. Surveillance cameras had been set up in the house so Benita could always keep an eye on them.

Benita observed Grace, Wes, and Deon watching local news reporter Tonya Murray giving an update on the upcoming trials of Carl Johnson, his artist Don "Bobby G" Jackson, and Johnson's bodyguard, Warren "Big Boy" Paine.

Reporter Tonya Murray revealed, "Carl 'Holiday' Johnson was charged with murder, conspiracy to commit murder, bootlegging, racketeering, and domestic terrorism. In addition, it has been brought to light that Johnson is allegedly linked to a string of harassment and assaults against Brooklyn business owners, including Deon Wright, owner of Deon's Hair Salon, who was hospitalized after being attacked. In a related investigation stemming from the attack on Mr. Wright, his cousin, Benita Renee Jenkins, who had been falsely implicated in a crime, was later cleared of charges related to conspiracy to commit murder."

Grace patted Wes's leg as she cried tears of joy. "Praise Jesus! Thank you, Lord, for watching over my baby. I always knew she was innocent and was taken for a bigger purpose."

"You were right, Grams."

"I wish I could tell Benita how thankful I am. She saved my business. And she saved my life. I'll never forget what she did for me." Deon wiped back a tear and continued watching the television screen.

"I'm sure she knows," Wes said.

As they continued discussing Benita being cleared of the ridiculous conspiracy charges, she fought back the urge to walk down the street and speak to them. At least Wes knew the truth, and he would reassure his family she was okay.

Benita was happy that Perkins had kept his promise of clearing her name and even allowing her to send a postcard to her grandmother a few weeks ago. She smiled when she thought of Grace seeing that she was following her dreams to save the world.

With tears streaming down her face, she shut down the computer. Now she knew her family was safe, and she could work for a secret organization created to bring down the bad guys. She started the car and sped off down the streets of Brooklyn, bopping to the beats of DJ Master Mic.